PENGUIN BOOKS

# The Market Girl

Libby Ashworth writes sagas set in Lancashire, England where she was born and brought up. Libby still lives in Lancashire and is passionate about its history. She can trace her direct ancestors back to the village of Whalley in the Middle Ages. Many of her ancestors worked in the cotton industry – first as home-based spinners and hand loom weavers, and later in the mills of Blackburn. It is their lives Libby has drawn on to tell her stories.

T0322292

*By the same author*

The Rag Maiden

# The Market Girl

### LIBBY ASHWORTH

PENGUIN BOOKS

PENGUIN BOOKS

UK | USA | Canada | Ireland | Australia
India | New Zealand | South Africa

Penguin Books is part of the Penguin Random House group of companies
whose addresses can be found at global.penguinrandomhouse.com.

First published 2024

001

Set in 12.5/14.75pt Garamond MT Std
Typeset by Jouve (UK), Milton Keynes
Printed and bound in Great Britain by Clays Ltd, Elcograf S.p.A.

The authorized representative in the EEA is Penguin Random House Ireland,
Morrison Chambers, 32 Nassau Street, Dublin D02 YH68

A CIP catalogue record for this book is available from the British Library

ISBN: 978-1-405-96204-9

www.greenpenguin.co.uk

*For Anne Cavanah*

# Lancashire 1852

# I

Agnes Cavanah folded the last of the white cotton rags into a sack for the paper mill and tied the top. It was surprising, she thought, how working with supposedly clean rags left her hands and apron so soiled. Her fingers were filthy and her nails, although cut short, were ringed with black around the cuticles and beneath the tips. She would scrub them with a brush and hot water when she got home, but they would be as bad tomorrow.

At least she'd been promoted from the tables where she'd first begun working for Mr Reynolds, sorting out bones. They stank with the remnants of rotting flesh and it was only after they'd been washed that they were sent on to be made into knife handles, or buttons, or boiled up for glue, or ground down to fertilize the fields. The stench of them sometimes made her nauseous and on the days that the smell was particularly bad, Agnes still had to go to the door and breathe deeply to prevent herself being sick.

Not that the air outside was much better. The acrid smell of burning coal clung everywhere and was nothing like the aromatic scent of the peat fires that she remembered from her childhood in Ireland. Here in Lancashire, she was surrounded by smoke and factories and streets thronged with people clattering along in their iron-tipped clogs, the women and lasses with their shawls pulled over their heads and their backs bent as if carrying an invisible burden. Agnes longed for the countryside, for clean, sweet air, for animals grazing in fields, and crops growing sturdily under the unshrouded sun. She wanted the life she remembered she once had, running through the soft grass in bare feet and tasting the distant, salt-laden sea before skipping home to the whitewashed, thatched cottage where her mother would be boiling or baking potatoes for their dinner.

When she'd described the scene like this, her mother had told her that she only recalled such happy times because she and Agnes's father had taken such pains to keep their troubles from their children. Her mother had spoken of different memories of Ireland – of spoiled crops, prolonged rain, endless demands from the bailiff for rent they had struggled to pay and the eventual tearing down of their cottage that had forced them to leave. Her mother remembered her father too, although she rarely spoke of him now, and whenever Agnes mentioned him her mother told her that the past was past and they must look to the future. But what future was there for her here? The thought of spending the rest of her life sorting through rags and grading them into piles of white, coloured, clean or dirty was not a prospect that gave her much hope.

It was Saturday and they were finishing at six o'clock, an hour earlier than their usual knocking-off time of seven. The shop and warehouse closed on Sundays and Agnes was looking forward to her day off. Tomorrow she would be able to wear her Sunday best – a blue gown that had been given to her on her last birthday by Mrs Anderton, the wife of their landlord. It was beautiful, barely worn, and for one day of the week at least she could feel like a lady as she walked to the morning service at St Alban's Church wearing it, even if having to wrap her shawl over the top in the cold weather rather spoiled the effect. The shawl stank of the warehouse even though she tried to air it at every opportunity. But the summer would soon be coming and then she could discard it and show off her gown to its full advantage.

Agnes walked across the warehouse and joined the line of women and girls waiting for Mr Reynolds to hand them their wages for the week.

She was surprised when he counted one shilling and tenpence on to her outstretched palm – fourpence more than she was usually paid.

'Is that right?' she queried, staring at the coins and wondering if the rag dealer had become confused.

Mr Reynolds smiled before raising a finger to his lips to warn her to keep silent.

'Tha's earned it this week,' he whispered. 'Tha's one of the few I can rely on to weigh in the rags and pay out the correct money. It seems tha has an aptitude for calculations.'

Agnes closed her fingers around her wages, feeling

proud of herself. She'd never had the opportunity to go to school, but since she'd begun work in the warehouse she'd always paid close attention when Mr Reynolds paid the gatherers who brought in rags and other items of value to sell. She'd quickly learned the names of the weights and the coins and how to add up the numbers in her head even though the calculations were complex – four farthings to a penny and twelve pennies to a shilling. She'd also watched as Mr Reynolds had written in his account book. Agnes knew that the marks on the paper represented the shillings and pence and farthings that he counted out. She tried to memorize the shapes of the numbers and she could recognize a few, but mostly the numbers stayed in her head where she could reckon them with ease.

'Besides, we've done well this week,' continued Mr Reynolds as Agnes carefully put the money away in her purse. 'Thy mother fetched a good bundle t' other day.'

'Yes. She was lucky,' Agnes replied.

'And where's tha off to tonight? Hast tha found a young man to walk out with yet?' He grinned. He asked her the same question every Saturday night and every week Agnes shook her head and told him she was going straight home.

'Tha's a good lass,' he said as she turned to follow the other workers out on to the street where they were calling their goodbyes and setting off either for their houses or to do their errands.

'I'm going to the market,' said her friend Jane. 'My mam wants some cheese. Walk with me,' she invited as she lifted her shawl over her bare head.

'All right,' Agnes agreed. She knew her mother would be expecting her home, but she wouldn't be missed for ten or twenty minutes.

The sounds of the market drifted down King William Street as they approached. Both the outdoor and indoor markets were thronged with customers now that the working folk had their weekly wages in their pockets to shop for provisions, and on the food stalls the traders were shouting out the last of their bargains.

'Two a penny!'

'Three a penny!'

'Only tuppence a pound! Tuppence a pound!'

The men in their battered hats and brightly coloured cravats were thrusting out bargains to every passer-by who caught their eye, keen to clear their produce before it was time for them to leave. All the bruised fruit and potatoes with many eyes were being offered at knock-down prices, and women were filling their baskets before going home to cook a meal for their families.

Agnes and Jane pushed their way through the crush, past the fishy smell of the woman who had just sold the last of the shrimps she'd brought from Southport and towards the stalls where the farmers, who travelled in with produce from the countryside, were reducing the prices of what they hadn't sold.

7

There wasn't much remaining on the cheese stall. Just the remains of one huge wheel of Lancashire cheese and the weighing scales.

'A pound, please,' said Jane and Agnes watched as the cheesemonger drew his taut wire through the triangular wedge of creamy white and put the offcut on to the scales, adding his pound weight to the other side. The scales balanced beautifully, bobbing up and down in a pleasing fashion, and Agnes was impressed by his skill in judging how much to cut.

'Is that all?' he asked.

'Yes.' Jane nodded.

'Sixpence ha'penny,' he said as he handed Jane the cheese. 'And what can I get for thee?' he asked Agnes as he took his payment and dropped the pennies into the cotton pouch he wore tied around his waist above his white apron.

Agnes was about to shake her head and walk away, but the sight and smell of the cheese was tempting and she remembered the extra pennies she'd been paid.

'How much can I get for fourpence?' she asked.

'It's thruppence farthing for half a pound. I can't weigh owt else,' he told her as he reached for the cheese wire again. 'Though it'd be a shame to waste what's left. I'd rather sell it cheaper than take it back with me.' He picked up the remaining portion and held it out for her to inspect. The tang of it made Agnes, hungry for her tea, want to sink her teeth into it there and then.

'Three pounds left,' he told her. 'I can let tha have it all for one and fourpence.'

'All right!' agreed Agnes, quickly calculating that at less than thruppence a half-pound it was a bargain. 'I'll take it,' she said as her fingers scrabbled in her purse for the money and the stallholder wrapped the cheese in a fragment of muslin for her to carry it home.

'What are you going to do with all that?' asked Jane as they walked away. 'It'll be cheese for every meal until it goes mouldy.'

'It'll not go mouldy,' Agnes told her. 'I've got an idea.'

When Agnes reached the house on Mary Ellen Street where she lived with her mother and sister and brothers, she put the cheese on the kitchen table. Her mother stared at it and then at her as if she'd gone mad, and then Agnes saw the anger and disbelief cloud her face.

'How much did you pay for all that?' her mother demanded.

'One and fourpence. It was cheap.'

'But that's almost the whole of your wage!' Her mother stared at the cheese. 'What am I supposed to do with it? It'll be off before we can eat it all. And how do you expect me to pay the rent and get coal and candles now that you've spent all your wages?' Her mother sounded upset and worried, and Agnes felt guilty about what she'd done. Standing at the market stall it had seemed such a good idea, but now she wondered if she'd made a huge mistake.

'I still have sixpence. Mr Reynolds paid me a bit extra,' she explained, putting the silver-coloured coin down on the table beside the cheese. 'And it's not all for us. I'm going to offer it round the neighbours at thruppence for half a pound. It'll bring in one and six. That's tuppence clear profit.'

'And what if they don't want it?'

'I'm sure they will. Everybody likes a bargain,' said Agnes.

'And how will you weigh it?' asked her mother.

Agnes hesitated. In her enthusiasm it was something she hadn't thought of. Then she recalled the stallholder.

'I just need to cut it into six equal pieces,' she said. 'That won't be hard if you let me use the sharp knife.'

Her mother shook her head. 'I don't know,' she said. 'I wish you hadn't bought it.'

'It'll be all right,' Agnes reassured her, hoping that she had made the right decision.

Before she began to cut the cheese, Agnes went to the sink in the scullery to scrub her hands and nails. She'd noticed that the man who sold her the cheese had very clean hands and she'd felt ashamed of her dirty nails as she paid him. Agnes knew that no one would want to buy from her whilst her hands were still soiled from the rag warehouse, so she poured some of the boiling water from the kettle into a basin and picked up the scrubbing brush and the cheap soap that was all they could afford. It stung the cuts and nicks on her fingers and made her skin red and sore, but she was determined not to touch the cheese until her hands were spotlessly clean.

Once she was satisfied, she went to fetch the one sharp knife that they owned. Her mother had been using it to slice bread, so Agnes dipped it into the pail of water by the scullery sink and wiped it on a clean cloth.

Then she came back to the table and held the knife over the cheese. Now that the moment had come to slice it, she was beset by doubts. She was afraid that when she cut into it, the cheese would crumble, and no one would want to buy crumbs. But Agnes was aware that her mother was frowning with worry and her little sister Maria had come to stand on the other side of the table to watch. She couldn't back down now and admit that she'd made a mistake. She had to prove herself.

The first cut cleaved the cheese neatly into two equal portions and Agnes let out the breath she'd been holding. Judging the distances with her eye, she carefully reduced each portion into three pieces. There were some crumbs that fell away, but the slices didn't fall apart and she was content that she'd done a good enough job.

Agnes put the knife down and reached for the muslin. 'Bring me the scissors,' she said to Maria and her sister hurried across to the drawer where they were kept and brought them, handing them to Agnes, handles first as she'd been taught, and waiting to see what would be done next.

Agnes spread the muslin on the table and cut it into six pieces. She placed one portion of the cheese on each, adding the crumbs to the ones that looked a little undersized, and wrapped them tightly.

'Get the shopping basket,' she said to Maria. 'You can come with me and we'll go knocking on some doors to sell it.'

'You can bring one piece back if you don't sell it all. But no more than one,' warned her mother. 'We don't want to be eating nothing but green cheese for a week.'

Agnes nodded and wrapped her shawl around herself again before slipping the handle of the basket over her arm. She wondered if she would even dare to come home if she couldn't get her money back. She hadn't expected her mother to be so upset.

At the front door, Agnes met her brother, Timothy, coming home from his work. He was a post boy and general assistant for Mr and Mrs Sharples who ran the post office and hat shop on Church Street. Timothy was out and about in the open air for much of the day delivering letters. He was provided with a uniform: dark trousers and matching jacket, and a jaunty hat. And he wore a satchel slung over his shoulder to hold the post. But the thing that really made Agnes envious of her brother was that Mr and Mrs Sharples sent him to the Sunday school at the parish church, where he was learning to read and write and do simple arithmetic.

'Where are you off to?' he asked curiously.

'We're selling cheese!' announced an excited Maria before Agnes had a chance to reply.

'Cheese?' he repeated, looking into the basket. 'Where's that come from?'

'I bought it on the market. They were selling it off cheap at the end of the day and I'm hoping to make a profit,' Agnes told him.

Timothy looked doubtful. 'What does Mam say about it?' he asked.

'She's furious,' admitted Agnes as she went to knock on the door of their nearest neighbours, Wilf and Edna.

'Come in!' shouted Wilf, and when Agnes stepped inside she was met by a thick fug emanating from his pipe as he sat in a wooden chair by the fire, a cushion tucked into the small of his back and his stockinged feet perched on the fender where Agnes feared that a spark from the tumbling coals might suddenly set his socks alight.

'What can I do for thee?' he asked.

'I've some cheese for sale,' Agnes told him, holding up the basket. 'I bought too much at the market and thought I'd share it with any neighbour who might want a bit. It's fresh today,' she added. 'Proper Lancashire cheese from the farm.'

'Tha'll have to ask our Edna. She's in charge of such things,' said Wilf, waving his pipe in the direction of the stairs. 'She'll be down in a minute.'

Agnes stood awkwardly in the neighbour's parlour, trying not to cough until Edna descended the steep wooden steps.

'Thruppence for half a pound,' Agnes told her, holding out one of the small packages.

'Aye, I'll have one,' agreed Edna. 'Let me get my purse.'

With thruppence in her purse and only five wedges of cheese left, Agnes felt more enthusiastic as she knocked on the next door. Those neighbours, too, bought a piece, commenting that they'd seen it at fourpence on one of the market stalls that morning and had decided it was too expensive.

Agnes was only halfway down the street by the time she'd sold all the cheese and recouped the money she'd spent with tuppence profit.

'That was fun!' exclaimed Maria as she skipped beside Agnes, back to their own door. 'Can we do it again?'

'I don't see why not,' replied Agnes as a plan began to take shape in her mind. If she bought leftover cheese at a cheap enough price every Saturday and then sold it on, she could make herself a few extra pennies every week, and her mother couldn't be angry with her about that.

'Well?' asked her mother gloomily when she and Maria came back in. 'Is it going to be cheese for every meal?'

'No,' Agnes told her. 'I sold it all.'

She emptied the coins from her purse on to the table and counted out the shilling that she owed her mother.

'No need to give me a penny back this week,' she said, feeling elated. 'I made my tuppence profit!'

'Well, you should save it,' advised her mother. 'It does no harm to have a bit put by. And don't you dare do something so foolish again,' she warned her. 'You were lucky it turned out all right today, but it might not have done!'

Agnes didn't reply as she turned to put the basket back on the shelf and hang up her shawl. She could feel the tears welling in her eyes and didn't trust herself to speak. She'd thought that her mother would be proud of her and tell her that she'd done well, and agree that it had been a good idea after all. But her mother's words had made it very clear that she still disapproved, and Agnes felt angry and disappointed that she wasn't prepared to encourage the enterprise.

She was still feeling misunderstood when she sat down at the table with her sister and Timothy and her younger brother Peter. As her mother said grace she wondered if it was worth defying her and buying more cheese the following week anyway. Agnes was tired of the hand-to-mouth existence that they were forced to lead, and she could see nothing wrong in trying to make things better.

She still remembered that terrible day on the boat from Ireland after they'd been forced to leave their home. They were supposed to be going to a fresh life in the New World, far across the ocean – the land of opportunity, people called it – and her mother and father had said how lucky they were to have been given tickets by their former landlord. But the boat had been disgusting. The deck was full of animals and their dung and urine had soon spread to where the passengers were sitting as a storm had risen and washed seawater across the wooden deck. Then a bell had begun to ring and people had started praying and crossing themselves and saying that they were sinking. Agnes still shivered as she remembered the terror that had filled her when the mast had snapped in the relentless wind, and she couldn't rid her mind of the sound of the screaming boy who'd been trapped beneath it.

Her father had jumped up and pushed through the crowd of people to try to help raise the mast high enough to free the boy. In her mind's eye, Agnes could see him now as he bent to grasp the splintered wood and heave and heave along with some other men in an attempt to shift it.

It was her last memory of her father. She couldn't clearly recall what had happened next, but another ship had come and people had begun to slide and slither across the deck in a desperate attempt to reach it before the *Sirius* went down.

Agnes remembered the expanse of sea, the rolling grey waves, the salty spray lashing her face, and her fear as a man had shouted at her to jump. When she'd hesitated, she'd felt herself grasped and tossed into the air. The moments had lasted for ever. It was as if time had slowed right down and Agnes had looked at the sea beneath her and noticed that her petticoat was billowing out above it and that she could see right through a hole in it, and her feet looked an odd colour because they were so cold, and the people on the decks of both ships seemed so small and they were all staring up at her. She'd thought that this must be what it was like to be one of the seagulls who soared and circled in the sky, except that she wasn't soaring or circling, she was falling and then the deck was rushing up towards her and she was afraid and it jarred hard as she hit it, but hands had grabbed at her and pulled her up, although it had taken a while for her to recover her senses and realize that she'd been saved.

Timothy and Maria and little Peter had all been thrown on to the deck of the rescue ship, where they'd clung together and watched their mother, with the baby in her arms, as she'd stood on the *Sirius* with the waves around her knees. Her mother had refused to jump and a man had tried to throw her across, but she didn't make it and went into the water, and Agnes had felt such a panic that she would never see her again. But then her mother had appeared in the waves, gasping and flailing, and a man had grabbed her by the hair and pulled her into a lifeboat. But the baby had no longer been in her arms.

'Don't let your tea go cold. Get it eaten!' said her mother, bringing Agnes back to the present.

She picked up her spoon and filled it with the stew her mother had prepared. Potatoes, carrots, parsnips and some lumps of fatty mutton that Agnes knew would be chewy.

'Better than bread and cheese,' added her mother.

'It's good. Thank you,' said Agnes, knowing how hard her mother worked to earn enough to buy even a scrap of meat. She certainly wasn't ungrateful. She knew how difficult life was for her mother without a husband to provide for them. It was why she was determined to help ease her mother's burden.

## 2

The next day Agnes had the luxury of a little more time in bed before she got up to go to mass at St Alban's. They went as a family and had done almost every week since they'd come to Blackburn. The church was the one most of their friends attended too. Her mother clung to the other Irish residents, especially Aileen and Michael Walsh, who had been so good to them when they'd arrived penniless and forlorn in the unfamiliar town, in search of cousin Nan.

Agnes sometimes found the churchgoing tedious, but it was the only social life they had. Her mother didn't like them to mix with anyone who wasn't *one of them*. Agnes knew that this meant anyone who went to any of the other churches in the town. Her friend Jane went to the protestant church called St John's, but her mother had forbidden her to set foot in the place. Her fear was palpable, and Agnes had always gained the impression that her mother thought she would be cast into the fires of hell if she ever went inside. But Agnes knew that Jane was a good person and when her friend had confided that her mother said exactly the same thing about St Alban's, they'd laughed about it and Jane had invited her to go to the evening service with her.

But Agnes had made an excuse. She knew it was probably silly, but her mother's genuine fears preyed on her imagination and she was slightly afraid herself of what she might find behind the sturdy wooden doors of the town centre church.

Now, they filed into their usual pew and Agnes drew her shawl more closely around her shoulders against the chill. She knew Father Kaye well and the Latin words of the mass washed over her like a blessing. It was a peaceful hour in the midst of their busy lives, and today Agnes was content to sit awhile and not feel guilty about being idle.

As she allowed her mind to wander, she became aware of someone glancing at her from a pew on the other side of the aisle. It was Patrick Ryan, the eldest son of Rory and Bridie Ryan who all worked at the Pearson Street Mill.

Agnes tried not to smile, but knew she'd failed when she felt her mother nudge her with a sharp elbow. She clasped her hands and stared at them, trying to ignore her admirer, but the idea that a boy might find her attractive made her feel giddy inside. And even though she had no particular feelings for him in return, it pleased her to be the recipient of such attention.

After the service, they came out into the churchyard and her mother fell into conversation with their friends, Michael and Aileen. Agnes stood alone, keeping an eye on Maria and Peter as her younger brother, bursting with the frustration of having been kept sitting still for far too long, ran up and down the path with his sister chasing him.

Looking round, she saw Patrick standing a short distance away, also waiting for his parents to stop talking so they could go home for their dinner. He gave her a brief smile. Agnes knew that he was about the same age as her, though he looked younger. His frame was thin and gangling, as if his arms and legs didn't quite belong to the rest of his body. His hair was dark and slightly curly, springing in unruly tufts around his head where it had been inexpertly sheared, probably by his mother in their back kitchen. His Sunday best clothes seemed too small for him, and Agnes knew that as soon as there was money to buy him something bigger from the second-hand clothes stall on the market, what he wore would be passed down to one of his younger brothers who were milling around, threatening to begin a play fight.

She also knew that it was a distinct possibility that she might be married to Patrick one day. The problem was that there were very few young men in Blackburn who were part of the Catholic community, and it would leave her with a limited choice other than becoming an old maid and never having a home or family of her own.

'Come on,' urged her mother, her conversation at an end, sounding as if Agnes was the one who had been keeping them waiting for far too long.

Agnes caught hold of Peter's arm as he careered past her and dragged him to a halt.

'Dinnertime!' she told him to prevent any tears of protest, and along with Maria and Timothy they fell into step behind their mother to walk back to Mary Ellen Street and eat their Sunday meal, which would be nothing more than their usual potatoes and bread. Perhaps she should have kept back a piece of the cheese, thought Agnes, eager for the taste of something flavoursome.

After they'd had their meal and washed up the plates and put them away, Timothy went off to his class at the Sunday school. Their mother had been reluctant to let him go at first when she'd discovered it was held in a room that belonged to the protestant church, but the Sharples had insisted he must have some education if he was to work for them, and her mother had been forced to agree if Timothy wasn't to lose the opportunity they'd given him.

Agnes had to stay behind, beside the meagre fire, and mend the holes and tears that had appeared in their fragile clothing throughout the week. As she watched her brother walk down the street from the front window, Agnes felt consumed with jealousy. She wanted to learn how to read and write. And although she'd learned about weights and money at the rag shop, she longed to know more. She wanted a book like the one Mr Reynolds had where she would be able to note down what she paid for cheese and how much she sold it for, so that her profits would be marked for ever in indelible ink for all to see. Because she'd decided that she would buy the cheese again, no matter what her mother had said.

'Come away from the window. You're blocking out the light,' her mother told her.

Agnes returned to the stool by the hearth and picked up her work. Maria sat opposite, already industriously sewing with neat little stitches. Peter was playing on the floor with some toys that their mother had found when she was out gathering rags. The wooden horse was missing a leg and the tin soldier had only one arm and no musket, but Peter had pleaded to keep them and for once her mother had indulged him.

'Patrick Ryan seems sweet on you,' remarked her mother after a while.

Agnes paused, then continued to weave the woollen thread in and out of the warp she'd created to darn the sock she was holding.

'Does he?' she replied warily.

'He seems a nice boy. He has work. Decent family,' her mother commented.

'Don't you think I'm a bit young to be thinking of boys?' Agnes asked.

'You're going on for seventeen!' replied her mother. 'I was married with a child at your age.'

'But that was in Ireland.'

'What difference does that make? I'd like to see you settled and Patrick Ryan seems suitable. Would you like me to speak to his parents?'

'No!' Agnes exclaimed. 'I don't want to get married yet.'

'He'll wed some other girl if you let him get away,' warned her mother. 'There are more girls than there are boys here. You don't want to be left lonely.'

Agnes pursed her lips over her work and didn't look up. She knew that her mother's ambition for her was to be a happily married wife and mother, but she had other things on her mind for now, and if she found herself married to Patrick Ryan she'd never be free to follow her own dreams. There'd be a baby before the year was out and more would follow until there was a houseful of them and few wages to feed them all.

'I'm not in love with him,' she said.

'Love grows,' her mother told her. 'Security is more important. It's a hard world for a woman alone. I know that better than most.'

Agnes knew that what her mother said was true and she felt sorry for her. Life had been desperately hard for her since they'd arrived in this country. At first, her mother had clung to the hope that her father had been saved from the ship and would come and find them. But as the days and weeks had passed, she'd been forced to acknowledge that he was most likely drowned, the tickets to America lost along with him, and that she would have to bring up her four surviving children alone. Work had been hard to come by, and women were only paid a fraction of what men could earn. She'd never dared to ask for help or charity for fear that they would be sent back to Ireland for being a burden, and rag gathering had been the only way she could earn anything at all. It was difficult and tedious work. It meant getting up before first light to find the best of what had been lost or thrown out during the night. And there were others who scoured the streets beside her mother. The competition was fierce and there were sometimes fallings out, and it was always the men who came off best in a disagreement.

If it hadn't been for the Walshes, they would never have survived their first weeks here. Cousin Nan, on whom they'd pinned their hopes, had turned out to be an old woman who was barely better off than they were themselves. But help had come in the end, from the Andertons and the Sharples. Mr and Mrs Anderton, who owed them nothing, had gone out of their way to help them. They'd found them this house to rent and provided a bit of furniture, and Mrs Anderton was always giving them gifts. And John Sharples, who was Nan's son, had employed Timothy even though his wife had been disapproving at first, and Timothy had proved himself by hard work and application. But even so, Agnes knew that her mother's struggle would have been so much easier if she'd had a husband to share the burden.

Agnes fastened off the darning and snipped the excess thread away with the scissors. The darn looked bulky and she feared it would rub a blister on Timothy's heel, but there was no money to buy new socks at the moment and they had to make do and mend. She wondered whether to broach the subject of the cheese again but decided not to. She didn't want to spoil the peace of the Sunday afternoon with an argument. Instead, she folded the sock together with its partner, picked up the next item that needed attention and held up her needle to the light to thread it.

## 3

The next Saturday evening, when the other workers were leaving the warehouse, Agnes hurried to be at the front of the queue for wages.

'Tha's keen to get off early tonight,' remarked Mr Reynolds. 'Hast tha got a young man to walk out with?'

The tone of the question was more serious than the rag man's usual teasing and Agnes hoped he hadn't heard some rumour about her and Patrick Ryan. Despite telling her mother that she wasn't interested in any matchmaking, she'd caught sight of her chatting to his mother, Bridie, on the street corner. She'd prayed that nothing had been said about her, but she feared that her mother had ignored her wishes, thinking that she was simply too shy or didn't understand that her choices were limited.

Agnes was well aware that her prospects were limited, and that was why she was keen to leave her work promptly and get down to the market to see if she could repeat her enterprise of the week before and purchase some cheap cheese.

She didn't even wait for Jane, she was so keen to get there. As she hurried along in the fine mist of the evening that was turning rapidly to a persistent drizzle,

Agnes pictured in her mind the portion of cheese that she would buy – bigger and better and lower in price than it had been the previous week.

The market was busy, and when she reached the stall she saw that there was a queue and the stallholder was slicing and wrapping the cheese with his usual dexterity. Agnes hung back. She knew that he wouldn't sell the cheese off cheaply if he thought there were still customers who would pay full price. She'd been so eager to get here that she was too early. It would have been better if she'd waited for Jane and walked with her through the stalls, browsing what was on offer for a while until she saw the cheesemonger beginning to pack up his wares.

Feeling frustrated, she turned away and walked across the cobbles to the door of the market house. It would be dry inside, at least, and she could wander about until she thought it was a better time to ask for a bargain. The smell of the indoor market was familiar, but one which Agnes couldn't have explained if asked what it consisted of. It seemed to be a mixture of the cloths and fabrics, the raw meat on the butcher's stall, the cold sliced hams, the sweet stall, the stall that sold coffee by the cup along with glasses of sarsaparilla, all mixed with the pungent smell of fish from the far side of the building. She wandered through the crowd of women with baskets over their arms, who were asking the prices of the apples and potatoes and cabbages as they went from stall to stall to see where the best purchases could be had.

Agnes paused by a stall selling printed calico. She would have loved to buy a length of the material to make a new summer gown. Stitching something new for herself wouldn't seem so tedious as mending, she was sure. But for now she was determined that any extra pennies she made would be used to buy more produce to sell on. It would be silly to squander her small profit on luxuries when it could be put to better use.

It was only when she reached the far side of the market, a place she usually avoided because she hated the smell of the fish, that she saw there was another cheese stall, not so large as the one outside. It was devoid of customers and she approached it cautiously, wanting to compare prices. The stallholder was a young man. Not much older than herself, thought Agnes as she was momentarily distracted from her task by his eager smile.

'Can I help you?' he enquired as he got up from the stool where he'd been sitting.

'How much a pound?' she asked.

'Sixpence,' he said.

Agnes quickly calculated that she would need to buy at a cheaper price than that to make any profit. Thruppence for half a pound was what she'd charged her own customers the previous week, and she knew they wouldn't pay more this time.

'My mother makes it herself,' said the lad. 'All the milk comes from our own cows.'

Agnes nodded. 'You've got quite a lot left,' she

observed as she pointed to the wheel of cheese. She reckoned that there must be about six pounds in weight.

'I know.' His smile faded and he looked serious. 'It's the first time we've come to this market,' he confided. 'We usually have a stall at Preston where my father stands, but he said I should try my hand at selling too, but there's another cheesemonger outside and everyone seems to be going there.'

'I don't suppose they'd think to come inside for cheese,' Agnes said. 'It's all fish at this end.'

The lad wrinkled his nose in agreement. 'Aye. I've been standing next to it all day,' he said. 'I think I'll stink of it for weeks.'

Agnes couldn't help but laugh at his gloomy face. She felt sorry for him and wanted to buy a piece of his cheese to cheer him up. But good sense prevailed as she reminded herself that she'd come looking for a bargain, not to be taken in by a morsel of charm and a sorry countenance.

'I doubt I'll be able to sell it all now,' said the lad. 'And my father won't be pleased if I go back with so much . . .' He stopped speaking and Agnes realized he suddenly regretted opening up to her. 'How much would you like?' he asked hopefully.

'How much for all of it?' she asked, wondering if she would have enough money. Mr Reynolds had paid her extra again and she still had her tuppence from last week. But that was only two shillings in total.

The lad stared at her as if he thought she was crazy.

'All of it?' he repeated.

'Aye,' said Agnes. 'I'll consider taking it all – at the right price.'

The lad looked doubtful. 'I suppose I could reduce it to fivepence ha'penny a pound,' he said.

Agnes knew that she didn't have enough to pay that. It would have to be reduced by more than a whole penny a pound for her to be able to afford it. She knew that was too much to expect and she began to regret asking for it. She didn't want to look foolish in front of this lad by having to withdraw her offer.

'I can't go any lower,' he said. 'My father'll probably kill me as it is.'

'Weigh it,' said Agnes, hoping that it might be less than the six pounds she'd guessed.

She watched, biting her bottom lip as the lad placed it on the scales and began to add the weights to balance them.

'Five pounds and eight ounces,' he announced as the cheese on the pan rose in response to his last placement. 'That's . . .'

'Two shillings and sixpence farthing,' said Agnes before he could calculate the right price. He stared at her in confusion, then searched for a scrap of paper and a pencil to scribble down the figures to check that she was correct.

'That's right!' he said after a minute or two. 'How did you know?' he asked, as if he was accusing her of some sort of trickery or magic.

She ignored his suspicions, wondering if she could borrow the extra money. If only she'd waited for Jane she might have been able to persuade her friend to lend it to her. She could have paid her back before bedtime.

'Well? Do you want it?' he wanted to know as she stood thinking. She knew he wouldn't keep a portion of it back. It would have to be all or nothing to get the bargain she wanted.

'You'll knock off the farthing, won't you?' she said with as much confidence as she could muster. 'Everybody does,' she told him. 'Stallholders can't be bothered with them. Call it two and six?' she ventured.

'All right,' he agreed.

'Can you give me five minutes?' she asked.

His face clouded over and he looked morose. 'I might have known you were just messing me about,' he grumbled as if he thought she'd been playing with him all along.

'No, I'm not,' she protested. 'I haven't got quite enough,' she confessed, deciding that truth was her best option.

'Well why say you wanted to buy it then?' he asked. Agnes could see that his hopes of pleasing his father by selling all the cheese were plummeting with each passing second. He'd hoped she was his salvation and now he thought she'd let him down.

'Five minutes,' she pleaded. 'Just wait five minutes and I'll get the money. I promise.'

'All right,' he agreed reluctantly. 'But if you're not

here in five minutes, I'm packing up and going. I'm not going to stand around like a fool waiting for you if you've no intention of coming back.'

'I'm not playing a trick on you!' Agnes told him. 'Honestly, I'm not. I genuinely want to buy your cheese. I just need a few more pennies, that's all.'

He didn't reply and with a glum face took the cheese from the scales and began to wrap it up. He was obviously cross and thought he'd fallen for a trick, and Agnes felt bad.

'Five minutes,' she repeated. 'Don't go anywhere.'

As the lad began to take the weights off the scales and pack them into a box, Agnes turned away and dodged through the stalls as quickly as she could to the entrance of the market house. Outside, she began to run through the rows of stalls, desperately trying to catch sight of Jane. But her friend was nowhere to be seen.

Panting, Agnes hesitated. She guessed that her five minutes was up and she was no nearer to borrowing the money she needed. There were just two things she could do. The sensible one would be to go home with her two shillings in her purse and forget all about her enterprise. The other was to run back to the warehouse to see if Mr Reynolds was still there and beg him to lend her sixpence until Monday morning.

It wasn't a difficult decision. Agnes ran as fast as she could, as if her life depended on it, until she turned the corner into Clifton Street and saw the tattered effigy that was the sign of the rag shop, illuminated by the sputtering gas lamp. Mr Reynolds had just turned his key in the door and was leaning on the handle to check it was locked when she arrived, gasping and unable to speak.

'Agnes? Is that thee? What on earth's to do?' he asked in alarm. He glanced up the street to where she'd come from. 'Is someone after thee?'

She shook her head as she waited to regain enough breath to speak. 'I need a favour,' she gasped. 'Will you lend me sixpence until Monday? Please?'

Mr Reynolds put his key away in his pocket and looked at her with concern. 'Why dost tha need sixpence?' he asked. 'Tha's just had thy wages. Tha's not lost them, has tha? Tha's not been robbed?'

'No. No,' she reassured him. 'I want to buy some cheese.'

'Cheese?' he repeated, as if he thought he hadn't heard her correctly.

Agnes nodded. 'A big piece,' she said, using her hands to estimate the size. 'It's to share amongst my neighbours. You'll get your money back,' she told him, hoping that she would indeed be able to repay him.

He stared at her for a moment, then put his hand into his pocket and brought out some coins from which he selected a sixpenny piece.

'I hope I don't regret this,' he said as he gave it to her. 'But I know tha's a sensible lass and I trust that tha knows what tha's doin' over this cheese business.'

'I do,' she told him. 'I'll pay you back. I promise I will. But I have to go. If I'm not back in a minute it'll be gone.'

Agnes set off running back up the street. 'Thank you!' she called over her shoulder as she went, leaving the curious rag dealer staring after her.

With the coin clutched in her palm and a stitch in her side, she ran and walked and jogged as fast as she could until she reached the market house, attracting a fair bit of attention as she pushed people aside to reach the cheese stall.

For a moment, she thought her mission had been for nothing. The stall looked empty and she feared the lad had gone. But then his head popped up from under the trestle table and he stared at her in disbelief.

'I'd given you up long since,' he said, sounding surprised.

'I know. I'm sorry. It took longer than I thought. Do you still have the cheese?' she asked, hoping that he wasn't going to say he'd sold it to someone else.

'I've packed it away.'

'Well, can you unpack it?' she asked. 'I have the money now.'

It was only when Agnes was walking home, with an empty purse, sixpence in debt and the cheese cradled in her arms, that she wondered if she could have bargained for an even better price.

As soon as she'd shown him the money, the lad had

eagerly given her the cheese. A smile of pleasure had lit his face and Agnes knew he was looking forward to telling his father of his successful sales. She smiled ruefully to herself. It would have been a bit cruel to reopen the negotiations and with luck she would make her profit easily. Her main worry was facing her mother. Agnes knew that she wouldn't be pleased.

'I cannot believe what you've done!' her mother exclaimed, staring at the huge amount of cheese that Agnes had placed on the kitchen table. 'I told you last week, so I did, not to be so foolish a second time.'

'It was cheap,' replied Agnes. 'I can make a profit again.'

Her mother was shaking her head and looked close to tears. Suddenly, Agnes was filled with regret. She knew how short money was, and she was sorry to add to her mother's worries.

'I suppose it's too late to take it back?' asked her mother, staring at the offending item.

'It is,' Agnes agreed. 'The stallholder was packing up to leave.'

'With a smug smile on his face, no doubt,' replied her mother. 'He must be laughing all the way home to have offloaded all this on to you.'

Agnes didn't think the lad would be laughing at her. She hoped not, anyway. But she knew that the only way she could pacify her mother was to get the cheese sold and prove her wrong.

She hung up her shawl, lifted the kettle from the hob

and took the hot water to the sink where she scrubbed her hands and nails. Then she washed the sharp knife and set about dividing the cheese into eleven neat portions. The half-pounds looked larger than they had the week before, she noticed, and she wondered whether the lad had weighed it incorrectly. Still, that wasn't her concern.

When it was all cut, Agnes wrapped the portions, placed them in the basket and went to the door.

'Can I come?' asked Maria eagerly. Agnes nodded.

They knocked on Wilf and Edna's door and Agnes was aware of her increasing heartbeat as she anxiously responded to the call to *come in*.

'I've got cheese again. Same price as last week. Thruppence for a half-pound.'

'Aye, I'll take some,' agreed Edna. 'We enjoyed it last week, didn't we, Wilf?' she asked her husband who was sitting with his feet on the fender again. Agnes could smell his socks.

She handed a portion to Edna, thanked her and on they went. She was knocking on the next door when she saw Timothy on his way home.

'Cheese again?' he greeted her.

'Yes. But Mam's upset about it,' she warned him as he headed for their own front door. 'Will you tell her that it's selling? It'll cheer her up.'

The door in front of Agnes opened and she showed Mrs Taylor her basket.

'Step inside a minute,' she said. 'I'll find you the money.'

With every sale, Agnes added the money to her purse with relief. She was only turned down twice, and by the time ten pieces had been sold she had the two shillings and sixpence that she'd spent. She could give her wages to her mother now and pay back Mr Reynolds, and if she could sell the last piece, she would be thruppence better off.

'Shall we try the next street?' she asked Maria.

'Yes. Let's go!'

Agnes was cheered on by her sister's enthusiasm. It helped to quell her own doubts. She didn't know the people in the next street and was worried that she might not be given such a friendly welcome.

Agnes knocked on the first door. A moment later there were steps and she heard voices in the lobby.

'Who's knocking at this time of night?' someone asked.

The door was opened a fraction and an elderly man peered out at her.

'Good evening,' she began. 'I live in the next street and I have some cheese for sale. Thruppence a half-pound if you're interested.'

'Who is it?' called a woman's voice from inside.

'Young lass selling cheese,' replied the man over his shoulder.

'Cheese?' came the voice and a moment later the owner of it appeared from the back of the house and scrutinized Agnes and Maria.

'Tha didn't tell me it were them Irish lasses,' the

woman accused her husband as if Agnes couldn't hear her. 'They belong to that woman that gathers rags,' she went on. 'Tell them to go away.'

'I fancied a bit of cheese,' complained the man.

'It'll be underweight and mouldy,' his wife told him.

'It's fresh from the market today and it's a full half-pound,' protested Agnes, wishing she hadn't knocked here. It was much harder to sell to strangers rather than friends.

'Aye. And I'm a monkey's uncle,' replied the woman with a sniff. 'Shut yon door, our Bert!' she ordered her husband.

The man shrugged. 'Sorry,' he said and firmly closed the door in Agnes's face. She turned away, feeling disappointed, but not entirely surprised. She knew it was why her mother insisted on them only mixing with the people they knew. There was often hostility from the Lancashire residents who made it quite clear that they weren't welcome here.

'Let's go home,' she said to Maria, wishing she could have shielded her sister from the woman's outburst.

'No,' protested Maria. 'Let's try another door.'

'No. I think we'll take the last piece home,' Agnes said. 'Cheese and bread will be nice for our tea tomorrow.'

'So you couldn't sell it all?' observed her mother when she got back.

'I could have,' Agnes told her. 'I just thought it would be nice for us to have some. You don't need to give me any money for it,' she added. She saw her mother soften at the gift.

'Thank you,' she replied, if a little ungraciously as she unwrapped the muslin and looked at the cheese. 'It seems nice.'

'It's made on a local farm. The lad on the stall said his mother makes it with their left-over milk.'

'A lad, was it?' said her mother and Agnes thought she heard a disapproving tone. It annoyed her. All she'd done was strike a bargain with him. She hadn't agreed to walk out with him.

He had been nice looking, though, she thought as she hung up her shawl and put the basket away, remembering his face, rosy cheeked from being in the fresh air, and his overlong fair hair. He was better looking than Patrick Ryan, that was for sure. She wondered if he would be at the market again on Wednesday, and she found that she was wishing away her Sunday off, to bring the day closer, in the hope that she might see him again.

# 4

'There's your sixpence,' said Agnes to Mr Reynolds as soon as she arrived at her work on the Monday morning. She pushed the coin across the shop counter towards him.

'It worked out then?' he asked. 'Tha sold the cheese?'

'I did.'

'Tha'll be turnin' into quite the businesswoman soon,' he remarked.

'It was only a bit of cheese,' she replied, her cheeks flushing.

'Little acorns and all that,' he told her. 'I only started out small,' he went on. 'I began by picking rags, but then I realized that the middle men, so to speak, were taking a fair whack of the profit when they sold stuff on. So I decided that I'd try dealing with the paper mills myself. It weren't easy,' he warned her. 'Some of them laughed at me when I first went to see them, saying they needed huge quantities, but I persuaded 'em I could send enough and I rented a little shed to store what I found until I had enough for my first sale. I went hungry,' he told her, 'because I was keepin' my rags myself rather than sellin' them on. But I were determined, and even though I had to borrow money to hire my first horse and cart to transport rags to the paper mill, I was sure I could turn a profit. It were a risk, of course,' he said. 'Business always is, but look at me now. It were worth it.'

Agnes began to sort out the morning's finds, looking for things that were good enough to go into the shop for sale. There were a couple of items: a rug that had only a small hole burned in it where a cinder had fallen from a fireplace, and a vase that was cracked – even though it would no longer hold water, it was still decorative and far too good, in Agnes's opinion, to be put in with the rubbish. It often surprised her what folks would throw out, especially the gentry who lived on King Street and Richmond Terrace.

She washed the vase and took the rug outside to hang it over a washing line and give it a good beating to remove the dust and dirt. They were serviceable objects that would fetch a decent price in the shop. When she'd first started this task she had always shown her finds to Mr Reynolds and asked him what price he wanted for each item. But now she knew that he trusted her to get the best price. The trick was, Agnes had learned, not to ask so much as to put potential buyers off, but to ask for a little more than you really wanted, so that customers could barter with you and go away feeling proud that they'd got a bargain.

She wondered if she really did have a head for business. Lots of people thought that only men could have a trade and that women didn't have the brains for it. But

Agnes knew this wasn't true. Take Mrs Sharples at the hat shop. Of course most people thought that Mr Sharples, the post master, was the one who ran both parts of the shop, but when Timothy came home from his work he often said it was Mrs Sharples who was the one who made many of the decisions and that Mr Sharples always listened to what she had to say. And there was Mrs Anderton as well. Agnes knew she ran her dressmaking business herself without needing to rely on her husband to add up her figures and keep her accounts. Then there were the women who ran the beerhouses in the town centre. And the washerwomen. And the woman who came to the market from Southport to sell shrimps. No one questioned their right to ply their trade. So why shouldn't she get into business? Agnes hoped that Mr Reynolds might encourage it. She had, after all, proved herself capable of borrowing a sixpence and paying it back.

As she worked, Agnes considered what her employer had told her. He'd known that taking only a handful of cloths to the paper mill had been no use. He'd had to work with bigger quantities to be taken seriously. And when she thought about the cheese she'd bought and sold, she wondered if the same principle were true. Buying a few pounds of cheese and selling it for a small profit had brought her in a few pennies, but it was hardly a business. If she wanted to take it seriously, she would have to find a way to buy and sell on a much larger scale.

On the Wednesday, which was the next market day, Agnes didn't go home as usual for her dinner, but went to look at the stalls.

The man who sold cheese on the outside market wasn't there, but his wife was, wrapped warmly against the cold March day in two shawls, a bonnet and some fingerless gloves that allowed her to work whilst still keeping her hands warmer than if they'd been bare. Her cheeks were a ruddy red with the broken veins prominent in the bitter wind. She was stamping her feet to bring back some feeling to them when Agnes approached, hoping to see what was for sale and at what price, but wary of approaching too closely and being mistaken for a customer.

The aromas and sight of so much food on the stalls made Agnes's stomach rumble with hunger. She wouldn't have time for her customary slice of bread and dripping and a cup of tea, but she remembered that Mr Reynolds had told her that he'd gone hungry when he first started his business and she decided that she must learn to discipline herself or fail before she even began, no matter how tempting it was to spend some of her precious pennies on a hot potato or a freshly baked pie.

There were several cheeses on the stall, along with butter and eggs. Agnes wondered if it was the produce of just one farm, or if the cheesemonger bought the produce from different places. She watched as a couple of women made a purchase, the stallholder's wife neatly slicing the cheese with a wire and weighing out the pats of butter on her scales, lifting them between the two wooden paddles that she'd shaped them with. The customers paid the money and turned away seemingly pleased.

'What can I get you?' asked the woman. Agnes caught her eye and blushed.

'I'm just looking,' she said, feeling embarrassed at being caught out.

'You'll not get better, or fresher,' the woman said. 'Or cheaper! We pride ourselves on our prices!'

Nodding, Agnes backed away, hoping the woman wouldn't think her rude. She wanted to go to check if the lad she'd bought from on Saturday had his stall inside.

It was slightly warmer in the market house as the smell of fish guided her to the right spot, but Agnes was disappointed to see that the place where the stall had been was empty.

'I was looking for the cheese stall,' she said to the nearest fishmonger.

He shook his head. 'There's just the one outside today,' he replied. 'There were a lad here t' other day, but I don't think he found it worth his while.'

Agnes was disappointed. Although she'd told herself that her trip to the market was purely to learn more about the business of selling cheese, she had to admit that the thought of seeing the lad she'd chatted to was also a draw. She'd been thinking about him since the weekend and had even dreamt about him. And in church, on Sunday morning, she'd closed her eyes and wished that it was him in the pew on the opposite side of the aisle glancing at her time and again during the tedious sermon.

'I bought some cheese from him on Saturday,' she told the fishmonger. 'I think he said he was from out of town?'

'Aye. Told me he came from a farm at Samlesbury Bottoms.'

'Do you know his name?' asked Agnes.

The fishmonger shook his head. 'We didn't talk that much,' he said. 'I were doin' a brisk trade even if he were sitting there twiddling his thumbs for most of the day. I'm surprised he sold owt at all. Never even tried calling out his wares. Waste of time,' he commented as he turned away to serve a woman with a fillet of haddock, telling her she'd not find better quality at his price no matter how many other stalls she visited.

Disappointed, Agnes walked back to the rag warehouse. She had to admit that she'd been looking forward to seeing him again, but if what the fishmonger had said was true, she feared that the lad would never come back to Blackburn market.

At the warehouse, she saw that a queue had formed of the rag gatherers bringing their finds to be weighed in. Her mother was there, with Maria and Peter.

'There you are!' exclaimed her mother. 'Why haven't you been home for your dinner?'

'I had an errand to run,' she told her. Her mother looked suspicious.

'What are you up to?' she asked. 'Not meeting some-one?'

'No!' said Agnes. She could be truthfully indignant, she thought, as she realized her mother's mind was still on her marriage and she was worried that Agnes had been meeting a boy. 'I have to get on with my work,' she added as she moved away to the front of the queue and popped the bag of nails that were handed to her on the weighing scales.

It wasn't long before her mother reached the front of the line and Agnes weighed the bags of cloth – one white, one coloured – and calculated the payment in her head. Fear of being accused of cheating made her extra careful and she always gave her mother the exact money she was owed and not a farthing more.

'I spoke to Bridie Ryan,' her mother told her as she put the money away. 'She said that Patrick's taken quite a shine to you.'

Agnes felt annoyed and frustrated as she listened to her mother. She knew that she was warning her against taking up with another lad – one who wasn't a part of their community.

'I don't like him,' she muttered, tight-lipped. 'I wish you hadn't mentioned it.'

'Don't go getting ideas. That's all I'm saying,' replied her mother as she turned to go.

Without answering, Agnes turned to the next person in the queue and pulled her face at the stench of bones in the man's sack. 'Take them over there,' she told him, more sharply than she intended. 'I can't weigh greasy bones on these scales.'

If her mother knew about the ideas she had, Agnes suspected she would be even more disapproving than if it had been about a boy. Agnes knew that if she was serious about selling cheese, she would need to borrow the money to buy in bulk and it was a risk her mother would not want her to take.

# 5

The next Saturday, Agnes once again went to the market after work with her money in her purse. The day before, on the Friday, she'd been tempted to go to the market in her dinner hour, although in her heart she'd known that the lad wouldn't be there. She was hoping that he might have returned for the weekend market.

She tried not to hurry even though she was keen to see if he'd come, and she waited whilst Jane collected her wages and got her shawl and walked with her across the cobbles to where the rain was dripping off the canvas roofs of the outside stalls.

'Are you buying cheese again?' she asked her friend.

'Aye. My mam likes a bit of cheese.'

'I could get it for you cheaper,' offered Agnes and explained that she'd cut up a large portion of a cheese for her neighbours for the previous two weeks. 'I've sold it for thruppence for half a pound. It seems a shame for you to pay more than you need to.'

'I wouldn't mind saving a ha'penny or two,' agreed Jane.

'Do you think any of your neighbours might be interested as well?' asked Agnes.

'Everyone likes a bargain.'

By this time, they'd reached the outside cheese stall, but Agnes was disappointed to see that most of it had gone. There wouldn't be any chance of cheap leftovers there tonight, she thought.

'Fivepence ha'penny a pound! Thruppence for half a pound!' called out the stallholder as they approached. 'You'll not get it cheaper!'

'That's a bargain!' Jane exclaimed, but Agnes grasped her arm and pulled her back.

'There's sometimes a better place inside,' she told her as she took her friend's arm to lead her towards the door to the market house.

Jane was reluctant. 'It's the best price I've seen for weeks and if I don't buy a piece now it'll all be gone and my mam will be disappointed,' she complained.

'Well, it's up to you,' said Agnes, eager to go inside. 'But you'll end up paying more than you need to.'

Jane trailed behind her as Agnes threaded through the crowd to the far side of the hall. Her heartbeat increased as she caught sight of the lad and her stomach turned a flip that surprised her with its intensity.

He recognized her and greeted her warmly. 'Hello. I was hoping you might come.'

'I was hoping you might be here,' said Agnes, trying not to smile too broadly.

'Have you come for cheese? I've got plenty,' he said, pointing to a half cheese that had been cut into and another one that was still whole. 'Trade's been a bit slack,' he admitted.

'I'm not surprised,' said Jane. 'Everyone goes to the stall outside. I didn't even know there was another cheese stall in here. How much are you charging?' she asked.

'Sixpence a pound.'

'The stall outside are selling for fivepence ha'penny,' she told him. 'I'm going back there. I just hope it's not all gone.'

'Is it true?' asked the lad as Agnes watched her friend pushing through the shoppers, obviously cross at being brought in here when she could have bought cheaper at the first stall.

'Yes,' Agnes said, turning back to him. 'He's shouting out that price to anyone who's near. I expected you to be selling for less.'

'I didn't know. I've been stuck in here all day wondering why trade was so bad. I didn't realize he was undercutting me.'

'He must have sent someone in to see what you were charging,' said Agnes as she realized what had been done. The cheesemonger outside, worried that he had competition, must have decided to cut his prices to discourage the lad and his family from coming again.

'Aye. He must. It seems a bit of a shabby trick,' complained the lad. He looked glum and didn't have to tell her that his father wouldn't be pleased with him if he took so much unsold cheese home at the end of the day. But whilst she sympathized with him, she was also wondering if she could turn things to her advantage.

'I could buy what you've got left,' she offered. 'I'll have to go and get the money. But I came back last week,' she reminded him. 'You can trust me.'

He looked doubtful. 'It's a lot of cheese,' he told her. 'That full wheel is twenty-five pounds and there's at least fifteen pounds left of the other one. That's forty pounds weight altogether.'

'I'll not pay more than fivepence a pound to take it all,' Agnes said, quickly calculating that she would need around sixteen shillings and sixpence, depending on the actual weight. She wasn't sure if Mr Reynolds would be prepared to lend her that much, but she decided it was worth a try. 'Surely it's better than having to take it all back with you,' she cajoled.

The lad shrugged his shoulders briefly as if he thought she was nothing more than an annoyance. 'I doubt you can get that kind of money,' he told her.

'But if I can get it and I come back, will you sell to me at that price?'

'I'll give you half an hour,' he told her. 'That's when my father's coming to pick me up.'

'All right,' Agnes agreed.

She hurried out of the market house, hoping that she could keep her promise. When she passed the outside stall, the cheesemonger was still calling out his bargain to potential customers. Agnes was worried that he might have reduced his price again, but he was left with so little cheese he had no need to, and word must have got round the market because she saw that there was still a queue to purchase what was left.

Knowing that she had little time to spare, she ran down the streets towards the rag and bottle shop, hoping to catch Mr Reynolds before he left and persuade him to lend her some money again. To Agnes, sixteen shillings seemed a huge amount of money to ask for, but she knew that Mr Reynolds dealt in much larger amounts than that and she hoped that he wouldn't refuse her, especially since he'd encouraged her to become a businesswoman.

Agnes turned into Clayton Street to find it deserted. The moppet was swinging above the door, but it looked like Mr Reynolds had locked up and gone. She put her face to the glass and knocked, but there was nobody inside. She ran down to the corner and around the back, but the high wooden gate that opened into the warehouse yard was closed and secured with a padlock. She was too late.

Her first thought was to go around to Mr Reynolds's house. She knew that he lived not far away on Mill Lane, although she wasn't sure which number. When she reached the right street, she chose a door where she could see a light and knocked. She stood hopping from one foot to the other and wishing she knew how much time had passed, and when no one came she knocked again more insistently.

'Who is it?' called a woman's voice.

'I'm looking for Mr Reynolds!' she shouted back,

praying that chance or providence had brought her to the right door.

Agnes heard the sneck being lifted and the door opened a crack. An old woman peered out at her.

'Reynolds?'

'Yes. Do you know him? I work for him at the warehouse and I need to speak to him urgently.'

'Number eleven,' said the woman, pointing a swollen and crooked finger towards a house on the other side of the street. 'Lives alone,' she whispered as if it were a sin. 'But he won't be there. He never comes back this early.'

'Do you know where he might be?'

The woman shook her head. 'No idea,' she replied and closed the door.

Agnes went across and knocked on number eleven anyway. She could feel the woman watching from behind her curtains, probably insulted that Agnes hadn't taken her at her word. She'd been right though. No one answered the door. There was nobody at home.

Disappointment washed over her. What now?

She walked back up the street desperately trying to think of a solution. Who else was there who would have that amount of money to spare? None of her friends, that was for sure. She doubted that Father Kaye would raid the poor box for her. If she'd had anything to sell she could have tried the pawnbrokers on Shorrock Fold, but she owned nothing of value. There was John Sharples, Timothy's employer. Or their landlord, Mr Anderton.

He and Mrs Anderton had been so good to them in the past and Mrs Anderton was always trying to help her mother. But did she dare go and knock at their door and ask for money? Agnes hesitated, feeling unsure of herself, but then she remembered Mr Reynolds telling her about his struggles to succeed. Nothing came easily, she told herself. If she was serious about making money then she must take some risks, and even if Mr Anderton refused her she would be no worse off – except for never being able to see that lad again. She didn't even know his name, she thought as she set off again at a run towards King Street. She ought to have at least asked him what he was called.

# 6

Agnes knocked on the door of the Andertons' house and then retreated down a couple of the steps that led up from the street. All the way here she'd been trying to plan what she was going to say, rehearsing the words in her head before dismissing them and thinking of better ones. She hoped that Mr Anderton would be at home and wouldn't ask too many questions. She was aware of the minutes ticking away and it was clear to her that she had no chance of getting back to the market house within the half-hour deadline. She was afraid that even if her mission was successful, the lad would be long gone before she returned.

The door was opened by the Andertons' maid. Agnes knew her name was Dorothy although she would never have dared address her in such a familiar way, so, not knowing what her surname was, she always avoided calling her anything at all.

'Is Mr Anderton in, please? I'm Agnes, Agnes Cavanah.'

'Aye. I know who tha is,' said Dorothy. 'Best step inside. It's not thy mother, is it?' she went on. 'She's not poorly?'

'No, nothing like that. I wanted to beg a favour.'

Dorothy looked doubtful. 'Wait there,' she said. 'I'll tell him tha's here.'

Agnes watched her climb the wide staircase. She'd climbed it herself once, a few years ago now, on the night before they went to live on Mary Ellen Street. Her mother had been so fed up with Blackburn that she'd decided they should leave and go to try to find work in Stockport, but the Andertons had come after them and persuaded them to return. They'd been brought here to spend the night until the house they could rent had been prepared, and Agnes still remembered the bed she'd slept in, in a room up those stairs. The mattress had been stuffed with feathers and it had been the softest bed she'd ever known. When morning had come she hadn't wanted to leave it, and even now she wished that she could go up there and lie down on it. She'd never known such luxury before or since, but it was something she aspired to. How she would love to have a home like this, she thought, as she looked at the polished bannisters and the framed paintings on the walls.

Her daydream was interrupted by Mr Anderton coming down the stairs.

'Is everything all right, Agnes?' he asked, looking concerned. 'Dorothy says you need a favour?'

'I do,' replied Agnes. 'Would you lend me some money? Please?' she burst out – the politely worded request she'd rehearsed in her mind forgotten in her desperation. 'I'll pay it back,' she added.

'What's this all about?' he asked her. 'Are you in some sort of trouble?'

'No!' she told him. It was the same question Mr Reynolds had asked. Why did people always assume she was in trouble? 'I want to buy some cheese,' she explained.

'Cheese!' Agnes could see that Mr Anderton was trying not to laugh at her. 'How much do you need for some cheese?' he asked, drawing out a handful of coins.

'Sixteen shillings,' she told him and watched an expression of disbelief and astonishment cross his face.

'How much cheese are you thinking of buying?'

'There's a full wheel and about half a wheel,' she said. 'It'll be around forty pounds in weight and I've struck a bargain to buy it for fivepence a pound. But I have to get back before the stallholder goes.'

'It's a lot of money to ask for,' he told her. 'And I don't think you can offer me any securities.'

'What's that?' asked Agnes, not understanding what he meant.

'It's something of value that you could give me so that I wouldn't lose out if you couldn't pay back the money. Do you have anything that's worth sixteen shillings?'

'No.' Agnes shook her head.

'And then there's the matter of interest,' went on Mr Anderton. 'Do you know what that is?'

'No,' admitted Agnes, beginning to regret that she'd come.

'Well,' he told her. 'When one person asks another

for a loan they usually pay back a little bit more than they borrow as a reward. That's interest.'

'I see,' said Agnes. It was clear that Mr Anderton was going to refuse after she'd demonstrated her ignorance. Maybe she wasn't clever enough to be a businesswoman after all. She turned towards the door feeling disappointed. Mr Reynolds had never asked for anything extra. He'd been pleased to help her out, but she supposed that borrowing sixteen shillings was a bit different from borrowing sixpence.

'No. Don't leave,' called Mr Anderton. 'That's not how to do business. You have to convince me it's a good investment of my money. What do you plan to do with all this cheese?' he asked her, obviously curious.

'I'm going to cut it up and sell it on to the neighbours,' she explained. 'I know I can make a profit because I've sold some for the last couple of weeks and had a few pennies left over, and this cheese is even cheaper. I borrowed sixpence from Mr Reynolds last week and paid him back on Monday morning, but he's gone home and I can't find him, otherwise I would have asked him. But I know I'll be able to pay you back by Monday,' she assured him.

He nodded as he listened to her. 'Well, you have a good idea,' he told her. 'So I've decided that it's a risk worth taking.'

'Really?

'Yes,' he said. 'I'm willing to take a chance and give you what's called an unsecured loan. That means if you can't pay me back I will lose all my money.'

'But I will pay you back!'

'We'll see. But I'm going to add a penny interest. So you'll need to pay me back sixteen shillings and a penny. Will you agree to that?' he asked.

'All right,' agreed Agnes. It was clear that she had a lot to learn.

'Wait there,' Mr Anderton told her. 'I'll be back in a moment.'

He was as good as his word and within minutes, he came back from his office with the money in a little cloth bag which he emptied on to the hallway table and counted out so that she could see he wasn't cheating her.

'Where are you going to buy this cheese?' he asked her when he was sure she had the money put securely away.

'A stall in the market house. He said he'd wait half an hour, but I think I might have been longer than that.'

'You could do with someone to walk with you,' advised Mr Anderton. 'Where's your brother?'

'I don't know.'

'I'll tell you what,' he said. 'If you wait just a moment whilst Miss Dorothy fetches my hat and coat, I'll walk with you. I wouldn't want to risk losing my investment to a petty thief.'

Minutes later, Agnes was walking up King Street with Mr Anderton at her side. In one way she was glad of his protection, but in another she was frustrated because she wanted to run all the way back to the market and she couldn't expect an important man like him to run. She was also concerned about what the lad would think. She'd been so keen to prove herself as a businesswoman that she didn't want him to think she needed a man to help her complete her purchase.

When they reached the market house she saw that the superintendent was waiting at the big double doors, a bunch of keys in his hand, waiting to lock up.

'Can't go in now. Everyone's gone. I'm shutting up,' he told them.

'But I've come back for some cheese. From the stall near the fish market,' Agnes protested, embarrassed to look foolish in front of Mr Anderton.

'Oh him!' exclaimed the man. 'He's the one I'm waiting for. Never known anyone take so long to pack up. Anyway, here he comes now,' he added as he jangled his keys impatiently.

Agnes heard the sound of a squeaky wheel on the barrow that the lad was pushing down the deserted aisles towards the main door. He'd put on a cap and fastened a muffler around his neck over a thick coat. He looked surprised when he saw her.

'I'd given you up,' he said as he glanced at Mr Anderton. 'Who's this?' he asked.

'Mr Anderton has agreed to loan me the money to buy your cheese,' Agnes replied.

'Him?' asked the lad as the superintendent ushered him clear of the doors so he could draw them shut and turn the key in the lock. 'Can you trust him?'

'Of course I can trust him! He's our landlord,'

explained Agnes. 'Look, I have the money. Let me take the cheeses.'

'Show me,' said the lad as he parked his cart under a street lamp so that he could see the coins that Agnes was offering him. He seemed wary and it was obvious he didn't trust her or Mr Anderton and suspected that they had set out to rob him.

'Here.' Agnes offered the money again. 'Count it. There's sixteen shillings for what cheese you have left over.'

'But sixteen shillings is less than fivepence a pound.'

'Do you want it or not?' she asked, feeling exasperated. She wanted a bargain and she was sure he didn't really want to take so much cheese home.

The lad looked at the money she was holding out and after a moment's consideration he agreed.

'All right then,' he said. 'It's yours.'

He lifted the whole wrapped cheese and the part cheese from his cart and set them down on the cobbles. Then he stowed the money inside his coat and picked up the handles of his barrow to go on his way.

'Wait!' said Agnes. 'I can't carry it home all on my own.' She looked around to see if Mr Anderton would do her another favour, but he had disappeared into the night now that he'd seen the transaction done. Agnes hoped he hadn't slipped away because he'd been upset by the way the lad had spoken about him. She knew that many people didn't trust black men, but Mr Anderton was as honest as the day was long.

'I don't live far away,' she told the lad. 'Would you bring it to my house in the barrow?'

'My father's expecting me. He's coming in the cart to pick me up.'

'But he's not here yet,' argued Agnes, waving a hand towards the empty market square where the outside stalls had been dismantled and packed away until the next market day. There was nothing left now except some piles of rotted fruit and a few scraps of material blowing in the wind. For a moment she wondered if she should run and gather them up for her mother to take to the warehouse, but she knew she needed to concentrate on her own affairs.

'It'll only take five minutes. Ten at the most,' she told him. 'I'll pay you sixpence,' she offered. 'When we get to my house,' she added, not sure that he wouldn't try to cheat her in return.

The lad looked doubtful. 'I don't know,' he said. 'Where's that man gone?'

'Home probably,' said Agnes. 'He's not waiting to rob you if that's what you're thinking!'

The lad didn't reply. It was clear that it was what he'd thought.

'Please? You wouldn't leave me stranded, would you?' she implored him.

'All right,' he agreed after a moment and Agnes bent to help him as he lifted the cheese back into the barrow.

'This way,' she told him as he pushed the squeaking barrow beside her.

As they walked to Mary Ellen Street, Agnes realized that if she was to buy so much in future, she would need to get a barrow like his, hopefully one that didn't make so much noise, she thought as she saw some girls laughing at them as they went by.

The town was growing busy again after the lull in which people had gone home to eat. Young couples were coming out again to visit the beerhouses and taverns, or to see the latest play at the Theatre Royal or to join in the singing at the assembly rooms. Agnes wondered what Mr Reynolds would say if he saw her. She allowed herself to imagine that she was walking out with this good-looking lad and as people passed them by and stared in their direction, she hoped that they would think they were indeed a couple, although she feared that it was the incessant squeaking of the barrow that was attracting the attention.

'I don't even know your name,' she said as they walked. She'd been longing to ask him before, but the moment had never seemed quite right.

'Jonas,' he told her. 'Jonas Marsden.'

'I'm Agnes Cavanah.'

'You don't sound local,' he said. 'Where are you from?'

'From Ireland,' she told him.

'Did your father come here to work in the mills?'

'No. We were going to America, but there was an accident. Our ship went down. My father was drowned.' She hated having to explain her circumstances to people. It always made her feel uncomfortable.

'I'm sorry,' said Jonas, keeping his eyes averted from her as if he regretted asking.

'My mother works hard to keep us,' Agnes went on. 'It's why I want to help her. I can make a few pennies' profit selling the cheese,' she confessed, hoping that he wouldn't think she was taking advantage of him.

When they reached the corner of Mary Ellen Street, Agnes slowed her pace. 'We're nearly there,' she said, wondering what her mother was going to say when she saw how much cheese she'd bought this week. 'I can manage from here.'

'I'll wheel it to your door,' Jonas replied. 'I may not get my sixpence otherwise.'

Agnes got out her purse and felt for the small silver coin.

'I'll pay you,' she reassured him, holding it out as they reached the door of number four. 'Just put the cheese on the doorstep,' she told him. 'I'll carry it inside.'

She would have loved to invite him in and offer him a cup of tea, but she quailed when she heard footsteps from inside and her mother flung open the door.

'There you are!' she exclaimed. Agnes heard the relief in her voice, but it was quickly replaced with horror when her mother saw the cheeses.

'What's all this?' she demanded as she looked from the cheeses to Jonas and then back to Agnes. 'What in the name of all that's holy have you done now?' she demanded.

Agnes's cheeks flushed and she was glad of the

darkness so that Jonas wouldn't see her shame. 'It's just some cheese,' she said, trying to sound as if it was of no importance and hoping that her mother wouldn't make a scene.

'Have you lost your mind, Agnes? Please tell me you haven't bought all this? Where did you get the money? And who are you?' she asked Jonas, glaring at him.

Agnes regretted not insisting that Jonas leave her at the street corner. She didn't want him to meet her family in these circumstances and feared he would want nothing more to do with her after this.

'I'm Jonas Marsden,' he said. 'Your daughter asked me to help her bring the cheeses, so I did.'

He reached to lift them out of the barrow and put them on the doorstep at her mother's feet. Then he touched his fingers to the brim of his cap, grasped the handles of the barrow and hurried away down the street. The sound of the squeaking faded, but never slowed as he made his hasty retreat. Agnes felt mortified and she was furious with her mother for making her look foolish in front of the farmer's son, but she knew that she needed to keep calm if she was to convince her mother that she hadn't made some terrible mistake.

'Where did you get the money to buy all this?' her mother asked again. 'How much did it cost?'

'Mr Anderton lent me the money. He thought it was a good idea,' replied Agnes, pleased that she'd gone to their landlord with her request. She knew her mother respected him and was less likely to keep shouting at her if she knew her purchase had come with his approval.

'Mr Anderton?' repeated her mother as if she couldn't quite believe it. 'How much did he lend you?'

'Shall we take it inside?' asked Agnes as she heaved the smaller portion of cheese into her arms. She didn't want to have this conversation on the doorstep where the whole street would be peeping out from behind their curtains to watch what was happening.

'How much did you borrow?' her mother asked again when the cheeses were on the kitchen table and the front door was shut.

Agnes was reluctant to tell her but knew she had no choice and that she would have to be honest. A lie would be too easily found out, and besides, she'd done nothing wrong. Once the cheese was sold she would pay her debt.

'Sixteen shillings,' she said quietly.

For a moment her mother simply stared at her and then, as the colour drained from her face, she clutched the edge of the table and sat down.

'And Mr Anderton gave you that much?'

'Yes. I explained to him why I wanted it and he thought it was a good idea.'

'Did he?' Her mother sounded as if she didn't believe it.

'Why would I say it if it isn't true?' asked Agnes. 'He wouldn't have lent me the money if he didn't think he was going to get it back. Once I've sold the cheese I'll pay him.'

'But how will you sell so much?' asked her mother, looking at the creamy white rounds that were stacked on the table.

'Same as last week. I'll take it around the neighbours once it's cut into pieces.'

Agnes hung up her shawl and went to scrub her hands. It would take a while to cut so much into portions and she was keen to get out and knock on doors with it before it got too late and folks locked up and went to bed.

As she washed the sharp knife, she thought again about a cheese wire and how much simpler it would make things. She needed to buy one, she realized, so that there would be less wastage, and some weighing scales too. It was all very well to estimate each piece, but she didn't want her customers to complain that they were being sold underweight portions.

'What are you going to wrap them in?' asked her mother as she watched her making her cuts. 'There's not enough cloth there for every piece.'

Agnes was silent for a moment, concentrating on her task, and then she wiped the blade of the knife to clean it between separating the slices as she considered her mother's question. It would add to her overheads if she had to buy more muslin.

'Do they need to be wrapped?' she asked, thinking out loud. 'If I put a clean cloth at the bottom of the basket and cover them over with another one, they should be all right. When people buy it at the door they can put it straight on to a plate.' It would work well enough for now, although she was beginning to realize that her enterprise was much more complex than she had first thought.

'I suppose so,' said her mother as she went to a drawer and took out two clean white cloths. 'You can use these,' she offered.

'Thank you,' said Agnes and watched as her mother lined their wicker shopping basket with one. She was pleased that her mother had decided to help. 'I know it seems a lot of money,' she said, wanting to reassure her. 'But I can make a profit. I know I can.'

'I hope you're right,' said her mother as she sat down again. 'Sixteen shillings is a fortune. We'd never be able to pay back that amount.'

'Don't worry. It'll be all right,' Agnes told her, hoping that she had made the right decision. There were a lot of portions of cheese to arrange in the basket and she began to doubt that she could sell every last piece tonight. She thought about Jonas, sitting at his stall all day with no customers. She could see that he'd been relieved when she'd bought everything he had left, and she prayed that she hadn't been a fool.

'Who was that lad?' asked her mother.

'He was just the stallholder,' she replied.

'So why had he not sold all this on the market?'

'He wasn't in the right place. And the stall outside was undercutting his price, but he didn't know.'

'Maybe everyone who wants cheese has already bought it cheaply,' suggested her mother.

Agnes hesitated with the knife held over the last part of the wheel. The less there was, the more difficult it was to cut, and she knew she needed a steady hand.

'Not everyone goes to the market on a Saturday,' she said, hoping that she was right and there would still be customers eager to buy from her.

Once the basket was full, Agnes set off with Maria to go door to door. Wilf and Edna were enthusiastic when she knocked.

'I hoped you might come,' Edna told her as she fetched her purse. 'There was none left on the market tonight.'

Agnes didn't tell her that there had been another stall in the market house. It made no difference now anyway. She simply murmured that she was pleased to help out, put a portion on Edna's white plate and stashed the payment in her purse.

She and Maria made their way down the street. Many of the neighbours knew why she'd come when they saw her on the doorstep and only one refused the offer of a bargain. But after they'd knocked on the doors of Mary Ellen Street, there was still so much cheese left that Agnes began to have serious doubts. Where was she going to sell the rest of it? The memory of the vile words that had been aimed at her and her sister the previous week once they strayed beyond their own street still rang in her ears and she was reluctant to expose Maria to that sort of hatred again. But Agnes knew that she couldn't let her mother or Mr Anderton down.

'I think you should go in now,' she told Maria. 'I'll just try a few more houses.'

'But I want to come!' protested Maria.

'It's getting late. It's nearly your bedtime,' Agnes said.

'I don't want to go to bed yet! I want to come with you. Why are you being so mean?'

'I'm not being mean.'

'Then why can't I come?'

Agnes didn't know how to reply. She couldn't tell her sister the truth, that she didn't want her to hear more abuse.

'Perhaps we should both go in,' she said at last. 'We've sold quite a lot and it is getting late. We could go round some more streets tomorrow, after church, when it's daylight.'

Maria was still reluctant, but more willing to go home if Agnes went with her. And maybe it was for the best, thought Agnes. Folk were bound to be suspicious if someone knocked on their door so late. It might be better to go tomorrow, and the cheese would take no harm on the stone slab overnight.

# 7

Next morning Agnes sat in their usual pew and wished that Father Kaye would finish his sermon. Even knowing that Patrick Ryan was desperately trying to catch her eye didn't amuse her today. She kept looking straight ahead as if she was concentrating wholly on the priest's words when she was, in fact, making a mental list of the streets and courts where the members of the Irish community lived so that she could go there first to sell her cheese that afternoon.

At last the service was over, and they spilled out into the fresh spring morning. There was a keen wind whipping down from the surrounding hills, and Agnes still needed to keep her shawl wrapped over her best dress for warmth, but there was a promise of better weather in the air and as soon as she thought she wouldn't freeze she knew she would discard the garment.

She was restless as her mother chatted with Michael and Aileen, sharing tales of who had found what and where during the previous week. There'd been great excitement about the rug that had been discovered in a back alley off Heaton Street. Agnes already knew all about it. Old Tatty Barnes had brought it into the warehouse and she'd given him a good price for it, but apparently there was now speculation that it hadn't been put out for the rag gatherers after all, but had been hung over a line to be beaten and had dropped to the floor whilst the maid had gone to answer a knock at the front door. Michael was telling them the house owners were furious and were threatening to bring in the constable. Not that anything could be done, thought Agnes. The rug had been sold and was no longer in the rag and bottle shop, and even though she knew the name of the purchaser she would never reveal it. Mr Reynolds had taught her that much.

'Well, we'd better be going,' said her mother at last. 'We're off out to tea this afternoon with the Ryans.'

'Are you now?' replied Aileen as her attention turned to Agnes. 'Are you going to be sharing some good news with us soon?' she asked.

'I'm hoping so,' said her mother.

'They'll make a lovely couple,' observed Aileen as she beamed at Agnes. 'He's a nice lad.'

'What's this about going to tea at the Ryans?' burst out Agnes as soon as they'd moved out of earshot.

'Did I not tell you?' asked her mother, acting the innocent.

'You know you didn't tell me!'

'I'm sure I did.'

'You did not!'

'Well, it's all arranged.'

'But I'm going out selling the rest of the cheese this afternoon.'

'You can't do that!' her mother told her. 'It's Sunday. You can't go out selling on a Sunday.'

'Why not? I've been to church.'

'Well, it's not right. You can't trade on a Sunday. That's why the shops have to close.'

'I was going to go door to door.'

'People won't buy on a Sunday. There'd be no point. Anyway, I've accepted Bridie's invitation so we'll have to go. She'll have got everything ready.'

'Is Timothy coming?' asked Agnes.

'No. He'll be at his class. But we'll have to take Maria and Peter. I'll make sure they eat plenty of potatoes before we go so they won't be hungry. I don't want them to look greedy. And don't you eat too much either,' her mother warned.

'I'm not going,' replied Agnes. She was furious that her mother had played such a trick on her. There was no way she was going to be forced into a marriage with Patrick Ryan.

'You will go,' her mother told her. 'It's time to think of your future.'

Agnes didn't reply. She dropped back so that she was walking behind her mother and didn't have to speak to her as she wondered how she could get out of the ordeal. The thought of having to spend hours in the Ryans' small parlour with Patrick grinning at her was more than she could bear.

Whilst her mother dished out the stew that had been keeping warm in the small oven beside the fire, Agnes went to check on the cheese. It still looked fresh, but she knew that if it began to show any signs of mould she would be unable to sell it and then she would be in debt to Mr Anderton with no way of paying him back. She said as much to her mother, but the answer was the same – people wouldn't buy on a Sunday and they were going to tea with the Ryans.

After they'd eaten and Timothy was getting ready to go to his class, Agnes wondered whether to entrust the sale of some of the cheese to him.

'Who would I sell it to?' he asked after she'd whispered her plan, not wanting their mother to overhear.

'Shh!' She warned him to be quiet.

'They're all like me at the school,' he muttered to her. 'They've no money. And they're not interested in cheese. Most of them can't wait for the class to finish so's they can run outside and play football.'

Agnes saw that it was hopeless. Part of her wanted to defy her mother by taking the basket of cheese and going around the streets with it anyway, but she couldn't bring herself to do it. She'd never disobeyed her mother. They'd always been supportive of one another before, especially in the early days after her father had been lost when her mother had needed her to be strong. Agnes had thought that her mother saw her as a friend as well as a daughter, but over the last few weeks their relationship seemed to have shifted as her mother had become determined to marry her off.

At four o'clock, after Agnes had spent the afternoon

sitting and fuming as she did the mending, her mother said it was time to go.

'Brush your hair,' she told her. 'You need to look nice.'

Agnes put away the needle and threads she'd been working with. She said nothing but brushed her hair anyway, wondering if she could sneak out with her basket after they came home. There might be some potential customers who would buy from her on a Sunday evening.

'Wrap some cheese for the Ryans,' her mother told her. 'Make it a full pound.'

'I didn't bring it home to give it away,' snapped Agnes as she threw her shawl around her shoulders then fastened the ribbons on her bonnet.

With the cheese neatly wrapped in a scrap of muslin, she walked sulkily beside her mother to Pearson Street. The houses there were recently built, unlike their home on Mary Ellen Street which was an ancient cottage. They all belonged to the mill owner who'd built them for his workforce and allocated them to those workers he knew would keep them in good order, with scrubbed steps and sills, freshly washed windows and clean curtains. The street itself was much wider than Mary Ellen Street and paved with flags outside the houses and setts in the road. There were gutters that took the rainwater down into the new drainage system, and all along the street were gaslights that would be lit when dusk came. At the top of the street was the mill – a huge building constructed from red brick, like the houses, that seemed to dominate them with its tremendous size. Its rows and rows of windows were lit like fire as the low sun caught them and for today at least it was silent and its tall chimney clear of smog. But Agnes knew that everything would change by six o'clock the following morning. The pounding of the mill engine would reverberate through the walls of the terraces, dirty smoke would billow from the chimney and the street would be filled with the sound of workers' clogs clattering on the stone as they hurried to their work, keen to arrive before their pay was docked for being late.

Agnes's mother knocked on the door of number twenty-eight. The door was black but looked newly painted, and behind the net curtains that framed the front window was a leafy green plant on a tall wooden stand. The door was opened immediately and Bridie Ryan greeted her mother with a kiss to her cheek before ushering them all inside.

'Come into the parlour,' she invited them, opening the dark wooden door that led into the front room. Here there was a crackling fire, newly lit in the fireplace. Not a range like the one they had in the kitchen at home, but a grate, surrounded by green tiles and framed by a mahogany surround and mantelpiece, partly obscured by Mr Ryan and Patrick who were standing with their backs to the warmth.

'Sit down,' said Bridie, pointing to the horsehair sofa that was pushed against the wall.

Agnes, her mother, Maria and Peter arranged themselves in a row and Mr Ryan took one of the chairs on either side of the fire.

'Sit down,' Bridie told her son, pointing to a three-legged stool. Agnes watched as Patrick picked it up and came to sit beside her at the far end of the sofa, near the window. He looked bashful but managed a smile that Agnes didn't return. The sooner she could get away from here the better.

'I'll fetch the tea,' said Bridie and went to another room at the back of the house. Moments later, she was back, pushing a wooden trolley on castors that held a large brown teapot with steam gently wafting from the spout, cups and saucers with a pattern of roses, a platter of sandwiches on thinly cut bread, a yellow jelly and a seed cake.

'The cheese!' exclaimed Agnes's mother. 'Don't forget to give Mrs Ryan the cheese!'

Agnes reluctantly proffered her gift. 'I thought you might like this,' she said. 'Lancashire cheese.'

'That's very kind,' said Bridie. 'I've made ham sandwiches,' she added as she took the cheese, seeming unsure whether or not she was intended to add it to the tea.

'The ham sandwiches look delicious,' Agnes's mother told her. 'The cheese is for you.'

'Thank you,' said Bridie. 'I'll just pop it in the kitchen.'

Agnes watched as a penny of her profit was taken away.

Her mother simply didn't understand what she was trying to do. She was trying to help her, but in practice everything her mother did merely put obstacles in her way.

When she came back, Bridie poured the tea and she told Patrick to pass round the sandwiches.

Agnes took one and put it on her plate, avoiding meeting his eyes. She knew that her coming here was encouragement enough for him, and she was at a loss to know how to make him realize that she wasn't interested in him but had been coerced.

'What did you think of Father Kaye's sermon this morning?' asked Bridie.

Agnes hurriedly bit into her sandwich so she wouldn't be expected to reply. The truth was that she had no idea what had been said.

'Ephesians 5: 21 to 22,' said Mr Ryan. '*For the husband is the head of the wife as Christ is the head of the church.* But I often think you're the boss in this house,' he teased his wife.

'That's nonsense and you well know it,' she said as she passed him a cup of tea. 'All I do is remind you to put on your clogs and cap before you go out. You'd be going to work half-dressed if I didn't keep my eye on you, so you would.'

Mr Ryan laughed as his wife held out the sugar basin to him and he picked out two large lumps with the tongs then dropped them into his tea and stirred it. 'Marriage has to have some give and take,' he said. 'That's what keeps it sweet.'

Agnes wondered if they spoke to one another like this all the time, or if it was a performance, put on like the ones at the theatre, to bring the subject around to matrimony. She had little experience of married couples. Her memories of her father and mother together were hazy, and the only other example of marriage she was familiar with was Mr and Mrs Anderton. They seemed to like one another, but she rarely saw them together and never in an intimate setting like this.

'So, Agnes,' said Bridie, holding out a cup to her. 'You and Patrick are both of an age to marry and I know that Patrick likes you. What do you think of him?'

Agnes stared at her, too stunned to accept the teacup. She'd never imagined that Mrs Ryan would be so forthright. She glanced at Patrick who had turned a bright red and she felt her own cheeks flushing.

'I'm a bit young to be thinking of marriage just yet,' she stuttered.

Mrs Ryan looked confused and glanced at Agnes's mother.

'She doesn't mean that,' her mother told Mrs Ryan. 'Of course you're old enough to be thinking of marriage,' she told Agnes. 'What a silly thing to say.'

Agnes kept her eyes on the pattern of the hearthrug and wished that she was somewhere else. Anywhere but in this stuffy parlour, with these adults, who seemed determined to foist her off as a wife for Patrick Ryan.

# 8

Tea with the Ryans was excruciating for Agnes. The ham was tough, the seed cake dry and the jelly tasted of some fruit that she didn't recognize but disliked the taste of.

After the cups and plates were cleared away and Mrs Ryan had refused her mother's offer of Agnes's help to wash up, they had sat by the fire and Mr and Mrs Ryan and her mother had chatted as if she and Patrick weren't even in the room.

'He's a hard worker and brings in a decent wage. I'm sure if we speak to Mr Yates, the mill manager, he'll put them on the list for a house as soon as one comes vacant,' Mr Ryan said.

'Meantime they could live here and have the back room upstairs. It'll take a double bed,' added his wife.

Agnes shuddered at the thought of sleeping in the same bed as Patrick. But the discussions went ahead as if it was something she'd agreed to, and she couldn't help but wonder exactly what her mother had said to Bridie before this tea invitation had been extended. She was beginning to fear that the wedding would be arranged without her being able to do anything to prevent it.

'That went well,' her mother said as they'd walked

home by the light of the recently lit lamps, the air pungent with the smell of gas.

'It was a waste of time,' Agnes grumbled. 'Surely you don't expect me to agree to marrying him?'

Her mother sighed. 'I'm trying to do what's best for you, Agnes,' she said. 'It's no good having a dream of some shining knight coming to sweep you off your feet – life isn't like that. We need to be practical. Patrick's a nice, decent boy with a good job as a weaver at the mill. And you heard what they said about getting you a house. You'll not do better, so you might as well accept it. You'll look back and thank me in a year or two.'

I won't, thought Agnes, wondering why her mother was being so unreasonable. Besides, she'd never even considered a knight in shining armour. She knew that was a fairy tale. But there were other lads. Jonas Marsden, for example. Now if her mother had been keen to discuss a marriage with him she might have shown more interest.

Timothy was home by the time they arrived back. He had a fire going and was eating the cheese sandwich their mother had made for him – more profit going to waste, Agnes thought irritably.

Without even taking off her shawl, she picked up the basket and began to transfer the cheese into it.

'I'm going out,' she said, determined not to be thwarted again. She saw her mother hesitate but, now that the tea party was behind them, she nodded her head briefly. Agnes knew that she was worried about Mr Anderton getting his money.

'Can I come?' pleaded Maria.

'No,' Agnes told her sister firmly. 'It's too late. You need to go to bed soon.' She turned away because she hated to see the disappointment on Maria's face. It wasn't all that late, but she wanted to try some of the neighbouring streets and she was determined to protect her little sister.

As she stepped out of the door into the darkness – there were no lamps on Mary Ellen Street – Agnes lifted her shawl over her head. It was chilly now the sun had gone down.

She walked to the next street but avoided the house where she'd knocked previously. She began on the other side of the road.

It was much harder than she'd anticipated. At the houses where someone did answer the door, the response was always the same. A glance at the basket, then a shake of the head before the door was closed again. Some people managed to say they were sorry but they didn't need any cheese, but she found that she was mostly met with suspicion and she wondered if her mother had been right when she'd said that folk wouldn't buy on a Sunday, or if it was simply a reaction to her Irish accent that made them turn her away so quickly.

When she reached the last house and hadn't sold a single portion, Agnes decided to try something different and walked into the centre of the town, towards the empty marketplace. It was much quieter than it had been the night before. The theatre didn't open on a Sunday and the beerhouses kept their doors closed.

She walked down King William Street with the basket in front of her.

'Cheese!' she called out to anyone who passed her by. 'Fresh Lancashire cheese! Only thruppence a half-pound!'

Most people hurried by as if she was invisible, but one or two stopped and she sold four portions; it was nowhere near enough to empty the basket.

She was considering giving up and going home to face her mother when a man in a tall hat and frock coat, with his wife on his arm, came up the street. Probably on their way home from the evening service at the parish church.

'You, girl!' barked the man. 'What are you doing?'

'I'm selling cheese. Would you like some?' she asked, hoping that she might make another sale, even though the man looked unfriendly.

'I most certainly would not!' He stood over her in a threatening manner. 'You can't sell on a Sunday. There are laws against it. Best get on your way before I call out the constable.'

'Irish,' Agnes heard his wife mutter as she hurried away. The threat of the constable was one that terrified her. Her mother had always avoided anyone in authority from fear that they would all be returned to Ireland if they were ever brought to court and issued with a fine that they were unable to pay.

Agnes felt worried as she pushed open the door of her home. It would have been so satisfying to show her mother an empty basket, but her failure only reinforced her mother's view that she'd been foolish. And perhaps she had. Maybe trading in cheese hadn't been a good idea after all, and all she'd done was plunge them into a debt to their landlord that they could never repay.

Her mother looked up when she went in and Agnes saw the worried frown that creased her brow as she put the basket on the table without a word.

'Did you sell it?' her mother asked.

'I sold some,' replied Agnes, unwilling to admit that only four pieces had gone. The shilling in her purse was a long way from the amount she'd been so sure she could pay back the next day. Even added to what she'd made the previous evening, it was nowhere near the sixteen shillings she owed.

'Maybe you could sell some to the women at the rag warehouse,' suggested her mother. It was something that hadn't occurred to Agnes and she felt relieved and grateful.

'I might try that,' she said. 'I'll go in early.'

Agnes put the cheese on the cold slab. If she could sell it the next day, she would be able to pay Mr Anderton that evening.

'I think I'll go to bed now,' she said after she'd hung up her shawl. 'I'm tired.'

'We've had an exciting day,' agreed her mother. 'I'll

lock up and cover the fire, then I think I'll come up too. Monday again tomorrow,' she sighed.

Agnes went up the steep winding stairs ahead of her. The next morning would bring another busy week filled with long hours of hard work for all of them. The precious Sunday that she had looked forward to all week had been spoiled by having to visit the Ryans rather than selling her cheese. And Agnes worried that she would be expected to spend time with them every week from now on. It was too soon to consider being a married woman, she thought as she undressed quickly and slid into the bed beside Maria, who was already asleep. It wasn't fair to expect her to give up her freedom just yet, not when she thought she could make something of herself. She was sure if she'd been able to take the cheese out that afternoon, she could have sold it easily, and she felt resentful towards her mother for her interference – no matter how well intentioned it was.

Agnes plumped the pillow, making Maria turn and mutter a few words of irritation without even waking. Their mother would be up in a moment to get into the other side of the bed she shared with her daughters; Timothy and Peter slept together on a mattress tucked under the window. It wasn't that she minded sleeping in the same bed as another person, Agnes thought as she closed her eyes tightly, trying to rid her inner eye of the image of Patrick Ryan and his spotty chin; it was just that she preferred to imagine Jonas Marsden lying beside her.

# 9

Next morning, as soon as her mother stirred, Agnes got out of bed. It was still dark outside, but the first faint rays of morning light had been enough to waken her mother who knew that getting out on to the streets early was the only way to make a living from rag gathering.

Agnes pulled on her working clothes, still slightly damp from being washed, and went downstairs where the stone floor struck up cold through her feet as she poked at the remnants of the fire. It had gone out and there was neither time nor fuel to light it now. Their breakfast would be oatcakes smeared with a little of the precious treacle from the jar on the shelf and a drink of cold water.

By the time her mother came down with Peter and Maria, bleary-eyed and complaining about being dragged from their beds, Agnes was putting the cheese into the basket.

'Go and give Tim another shout,' said her mother as she put food into the children's hands to soothe them. 'We don't want him falling back asleep after we've gone and losing his job for being late. Make sure he's out of bed.'

Agnes clattered up the stairs in her clogs. Sure enough,

her brother was on his back, snoring gently. She reached for the blanket that covered him and pulled it away, but he didn't respond. She poked him in the ribs and he jumped and swore at her in protest.

'Don't let Mam hear you saying those words,' she admonished him, wondering where he'd heard such language. It certainly wasn't the Sunday school, or not until the lads were out of earshot of their teachers anyway. 'You need to get up,' she told him as she pushed him roughly off the mattress. 'I have to go. Don't fall back asleep again,' she warned as she went back down the steep, twisting steps.

Agnes hurried through the quiet streets towards the rag warehouse with her basket over her arm. She was so early that the doors were all still locked when she arrived and she waited impatiently, watching for Mr Reynolds as the boilers in the mills were coaxed into life and the smoke and steam began to billow over the rooftops.

'Tha's early this mornin',' Mr Reynolds observed when he eventually came down the street, whistling a tune. He stood for a moment as he looked through the keys on his ring until he selected the right one and slotted it into the rag and bottle shop door. 'What's tha got there?' he asked as Agnes bent to pick up her basket.

'Cheese,' she told him.

'I thought tha'd sold it all last week.'

'This is more cheese that I bought on Saturday. Do you want a piece?' she asked, turning back a corner of the cloth that covered it.

'Tha bought all that! How much did that cost thee?'

'It was a bargain,' she told him. 'I did come to see if you would lend me some money again,' she explained, not wanting him to be offended that she hadn't sought out his help. 'But you'd locked up and gone, so I asked Mr Anderton.'

'How much is tha sellin' it for?' Mr Reynolds asked as Agnes put the basket on the counter.

'Thruppence for half a pound.' She hesitated for a moment. 'I thought some of the other lasses might be interested,' she said. 'I was thinking of taking it over to the warehouse. Before we begin work,' she added, not wanting to take advantage of his good nature.

'Aye. That's all right,' he said. 'And put a piece to one side for me.' He plunged a hand into one of his deep pockets and then counted out three pennies from the change that was grasped in his hand. 'Full weight, mind!' he added.

Agnes knew that he was teasing her, but she took the opportunity to beg another favour from him.

'Is it all right if I use the scales? Just to check?' she asked. 'We don't have any at home so I had to use my eye to cut it up.'

'I'd give 'em a wipe first,' he advised her. 'There's been all sorts on there.'

Agnes was well aware of the many objects that had graced the scales in the warehouse, and once she'd boiled a kettle of water over the fire in the little cubby that Mr Reynolds called his office, she kept some back from the teapot and scoured the pan from the smallest set of scales. Then she selected eight ounces in weights and set a piece of the cheese on the pan. It was underweight and when she tried a few more pieces she realized that her guesses were not as good as she had thought. Although some of the portions were over the half-pound, some were short, and she began to worry about accusations of cheating. There wasn't much she could do about these pieces though. If she tried to cut bits off some to add to others, all she would end up with was crumbs and that wouldn't look good. She decided that she would just have to make the best of it for now and hope that no one noticed. But it was clear that she would need to use scales in the future – and that would be a huge expense, probably more than her small profits. Once again her mother's warning echoed in her head. But she closed her mind to the words. She would find a way, she told herself.

When the other workers began to arrive they came across to see what Agnes was doing. She showed them the cheese, popping it on to the scales to show them that they weren't being cheated. If she sold the full weight portions here, then she would have to try to sell the smaller ones on the street where customers couldn't expect them to be weighed in front of them.

'Thruppence a half-pound,' she repeated as her friends gathered round.

'Aye. I'll take a piece,' most of them replied, and as the basket began to empty and her purse filled, Agnes was grateful to her mother for her suggestion.

'Time to get to work!' Mr Reynolds told them after they'd been standing around chatting for a while. 'It's not a market,' he added.

Agnes quickly put her wares and her money away. She would count it up later, but she'd mentally reckoned that she'd taken three and sixpence that morning and was beginning to believe that she would be able to repay Mr Anderton before very long.

She returned to the rag and bottle shop and put the basket on the counter. Any customers who came in would be offered cheese. Mr Reynolds didn't need to know.

As it turned out, the shop wasn't that busy, but she managed to get rid of a few portions along with the sale of some cups and saucers and a picture frame. At dinnertime, she put down the sneck on the door and went towards the market square. There was no outside market on a Monday although a few of the stalls in the market house were open. There was no cheese stall to compete with her business and at the end of an hour perched on a stool she'd borrowed from the shop, Agnes had sold a decent amount of cheese from her basket and treated herself to a pie.

She was taking goods for weighing when her mother came in that afternoon. Her finds today were sparse and she seemed frustrated by the fickleness of her work. Agnes weighed everything and paid her.

'Did you get rid of the cheese?' her mother asked.

'Most of it. I sold some here and then went on the market square in my dinnertime.'

'I thought you must have done when you didn't come home. Have you eaten anything?'

Agnes nodded. The price of the pie was still on her conscience. She'd been determined not to waste any of her profit, but her hunger and the enticing aroma had broken her resolve. If she went to sell on the market again, she thought, she must make sure to take a slice of bread and dripping with her to eat.

When she arrived home that evening, she counted up what she had left. There were about a couple of dozen portions, so she decided she would go out again and take them round the courts where the Irish families lived. She knew that they were poor and probably couldn't afford such luxury, but she was reluctant to go knocking on strangers' doors again. That would have to be a last resort.

By the time she'd tried everywhere, the cheese was almost all gone, but what was left in the basket would make the difference between having a profit and maybe having to use the money she'd made the week before to pay back Mr Anderton.

She knew that it was late as she walked towards King Street, but the longer she had the cheese the higher the chance was that it would begin to go off. Agnes knew that she needed to sell it whilst it was fresh.

Outside the houses of the gentry she saw horses and carriages bringing home the residents from the assembly rooms where there had been a musical recital. Agnes knew that knocking on the front doors here wouldn't be welcomed, so she turned into the backs, where she'd once helped her mother gather rags, and she descended the steps to the rear door of the first house. These doors led into the basement kitchens of the houses and it was here that the cooks and the maids would be finishing their work before they went to bed.

Timidly, Agnes knocked and waited.

'Who is it?' called a voice.

'Cheese!' she called, feeling slightly foolish. 'Fresh Lancashire cheese!'

She heard the door being unlocked and a pale face peeped out.

'Did tha say cheese? At this time of night?' asked the woman warily.

'I've a bit left over. It's still fresh. Only thruppence a half-pound,' ventured Agnes, wondering if she was going to be sent away with a threat to call the constable.

'Show me!'

Agnes lifted the cloth on the basket and the cook seemed satisfied.

'I'll take a pound,' she said.

'Can I come again?' asked Agnes after she'd been paid. 'I can let you have it cheaper than the market stall,' she said, hoping that she could fulfil her pledge.

'Aye. Tha can come again,' agreed the cook. 'I'm not promising to buy any,' she warned, 'but tha can call again. Make it earlier in the day next time though.'

'I will,' agreed Agnes, feeling pleased with herself.

\*

As soon as she had sold the last of the cheese, Agnes counted her money twice to make sure it was all correct. She slid the three shillings and fivepence profit into her purse and bagged up the sixteen shillings and a penny that she owed to Mr Anderton. She was looking forward to paying her debt.

She went to the front door of the Andertons' house and knocked. It was the only house on the street where she hadn't offered any cheese. The truth was that she was slightly afraid of Dorothy, and it had seemed a bit unfair to expect the Andertons to buy from her anyway.

It was Dorothy who opened the door.

'I've come to see Mr Anderton,' Agnes said. 'Is he in?'

'Step inside,' said Dorothy holding the door wider as she glanced up and down the street as if to check no one was watching. 'Was it thee going door to door with cheap cheese?' she asked when the door was closed.

'Yes.' Agnes prepared herself for a telling-off from the woman, but it didn't come.

'Tha never called here,' she grumbled.

'I didn't like to,' admitted Agnes.

'Well, tha can next time,' Dorothy told her before she went to fetch Mr Anderton. 'A bit of cheese never goes amiss.'

Surprised, Agnes watched her climb the stairs and moments later she came back down, followed by Mr Anderton.

'I've brought your money,' Agnes told him, holding up the bag. 'It's all in change. I hope you don't mind.'

'Well, I hope you won't be offended if I check it,' he replied. 'That's how business is done. Come into the parlour,' he invited her. 'Miss Dorothy, will you bring a pot of chocolate for Miss Cavanah to drink whilst she waits?'

Agnes stepped through the door on to a carpet that felt so soft under her feet she was reminded of the soft Irish grass of her home. She looked around the parlour, at the plush chairs and polished tables, and the fire that was blazing in the hearth even though the room had been empty, and was amazed that the Andertons could afford such luxuries.

'Sit down,' Mr Anderton said. 'Take a chair by the fire. You look cold.'

Agnes perched on the edge of the seat, reluctant to lean back and spoil the perfectly embroidered cushion that was propped there. She watched as Mr Anderton brought a small table from the side of the room and put it between them, in front of the fire. He tipped out the contents of the bag and Agnes stooped to retrieve a fallen coin, anxious that he might think she'd tried to short-change him.

With dexterity Mr Anderton piled up the pennies and threepenny bits into stacks that each totalled a shilling, and when there were sixteen of them and one penny left over, he smiled and tumbled the money back into the cloth bag.

'Well done,' he said. Agnes smiled at his praise. 'Are you going to do it again next week?' he asked her.

'Would you lend me the money again?' she ventured. 'I've made some profit, but not enough to buy a whole wheel of cheese.'

'I would,' he told her, leaning back in his chair. 'But I'm wondering if there's a better way for you to trade your wares. The first thing you have to remember,' he advised her, 'is that you need to buy as cheaply as you can, and I'm wondering if you would be better off buying directly from the farm. If you buy from a market stall then the stallholder wants his share of the profit,' he explained. 'But if you were to buy straight from the farm, that profit would be all yours.'

'Well, Jonas – the stallholder I bought from – is from a farm,' she told him.

Mr Anderton nodded. 'He would have had to pay rental on his stall in the market house,' he said. 'If you buy directly from him that wouldn't be necessary.'

'Would the farmer sell it to me?' asked Agnes, feeling doubtful. She knew that Mr Anderton was trying to give her good advice, but she wasn't certain how it would work. 'And I'd need a way to bring it home,' she said.

'A pony would be ideal,' replied Mr Anderton.

Agnes shook her head in bewilderment. 'I couldn't buy a pony. Where would I keep it?'

'You couldn't afford one straight away,' Mr Anderton agreed. 'I'm thinking of the future. Perhaps you could settle for a barrow in the meantime – and a strong constitution to push all that weight back into Blackburn.'

Agnes recalled that the fishmonger had told her the Marsdens' farm was at Samlesbury Bottoms. She wasn't sure how far away that was. Unlike the people who had lived here all their lives, she lacked the knowledge of the exact location of all the surrounding villages. And she wasn't sure when she could go. Sunday was the only day of the week when she didn't have to work at the rag warehouse, but there was church in the morning and she feared that her mother would expect her to walk out with Patrick Ryan in the afternoon unless she could find a way to get out of it.

'Think about it,' said Mr Anderton as Dorothy came in carrying a tray on which there was a tall jug and two tiny cups and saucers. The steam from the spout filled the room with the delicious aroma of chocolate and Agnes watched as the creamy brown liquid was poured for her. She thanked Dorothy and put the cup to her lips to take a sip. The taste didn't disappoint. If anything, it was better than Agnes had ever imagined – sweet and thick on her tongue.

## 10

When Agnes had arrived home the previous evening, she hadn't repeated everything that Mr Anderton had said to her mother. She knew her mother was relieved that the money had been repaid and that she would be horrified at the idea of borrowing more.

Perhaps it was a foolish idea, thought Agnes, as she walked through the early morning drizzle to her work. There were so many factors that she'd never considered in setting up a cheese selling business. It would be easier to give up the idea than pursue it. That would take the worries away from her mother and if she agreed to be married to Patrick Ryan that would help her mother with her money problems too, because there would be one less mouth to feed. But the notion that she could make a success of her idea wouldn't let her give it up. Agnes knew she would always have regrets if she didn't try.

She knocked on the door of the shop and Mr Reynolds let her in.

'Miserable mornin',' he observed as Agnes hung up her soaked shawl to dry. 'We'll not get many customers or much in the way of rags today. Half of 'em are too soft to turn out in this weather,' he grumbled.

Agnes nodded in agreement. She knew buyers would be reluctant to come out, but most of the gatherers worked in all conditions, even if there was little to scavenge.

As Mr Reynolds had predicted, the steady rain resulted in the shop being quiet. There were only a couple of customers and only one of them actually bought anything. It gave Agnes time to tidy up and sort out some items that had been hanging around for a while. It was clear that they were unlikely to sell, so she decided that they could go back to the warehouse.

After dinner, Agnes went across the yard to help with the weighing in. Instead of the usual orderly queue, she saw that several people were crowded around something interesting that had been found and she went to see what it was.

'I thought it would help me to carry stuff, but the wheel's so wobbly it'll do nowt but go around in circles,' complained Tatty Barnes. 'But I'm hoping they'll give me summat for it.'

Agnes stared at the barrow as if it had been sent as a sign. It was old and battered, and it was true that the wheel needed mending, but it was a barrow. The very thing she needed.

'I'll buy it from you!' she said.

Tatty Barnes stared at her for a moment looking doubtful. 'Shouldn't tha ask Mr Reynolds first?'

'No. I didn't mean I'd buy it for the warehouse. I want to buy it for myself.' She quickly reckoned up in her head how much of her profit she was willing to part with. 'I'll give you tuppence,' she offered.

'Nay. I'd want more than that.'

Agnes could have kicked herself. She ought to have offered much less than she was really willing to pay. In her excitement, she'd forgotten that Tatty Barnes was a wily character who enjoyed driving a hard bargain as much as she did.

'But you've just said that it's useless,' she pointed out.

'It can be mended.'

'Get it mended then and bring it back and I'll give you thruppence,' she offered, hoping that he might agree.

'Nay.' He shook his head. 'If I could afford to get it mended then I'd keep it.'

'Take my tuppence then,' said Agnes. The crowd who'd gathered around them waited silently to hear what Tatty Barnes would say next. The man puffed out his cheeks and hummed and hawed for a while then decided that tuppence in his pocket was a better bargain than a broken barrow.

'All right,' he agreed at last, as if he were doing Agnes some great favour. 'It's thine.'

Agnes reached into her purse and gave him two penny coins before trying to push the barrow away. But as soon as she lifted the handles and put her weight to it, it veered off in a snaking fashion that she had no control over. The onlookers laughed and she felt cross to be the object of their mirth. It was clear they all thought

Tatty Barnes had come off better in the encounter and that she was a silly lass who'd been robbed of her pennies. She tried to pull rather than push with limited success, but eventually managed to park it near the door. How she would get the barrow home, she had no idea, and who she could ask to mend it was even more of a puzzle. But with her head held high she walked back to the scales and began to weigh in the cloth. Agnes was aware that the scavengers were still amused by what they'd witnessed and she found herself irritated and didn't allow them a farthing more than they were entitled to.

'What do you want that barrow for?' asked Michael Walsh when it was his turn. 'You must have had a reason to buy it.'

Agnes lifted the bag of nails that he'd brought on to the scales and reckoned up the price, pleased that at least he acknowledged she wasn't stupid.

'I want it to carry cheese in,' she told him.

'I've heard about your cheese selling,' he said as she counted his payment into his hand. 'I thought it was just something you'd done on a whim. I didn't think it was serious. I'd heard that you were getting wed to the Ryans' boy, Patrick. Are you going to be leaving here and selling cheese instead when you're married?' he asked.

'I'm not getting married!' she told him emphatically.

'I must be mistaken then.' He looked crestfallen. 'I hope I haven't offended you. I didn't mean any offence.'

'No. It doesn't matter,' replied Agnes, guilty for having been so short with him. The Walshes were good friends and she didn't want Michael to think she was rude. 'I hate the way these rumours get about,' she told him, realizing that everyone in the Irish community knew about her visit to the Ryans' house and that they would all be looking forward to being invited to a wedding. Well, they would have to get over their disappointment.

'The wheel looked a bit wobbly,' said Michael, as he nodded his head towards the barrow. 'I could take a look at it, if you like.'

'Would you?' asked Agnes, full of gratitude now. 'I wasn't sure who to ask.'

'It probably won't take much to fix it,' he said. 'It's surprising what some people will throw out. It's a sturdy barrow. I'm surprised Tatty Barnes didn't keep it.'

'I think he was just after the cash,' said Agnes, although a sudden dark thought troubled her. What if it was like the rug all over again and Tatty had 'found' the barrow when it hadn't really been put out as unwanted? It would explain why he wasn't keen to keep it. She hoped her suspicions weren't true. She didn't want to be two pennies down and have the constable come after her and accuse her of stealing it.

'I'll take it now,' offered Michael. 'I'm done here for the day. Call round later this evening for it.'

'I will. And I'll pay you something for your trouble,' Agnes offered.

'No, you won't,' Michael told her. 'If friends can't help one another out then what's the use of them?'

He smiled, his blue eyes twinkling beneath his thick, dark brows. Agnes thanked him again, genuinely grateful, and made a mental note to reward him and Aileen with a piece of cheese next time she had some.

## 11

'Good as new!' declared Michael Walsh later that day when Agnes called to see if he'd been able to mend the barrow. He pushed it up and down the narrow court to demonstrate his repairs. The wheel was running straight and true, even over the bumps and puddles, and Agnes saw that he'd done a good job.

She offered him some money. 'Just for your expenses,' she told him, but he wouldn't hear of it. Agnes felt guilty. She knew the Walshes were not much better off than her mother. In fact, the cellar where they lived was cramped and damp compared with the house that the Andertons had found for her own family.

'Go and get your cheeses,' Michael told her. 'You don't want to be working with the filthy rags if you can do better – and I'm sure you can. Some of us need to rise above this,' he said as he waved his hand around the dire living conditions in Butcher's Court where the waste and offal from the slaughterhouses often ran down the cobbles and sometimes into the dwellings below. 'I have the money to move out of here,' he confessed, 'but no one will rent me a better house because I'm Irish. Then they complain about us living in squalor. We can't win.'

Agnes knew how hard it was. It had been a harsh lesson from the moment they arrived in this country – the knowledge that they weren't welcome and that the English accused them of bringing disease with them and hated them and distrusted them.

The families who worked in the mills were better off. The mill owners would rent them a house, like the Ryans had. Agnes thought about it as she pushed the barrow home. She understood that her mother thought a marriage to Patrick Ryan would be a way for her to improve her life, but she wanted to help herself rather than having to rely on other people to make things better.

It wasn't until she reached home that she realized the barrow wasn't going to fit easily through the door. She was trying to manoeuvre it around the doorposts when her mother came up the street.

'What on earth have you got there?'

'It's a barrow.'

'I can see that! Whose is it and why are you bringing it in here? We've no room for it.'

'It's mine. I can't leave it outside. Someone might steal it,' said Agnes, as she managed to get it through the door and into the kitchen.

'It'll help me to gather rags!' exclaimed her mother, looking at the barrow with new enthusiasm. 'Did you bring it from the rag shop? What did you pay for it?'

'It's not for you!' Agnes watched as her mother's face fell. 'I'm sorry,' she said, feeling mean for having given her mother false hope. 'I bought it to carry cheese.'

'Not cheese again! No, Agnes. It'll do me well for gathering, but I'll not have you buying more cheese, or borrowing money again. You were lucky to be able to pay back Mr Anderton, but it may not be so easy next time. And I'll not risk us being turned out of this house. I forbid it!' she told her daughter emphatically.

Agnes felt her anger rise at her mother's words.

'It's my barrow. You can't have it!' she shouted, feeling tears of frustration well in her eyes.

'Don't speak to me like that!' Agnes was taken aback at the anger in her mother's voice and the look on her face. She didn't recall ever having seen her mother so furious with her before. 'You need to give up this nonsense about cheese. Patrick will have none of it when you're married and I'll not have you plunge us into debt in the meantime. The barrow will do me well and I'm grateful to you for bringing it, but it's for rags and nothing more and let that be an end to it.'

'No!' protested Agnes. 'I'll not give up buying and selling cheese. I can make money from it. Michael Walsh said I could rise above all this!'

Her mother was shaking her head. 'I wish your father were here,' she said. Agnes watched as her mother appeared to crumple and reach for a chair to sit down as tears flowed. She raised her apron to her eyes as she began to sob, in huge, convulsive gasps. 'I wish your father were here,' she repeated as she wept.

Agnes stood, holding the handles of the barrow, and didn't know what to do. She was frightened. Her mother rarely mentioned her father these days, but her grief reminded Agnes of the first days when they'd got off the boat that rescued them, when her mother had been bewildered and afraid. But even then, she hadn't cried like this, and Agnes was worried that her mother would never stop weeping now that she'd begun.

'Don't,' she pleaded quietly. She could see Maria and Peter staring up anxiously from their places on the thin rag rug that covered the stone floor in front of the fire-place. Agnes propped the barrow against the wall and went to her mother. She put a hand on her shaking shoulder and wished that Timothy would come home. She wasn't sure how to deal with this situation on her own. 'Don't,' she repeated as she knelt by her mother's side. 'I'm sorry,' she said. She wished she could promise that she would marry Patrick and forget her ambition to be a cheese seller, but she couldn't. She just couldn't. Because it wasn't fair.

After a time that seemed to stretch to an eternity, her mother's sobs grew quieter and she began to take deep breaths and dry her eyes.

'I'll make a cup of tea,' said Agnes, not knowing what else to do, or say. The outburst had shaken her. She'd always been so sure that her mother was strong and resilient, and it was alarming to realize that it wasn't always true.

When her mother had recovered her composure, Agnes handed her the tea and they were silently drinking when the door opened and Timothy came in. He stopped short in the doorway, taking in the atmosphere and the barrow.

'What have you done now?' he asked Agnes.

'I bought a barrow,' she replied. Now that he'd arrived she saw that he wasn't going to be much help after all.

'Are you going to leave it there?' he asked.

'It's doing no harm,' she told him. 'There's hot tea in the pot if you want to drink some whilst I help Mam.'

Timothy looked at their mother. He could see something was wrong. 'Are you poorly?' he asked her. 'Do you want me to fetch the doctor?'

'Of course not,' their mother replied, getting up off the chair to check on the contents of her pan. 'I'm quite well.'

The next morning, Agnes agreed to let her mother take the barrow.

'Don't get it dirty,' she wanted to say, but she kept quiet. Even though she was determined to visit the farm at Samlesbury Bottoms on Sunday afternoon, the argument of the previous evening had made her realize that confrontation was not the best way to make her mother see reason. And maybe sharing the barrow with her mother was a good idea. She wouldn't need it every day.

# 12

After work the next Saturday, Agnes walked across the market and saw that the man on the cheese stall had raised his prices to their previous level. She went into the market house, but there was no sign of Jonas. The hope and anticipation that Agnes had been feeling all day dissipated into disappointment that surprised her with its intensity.

'Looking for the cheese lad?' asked the fishmonger she'd spoken to before. 'He's not come today. Doubt he'll come again,' he predicted.

Agnes turned away so that the man wouldn't see the tears welling in her eyes. She brushed them away with the back of her hand and told herself not to be too disheartened. Even though she'd been grasping at the chance that he might come, the sensible side of her had always known that it was unlikely and that if she wanted to see him again, she would have to go to his farm.

She walked away, pausing by the outside stall to see if she could purchase a bargain, but the stallholder was still doing a good trade and Agnes saw that there would be no cheap cheese tonight. It was clear that if she was to make a success of this business she needed to follow Mr Anderton's advice and buy direct from the farm.

That meant borrowing some more money. She didn't enjoy being in debt, but there was no other way, so she turned her steps towards King Street and knocked on the door.

Dorothy answered.

'If it's the cheese, tha should have come to the back door,' she reprimanded Agnes. 'My legs are getting too tired to be climbing those stairs from the kitchen for nowt!'

'I'm sorry. I don't have cheese today,' said Agnes. 'I've come to see Mr Anderton.'

'Come in,' Dorothy told her and sighed as she climbed more stairs to find her employer.

'Agnes!' Mr Anderton greeted her with a welcoming smile. 'Come into the morning room,' he said. 'My wife is in the parlour.'

He opened the door to a room at the back of the house. It was chilly. The fire in the grate was freshly laid, but Agnes guessed it wouldn't be lit until the next day.

'Sit down,' invited Mr Anderton. 'I take it this is a business call?' He raised an eyebrow.

'It is,' confirmed Agnes.

'You want to buy cheese again. From the same lad as last week?' he asked.

'No. He isn't there today,' replied Agnes, trying to make it sound as if it was of little consequence. 'So I'm going to buy from the farm tomorrow. I got a barrow!' she told him.

'Well done! You sure don't allow that grass to grow under your feet, do you?' Mr Anderton smiled his approval and Agnes wished that her mother could be half as encouraging. 'So, how much do you need to borrow?'

'I'm not sure yet,' said Agnes, hoping that when she found the farm Mr Marsden would be willing to sell to her. Otherwise, the long walk would be for nothing.

'Maybe another sixteen shillings?' suggested Mr Anderton.

'I think sixteen will be enough,' said Agnes, loath to ask for more, but worried that it might not be enough to buy two whole cheeses.

'Plus interest?'

'Of course,' said Agnes, wanting to seem professional. 'The same rate as last week?'

Mr Anderton studied her for a moment, then nodded. 'You drive a hard bargain, Miss Cavanah,' he told her. 'Wait there.'

Five minutes later, Agnes was walking home with a bag of money in the purse that hung at her hip. She kept one hand clutched over it and walked fast. Mr Anderton hadn't offered to escort her today and she was wary of some of the ne'er-do-wells that loitered around the pubs at this time in the evening, spending their wages instead of going home to their wives and families.

When she went in through the door on Mary Ellen Street, her mother looked round sharply, then visibly relaxed when she saw that Agnes hadn't brought any cheese with her.

Agnes placed one and sixpence on the scrubbed table and her mother slid a penny back towards her for her spending money.

'I'm glad you've seen sense,' she said.

Without a word, Agnes picked up the penny. She didn't tell her mother that Mr Reynolds had paid her extra again, and she certainly didn't reveal the huge amount of money that was weighing her down on her right-hand side. She climbed the steps to the bedroom and hid the purse under her clean linen in the drawer that was hers in the big chest. Then she went down to the kitchen where she scrubbed her hands before turning her attention to the barrow.

'I don't know why you're fussing over that,' her mother said. 'It'll be as bad again by Monday.'

Agnes pursed her lips as she scrubbed it clean and then set it near the fire to dry, despite her mother complaining that it was in the way. She wanted it to be spotless when she took it for the cheese the next day. In fact, she decided that she would borrow a clean cloth from the drawer to line it and to cover the cheeses. But she planned to take it whilst her mother wasn't looking.

Next morning, the weather seemed mild and Agnes decided she could dispense with her shawl and show off her best gown and bonnet. Her mother smiled in approval. She'd been so pleased when Agnes hadn't brought home any cheese the previous evening, and now she was convinced that her daughter was dressing to impress Patrick and the Ryans. But she couldn't have been further from the truth.

'Will you walk out with me this afternoon?' Patrick asked her eagerly once the service was finished.

Agnes could see her mother speaking to the Ryans near the church door. They all kept glancing towards her and Patrick and smiling amongst themselves as if they were very pleased. It was obvious they were all expecting her to say yes.

'I'm sorry,' she said to Patrick. 'I have an errand to run this afternoon.'

The smile faded from his face to be replaced by a look of suspicion. 'What errand?' he asked.

'Nothing for you to worry about,' Agnes told him. 'But I'll be gone until dark, probably.'

He frowned and seemed puzzled.

'I thought it had been agreed,' he said, glancing towards his parents.

'Nothing has been agreed,' Agnes told him. 'Please excuse me.'

She moved away and without waiting for her mother and the rest of her family she began to walk towards Mary Ellen Street. Inside, she was seething. How dare these people decide what she should be doing? Walking out with Patrick Ryan was the last thing she had planned for the afternoon.

117

'So, what time are you meeting with Patrick?' asked her mother as they were eating their dinner.

'I'm not,' said Agnes. She'd briefly wondered whether to tell a lie but decided that it wasn't worth it, because when she came home later with the cheese her mother would know that she hadn't been with him.

'Did he not ask you?'

'Yes. He asked and I said no.'

'Why?'

Agnes could see the disbelief on her mother's face and she dreaded the prospect of another row.

'I have something I need to do.'

'What?' demanded her mother. 'What do you have to do? If you're thinking about the mending then Maria and I will do it. You can meet Patrick.'

'Well, I've told him no, so it's too late now.'

'You could go and knock on his door.'

'Wouldn't that be a bit forward?' Agnes asked.

'Of course not. It was all arranged.'

'I didn't arrange it,' Agnes said.

'Why are you being so difficult? Don't you realize that I'm doing my best for you?'

'I know,' replied Agnes, hoping that her mother wasn't going to cry again. She didn't want to hurt or worry her, but she wished that her mother would acknowledge her feelings too and give her the chance to prove herself. 'I'm going to buy some cheese,' she said and flinched as she waited for the coming onslaught of her mother's tongue.

There was silence. Agnes looked at her mother and

her mother stared back at her, speechless. Timothy and Maria and Peter sat silently too as the tension grew until Peter's bottom lip began to quiver.

'I don't know what to say,' their mother confessed as she lifted Peter on to her lap to comfort him. 'I don't know what's got into you, Agnes.'

Agnes looked down at the crumbs on her empty plate. Her mother's silence was harder to bear than her anger.

'I'm only trying to help,' she whispered.

'No.' Her mother shook her head emphatically. 'You're not helping, Agnes. You're just being selfish and running after a dream that will end with us being put out on the street. Have you borrowed money from Mr Anderton again?'

Once more, Agnes considered telling a lie, but she knew there was no point. Her mother had already guessed that she had.

'He wouldn't have lent it to me if he didn't think he'd get it back,' she argued.

'So that's why you were scrubbing the barrow,' said her mother. 'I ought to have known. No good will come of this business, Agnes. And I'm at a loss to know how to make you understand that. I think you should go to see Mr Anderton and give him his money back and then knock on the Ryans' door.'

Agnes didn't reply. She had no intention of doing either of those things. Her mother simply sighed and put Peter back on his stool before starting to clear the table.

'I don't know what to do,' her mother whispered. Agnes heard the tremor in her voice. She wanted to go to her mother and put her arms around her and beg her not to cry again, but instead she went up to the bedroom and got the purse. She tied it firmly under her gown so she could reach it through the slit in the side of the garment, then she put on her bonnet and took the barrow to the door. As she did so she remembered the cloth and went back for it. Her mother watched her.

'You'll be the death of us,' she said quietly. 'I wouldn't be surprised if we end up being sent back to Ireland after I've tried so hard to make a life for us here.'

Agnes knew that being sent back was her mother's greatest fear, but she refused to be threatened by the words. She doubted it would happen.

'I'm only buying a bit of cheese,' she retorted irritably, but didn't wait to hear any more before she slammed the door shut and set off down the street.

She wheeled the barrow briskly across the market square and turned to climb the steep hill that would take her to the Preston road. She was soon panting and had to slow her pace as she felt her heart racing from the effort and the emotion. At the top she began to walk along the level track. Lots of people were walking out in their Sunday best and she wondered if this was where Patrick would have brought her if she'd agreed to meet him. It would have been the same as making a huge announcement that she had agreed to marry him, she knew. Walking out on a Sunday afternoon was almost as binding as a formal betrothal.

Leaving the curious onlookers behind, Agnes walked on at a steady pace, enjoying the fresh air and the freedom. At least she'd been spared an afternoon of mending, although she suspected that Maria would be cross and resentful later. Given the choice, her little sister would have chosen to come with her.

After about an hour and a half had passed, Agnes came to a pub, the Halfway House, closed on a Sunday, which had once been an ancient manor house. She knew that it wasn't much further to Samlesbury Bottoms from here and, as the road began to descend, she hoped that she would meet someone who could direct her to the Marsdens' farm.

Before long she passed a row of cottages where the occupants were working in their gardens, making the best of the spring weather to prepare the ground for summer crops. They watched curiously as Agnes approached with the empty barrow and greeted her with a smile.

'Nice afternoon,' ventured one man after he'd touched his cap.

'I wonder if you can help me,' said Agnes, watching as the friendliness faded when he heard her accent. It happened so often that she thought she should have become accustomed to it by now, but it always hurt, this distrust of anyone who was Irish. 'I'm looking for the Marsdens' farm. Am I on the right road?'

'Aye. Goosefoot Farm,' he told her. 'Go on up here and round a bend to the left, then you'll see a track. Follow it down. The farm's at the end.'

Agnes thanked him and went on her way, hoping that she would receive a warmer welcome there.

The man's directions were easy to follow and she saw the track he'd described before she'd gone much further. She turned down it, the handles of the barrow jarring her wrists as she struggled to guide it over the ruts in the narrow road. She soon saw the buildings in front of her: a small farmhouse surrounded by a jumble of outbuildings as if someone had thrown them down and left them wherever they landed. A dog began to bark as she came nearer to the gate and she hesitated, hoping that it wasn't running loose and vicious.

As she waited, a man came out and shouted at the dog to be quiet.

'What do you want?' he called out to her as he secured the animal with a length of rope.

'Are you Mr Marsden?' she asked, approaching the gate. She knew the answer already. His resemblance to Jonas was clear.

'Aye. What's it to thee?' he asked, looking from her to the barrow.

'I've come to buy cheese,' Agnes told him.

He looked puzzled for a moment and scratched his head before settling his cap firmly.

'Is my wife expecting thee?' he asked.

'No. But I bought some last week from your son,

Jonas, on the market in Blackburn, and I'd like to get some more,' she explained.

The man shook his head. 'Nay, lass, we don't sell it by the slice from here,' he explained. 'Tha's wasted thy time. We'll be on the market at Preston later in the week. Best get it from us then.'

'No. You don't understand,' Agnes told him, concerned that he might disappear into the house without hearing her out. 'I don't want to buy a portion. I want a full wheel. Or even two. That's what I got last week. Ask Jonas,' she said, wishing that her friend would come out and vouch for her. She hoped he was at home. It would be so disappointing if she didn't see him when she'd been counting down the days all week.

Mr Marsden frowned. 'Tha bought a full wheel?' he asked. It was obvious he didn't believe her. 'Our Jonas were at Blackburn market last Saturday, but on a stall selling by the pound.'

Agnes wasn't sure how to reply. Jonas must not have told his father about their arrangement. He must have allowed his parents to think that he'd sold the cheese to lots of customers, not just one. Perhaps he'd been embarrassed about his lack of success.

'I'd like to buy a full wheel of cheese,' Agnes persisted. 'Have you got one to sell?'

'I'll fetch my wife,' said Mr Marsden, still looking perplexed. 'Tha can speak to her. Best come through,' he added as his grimy fingers struggled with the knots in the rope that held the gate closed.

Once the gate had swung open, Agnes pushed the barrow into the yard. It was part cobbled, but in places the stones were missing and the gaps were filled with muddy water. Wisps of straw were blowing around or adding to the mess on the ground and the air was ripe with the aroma of animal dung. The smell conjured a vision of the boat from Ireland and she felt a wave of panic.

'Come up to the house. Tha can leave thy barrow there,' said Mr Marsden.

Agnes lifted the skirts of her best gown as she followed him across the yard. Perhaps it hadn't been such a good idea to wear it after all, she thought. Her work clothes would have been far more suitable.

'Mother!' Mr Marsden cried as he pushed open a stiff wooden door. 'There's a lass here asking about cheeses.'

A moment later a woman came out of the kitchen. She looked as if she'd been cooking. Her cheeks were flushed and her sleeves were rolled up to the elbow. She wore a coarse linen apron over her plain gown and Agnes felt overdressed as Mrs Marsden looked her up and down.

'She wants to buy a full wheel,' Mr Marsden told his wife.

'A full wheel?' she repeated. 'What do you want it for?' she asked Agnes.

'I'm going to sell it. In Blackburn. Door to door,' she said. The Marsdens looked doubtful and Agnes wondered whether it was a silly idea after all. They didn't seem impressed. 'I bought from your son last week, but he wasn't on the market yesterday,' she explained, wishing that Jonas would come.

'He sold that cheese too cheap. Cost nearly as much for t' stall rental as he made in profit so it weren't worthwhile goin' again,' said Mr Marsden. Agnes hoped she hadn't got Jonas into trouble with the bargain she'd struck.

'If you sell it directly to me you won't need to worry about paying for the stall,' she told him.

'Hast tha got a full wheel?' Mr Marsden asked his wife.

'I've two,' she told him. 'Milk's been quite plentiful this week. I made one on Tuesday and another on Friday. Jonas was going to take them into Blackburn until you decided it wasn't worth it.'

'Aye. That's right,' he said. 'What dost tha think?'

'They'll keep until we go to market at Preston. Or we could let this lass take them. It'd save us a journey and we're getting busy now with the spring barley to go in.'

'What about the price? We've never sold direct afore.'

'We couldn't ask full price. If we take off the cost of the stall we could maybe sell at four and three farthings a pound,' suggested his wife.

Mr Marsden turned back to Agnes. 'Dost tha have money?' he asked doubtfully.

'I've money.' Agnes nodded emphatically.

'I hope it's not stolen,' he muttered as he exchanged a look with his wife. 'We don't want any trouble.'

'It's not stolen!' Agnes told them, her patience at the never-ending prejudice wearing thin. 'I can pay.'

'Come on out to the cold room then,' said Mrs Marsden. 'I'll just fetch my shawl. Keep an eye on that pan,' she instructed her husband. 'Don't let it boil dry.'

Agnes followed Mrs Marsden to one of the stone buildings. A chill met her as she stepped inside and it took a moment for her eyes to become accustomed to the gloom. As she looked around she saw a big stone trough that was clean and empty, a cheese press in the corner and sitting on the shelves were two wheels of cheese, their tangy aroma drifting towards her.

'We don't have enough surplus milk to make a full one every day,' explained Mrs Marsden. 'So what we do is turn it into curds, then store them overnight and add them to the next day's curds. It's what gives Lancashire cheese its special taste. We've been making it like that for generations.'

Agnes nodded. She was learning something new all the time.

'You don't leave it to mature, then?' she asked. 'You sell it straight away?'

'Aye. This cheese is what folk call "white meat". It doesn't need to sit for months like the more traditional cheeses.'

'Will you sell them to me?' asked Agnes, still unsure if the farmer's wife was going to be co-operative.

'I can't split a wheel,' warned Mrs Marsden. 'It'll have to be a whole one.'

'Can I take them both?' asked Agnes, hoping that they wouldn't be too heavy for her to manage. It was a fairly steep incline back up to the main road.

'Have you come alone?' Mrs Marsden asked.

'Yes. But I have a barrow to take them in.'

The farmer's wife looked doubtful. 'They're heavy,' she said. 'There's twenty-five pounds in each one.'

Agnes did a quick mental calculation. At fourpence three farthings, each wheel would cost her almost ten shillings. Two would cost just under a pound and she didn't have that much money. She wished she'd asked Mr Anderton for more, but it was too late now.

'Perhaps I'll just take one then,' she said. One would be easier to transport and she was sure of selling it all, but it meant less profit. If she came again she would need to bring more money.

'Bring your barrow and choose which one you want,' said Mrs Marsden. 'I'll just reckon up the cost.' The woman closed her eyes and Agnes watched as she too calculated the price in her head rather than reaching for a pencil and paper. 'Nine shillings and tenpence three farthings,' she said when she opened her eyes again. 'Call it nine shillings and tenpence ha'penny. Have you got that much?'

Without a word, Agnes reached into her purse. 'I don't have the right change,' she said, offering ten of the shillings she'd borrowed. 'You'll owe me a penny ha'penny.'

'All right. Fetch your barrow,' the woman said again, 'and I'll just go into the house and get the change.'

Agnes went to bring the barrow to the door of the cold store and then selected one of the cheeses. She lifted it down, feeling the weight in her arms as she put it into the barrow and covered it with the cloth. As she did so, Mrs Marsden came out with her change.

'Can I come to buy more next week?' she asked her.

'You can come to see if we've any to spare,' she said. 'I can't promise. My husband might want to take it to Preston market.'

Agnes nodded. She would come. She knew she would, because she was keen to see Jonas again and even though the buying of the cheese had made her feel good, she couldn't shake off the huge gloom of disappointment that he wasn't at home this afternoon.

Telling herself that it was foolish to feel so morose about it, Agnes heaved her weight into the handles and trundled the barrow back up the rutted track. A few times she got stuck and had to back up to take a mightier push, but eventually she made it to the road, panting and with sore hands. She stopped to examine her palms. They were red. One was blistered and the other was deeply marked from the handle. No wonder the men she saw about town all wore thick gloves. She looked down at her gown, which was splashed with mud, and her boots, which were filthy, and she sighed. Her idea of looking nice to impress Jonas had come to nothing. All she'd done was ruin her best gown and make herself look silly rather than workmanlike. No wonder the Marsdens had been suspicious of her.

'Agnes?'

She looked round sharply, although she'd recognized his voice before she saw him. Her stomach did a somersault and she hated herself for blushing as he came towards her.

'I thought it was you!' said Jonas. 'What are you doing here? Is that cheese?' he asked as he noticed the mound in her barrow.

'You weren't on the market yesterday. And I wasn't going to buy from that man who tried to cheat you last week,' she explained.

'So you came all the way out here. Have you walked?' he asked.

'It's not far,' she replied, although they both knew it would take her going on for two hours to get home and by that time the sun would have set. It was already low on the horizon, gradually changing the sky from blue to a silvery yellow.

She wondered where he'd been. Unlike her, he was clean and his clothes were obviously his Sunday best. A sudden fear struck her that perhaps he'd been walking out with a girl.

'I see you got a barrow of your own,' he said.

'Yes. It doesn't squeak either.'

He laughed. 'I'm pleased to hear it. Although I put some oil on mine. It was embarrassing, walking through Blackburn with it making that noise.'

'It drew quite a bit of attention.'

'It did,' he agreed.

They stood and looked at one another. Their conversation had run out but neither seemed willing to move on.

'Well,' said Jonas after a moment. 'You'd best get on.'

'I had,' she agreed, but still didn't reach for the barrow's handles until he'd touched the peak of his cap and turned down the track towards his home. As she moved away she saw him glance back at her. Agnes considered waving, but thought it might be too friendly. She just hoped that he would be at home the next week.

# 13

It was dark when Agnes got back to Mary Ellen Street. Her mother came to the door with an anxious expression that melted into relief when she saw her, and Agnes felt guilty for having worried her.

She carried the cheese in and put it on the kitchen table, then struggled with the barrow until it was safely inside and the door was closed and locked for the night.

'I don't suppose you've had anything to eat,' said her mother as Agnes sat down and tried to hide a long yawn. She was exhausted but would never admit it. 'I've saved you something,' her mother said, putting a plate of bread and treacle in front of her and pouring a cup of tea.

'Thank you,' said Agnes, grateful that her mother wasn't going to tell her off again.

'You'd better wash your hands. They're filthy.'

Agnes looked down at them. They were covered in dirt from a puddle she'd stumbled into when the wheel of the barrow had caught on its edge and jarred her off balance. She went to the sink and the blisters stung as she washed them in the lye soap.

'You look like you've been in a mud bath,' observed her mother. 'Your lovely gown looks ruined.' She didn't add that she despaired of her, but Agnes understood that she did and was sorry to be the cause of so much anguish.

'I got the cheese. It was a good price,' she said. 'I'll take it to work tomorrow and ask Mr Reynolds if I can borrow the scales again to weigh it out. Can I borrow the sharp knife? It'll only be once. I'm going to get a cheese wire off the market or from the hardware shop. It'll make it simpler.'

Agnes stopped talking and looked around when her mother didn't answer. She was sitting by the fire with tears rolling down her cheeks. She looked desperately sad and Agnes wanted to cry too.

'I thought you were lost,' her mother confessed after a moment. 'I nearly went for a constable.'

'Of course I wasn't lost,' Agnes said as she came back to the table. 'What made you think that?'

'You'd been such a long time. I expected you back hours ago.'

Agnes could see that her mother had been badly frightened. She must have been very worried if she'd considered asking for help from the police. She always said that she didn't trust them and would even cross the street if she saw one of the constables walking his beat.

'Well, I'm back now,' said Agnes, picking up her food and realizing how hungry she was. If she'd thought that working in the rag warehouse was tiring, it was nothing compared to what she'd done today. Every muscle in her body ached and it would be worse tomorrow, she knew. But she would need to get up early to deal with the cheese before it was time to begin her regular work.

When Agnes got into bed beside Maria and tried to drift off to sleep she found that there were too many thoughts tumbling through her mind to allow her any peace. They were happy thoughts though, mostly about Jonas Marsden. She'd been afraid that she wasn't going to see him, but when he'd materialized on the road outside the farm, she was sure that all the prayers she'd sent up in the church that morning had been answered. It made her certain that Jonas was the one that God intended for her, not Patrick Ryan.

Agnes lay very still with her eyes closed when her mother came upstairs. She heard the door close and the old bedframe creaked as her mother sat down. Then there was a sudden cold draught as the blankets were lifted and Agnes shivered when her mother leaned to blow out the candle. She tried once again to fall asleep, but could think of nothing but Jonas's solemn hazel eyes and his eager smile as he'd called her name. He'd seemed happy to see her and the thought made Agnes smile, in the dark, where no one could see her.

Morning came too soon for Agnes. She felt heavy and lethargic as she forced herself from the warmth of the bed, encouraging herself with the thought of the business that she was going to do before her daily work began. Beside her, Maria was also yawning.

'Did you go selling cheese without me yesterday?' her sister wanted to know.

'No. I went buying cheese.'

'I wanted to come,' Maria complained.

'It was a long way. You couldn't have walked that far.'

'I could!' retorted Maria, wide awake now and eager for an argument that Agnes had neither time nor patience for. 'Where did you go?'

'I went to buy from a farm,' replied Agnes as she got dressed in her work clothes. Her best dress, which she'd left draped over the wooden chair, looked even worse in the early morning light. She would have to wash it and hope that it wouldn't be spoiled, but there was no time now.

Agnes hurried down the stairs and put some tea to brew then shoved a crust of bread into her mouth to eat as she manoeuvred the barrow out of the front door. She came back for a gulp of tea before lifting the wheel of cheese into her arms to load it into the barrow. Then she snatched up the sharp knife, grabbed her shawl and went out on to the street.

When she arrived at the warehouse, she had to wait on the doorstep for Mr Reynolds to come and unlock the door. She hoped that he would be quick because it would take her a while to cut and weigh the cheese into portions.

'Early bird again!' he said after he'd come up the street, whistling a tune that Agnes didn't recognize. She knew none of the songs that he whistled, and she missed the evenings back home in Ireland when the neigh-bours would gather to sing and play music that was familiar to her.

'Can I borrow the scales again?' she asked when they were inside.

'As long as tha's done before opening time,' he replied, and Agnes hurried to get things ready. It would be much easier to do it at home on some scales of her own, and she'd already decided that she would go out at dinnertime to enquire about prices. Even if she couldn't afford them straight away, she would know how much she needed to save before she could.

'How much today?' asked the women as they arrived at the warehouse and saw what she was doing.

'Same as last week. Thruppence a half-pound.'

Agnes was pleased and thankful that her offer was met with as much enthusiasm as it had been the previ-ous week, and when it was time to begin the warehouse work all the portions she'd prepared had gone and she had orders for more. The trip to the hardware shop would have to wait as her dinnertime would now be taken up with more cheese cutting.

It was late afternoon before she saw her mother arrive. Her arms were full to overflowing and both Maria and Peter were carrying stuff as well. Agnes felt a little guilty that she'd deprived her mother of the barrow on a day when she'd obviously had a good haul.

'Thy lass is becoming quite the entrepreneur with this cheese business!' Mr Reynolds grinned as he watched

Agnes weigh in her mother's finds, but his smile faded when he saw that her mother was not so enthusiastic.

'I suppose that's why you didn't come home for your dinner,' she said to her daughter. 'I had something ready for you.'

'I'm sorry. Everyone wanted cheese and I hadn't time to cut it all before I began work. I'll eat it for my tea,' she offered.

'I shared it between these two,' said her mother, indicating the younger ones. 'They've worked hard.'

Agnes nodded. She was distracted as she reckoned up the money owed to her mother and it wasn't until after she'd gone that she realized how awkward the encounter had seemed.

'Thy mother didn't seem right suited with this business tha has,' remarked Mr Reynolds.

'She worries about me borrowing money,' Agnes explained, trying to make an excuse for her. 'And she thinks I'm putting on you by asking to borrow the scales. But I'll be getting my own soon,' she added, in case Mr Reynolds also thought she was taking advantage.

'Aye. Well nowt's done without taking some risks,' he said. 'I take it tha borrowed money from Mr Anderton again?'

'I did. He seemed eager to lend it after I paid him back last time – with interest.'

'Interest?' said Mr Reynolds. 'What rate is he charging thee?'

'He asked for a penny extra.'

Mr Reynolds laughed. 'I was about to make thee a better offer, but I can't beat that,' he told her. 'But don't forget that I'm willing to help if tha ever needs owt.'

Agnes thanked him. Both he and Mr Anderton were so enthusiastic about her endeavour and wanted her to be successful. She felt sad that her mother couldn't be of the same mind.

# 14

Kitty Cavanah had watched as her daughter pushed the barrow up the street without a backward glance. She would miss the barrow when she went out to gather rags. It had made her life so much easier as they'd trudged from back alley to back alley.

Not for the first time, she wondered how she would have coped if she'd had the baby as well. Her body still ached for him even though nearly four years had passed since his loss. The pain she felt now came from deep inside her soul. It was an anguish she knew she would never shake off, because she was to blame for his loss.

He'd been a sickly babe, but she'd thought that if they'd been able to get on the ship to the New World, as they'd intended, he would have thrived with the better life and plentiful food that they would have had there. And even if he'd died in her arms she would have been able to bear it better. As it was, she knew that she'd failed him. She'd panicked when she'd fallen into the water and somehow she'd lost her grip on him. She'd let him go and the sea had swallowed him. For a long time she'd clung to the hope that someone must have pulled him from the waves. She'd prayed that he would be returned to her, but God had punished her for her carelessness and her youngest had been taken, never to be returned. She hoped he was with his father and that one day she would be reunited with them both and be able to beg their forgiveness. She'd said as much to Father Kaye and he'd been kind and encouraging, but Kitty suspected that she would spend long years in purgatory for what she had done.

And now there was all this trouble with Agnes. Kitty had thought that she could rely on her elder daughter; she'd been able to when they'd first arrived in England. Agnes had been her voice of reason. The one who had forced her to come to terms with their situation, who had made her realize that her husband wasn't going to find them because he'd been drowned in those awful, all engulfing waves that had washed over the deck of the sinking ship. But this nonsense with buying and selling cheese had taken hold of her and suddenly there was no reasoning with her. It made Kitty desperate. They'd been so lucky to get this little house and be able to earn enough to struggle by, but the thought of borrowing money made Kitty as afraid as she was of the sea. As afraid as she was of being sent back to Ireland, to a country that she loved, but where there was nothing left that would support them since the English had taken all the land and made it their own. If only Agnes would see reason and marry Patrick Ryan then Kitty would feel better. The Ryans were a decent family. Patrick was a steady boy, and there was the chance of them having a house of their own – something that Kitty had never even dreamt was possible. Yet Agnes had become suddenly stubborn and Kitty was afraid that she'd met someone who was putting ideas into her head. She wondered if it was the lad who had come to the door with her the previous Saturday. She suspected that was who her daughter had gone to see yesterday, in her best gown and bonnet, rather than spending the afternoon with Patrick. It wouldn't end well, that was for sure. She would have to find a way of putting a stop to it, and the only thing she could think of was going to speak to Mrs Anderton after she'd finished her work, to beg her to ask her husband not to lend Agnes any more money.

After Kitty had collected her payment from the warehouse she walked round to Aileen and Michael's home with her younger children.

'Come in,' invited Aileen. 'I was about to put the kettle on.'

'To tell you the truth, I've come to beg a favour,' replied Kitty.

'What's wrong?' asked her friend.

'There's nothing wrong. Not really. But I wanted to go and speak to Mrs Anderton about Agnes and I wondered if you'd mind these two for a bit. It would be easier to go alone. It's not for their ears,' she whispered as Maria and Peter settled themselves on the floor to help sort out a collection of nails and screws and separate them from the other, less valuable bits and pieces that Aileen had in a basket.

'Is it about this cheese she's been buying?'

Kitty nodded. 'She's borrowing money from Mr Anderton, and it's got to stop. But I thought it might be better to speak to his wife rather than approach him directly.'

'Is she borrowing a lot?' asked Aileen as she wound a length of string around her hand, secured it and popped it into a basket with some other bundles.

'Sixteen shillings!' Kitty confessed.

'That much!' exclaimed Aileen, looking shocked. 'I thought it was only a shilling or two at most.'

'I know. It scares the bejesus out of me,' Kitty told her. 'We've never been in debt like this before. Her father would have been horrified. He worried so much about us owing rent when we were back in Ireland that he'd rather have seen us all starve than not pay what we owed. And I'm that scared that come the day Agnes can't pay, Mr Anderton will come knocking on our door and we'll end up losing the house, because I can't pay back that amount if she loses it.'

'I can see why you're worried,' Aileen told her. 'But surely it's between him and her?'

'I'd rather not take that chance,' said Kitty. 'You know what the gentry are like about money. They'll not be out of pocket.'

'I wouldn't have thought of him as gentry,' Aileen remarked.

'His skin might not be the same colour as ours, but he has a big house on King Street and money to spare to encourage a girl in her silliness. That makes him above us. Although he ought to know better. I don't know what she was thinking of when she asked him in the first place, but it'll not end well. I need to put a stop to it.'

'Well, go and speak to Mrs Anderton,' said Aileen. 'These two are all right here for a while.'

Kitty felt herself trembling as she knocked on the door of the Andertons' house a few minutes later. Dorothy came to answer it and recognized her straight away.

'What can I do for thee, Mrs Cavanah?' she asked curiously.

'I wondered if Mrs Anderton was at home, and if I could have a word with her.'

'She's no scraps for thee today if that's what tha's after. Tha should have come round the back,' said Dorothy. It sounded like a reprimand. No one liked the Irish knocking on their front doors. But Kitty stood her ground.

'It's a private matter. It's important,' she insisted.

'Well, step inside and I'll ask.'

Kitty waited in the hallway. She looked up the stairs and could hardly believe that she'd once slept in one of the bedrooms up there. She doubted she would ever sleep in such a fine house again.

After a moment, Mrs Anderton came down the stairs. She looked concerned. 'What is it, Mrs Cavanah?' she asked. 'What's wrong?'

'I need to talk to you about Agnes,' she explained. 'She's been borrowing money from your husband and it's got to stop.'

Mrs Anderton didn't look surprised. She stretched out an arm and invited Kitty into the parlour. 'Sit down,' she said. 'Dorothy, bring us a pot of tea.'

Once Dorothy had gone down to the kitchen, Mrs Anderton sat opposite Kitty and smoothed her skirts under her hand. They were soft hands, Kitty noticed, with clean, manicured nails, not the hands of a woman who gathered rags for a living. She slipped her own under her shawl.

'I think it's Mr Anderton you should be speaking to,' Mrs Anderton began. 'It isn't really anything to do with me.'

'But you know about it?'

'Yes, I do. Agnes has been twice now and she's borrowed money to buy cheese. But she paid it back in full the first time and I'm sure she will this time.' Kitty watched as Mrs Anderton hesitated. 'Unless something has gone wrong. Has it?' she asked gently. 'Has Agnes lost the money?'

'No! At least I hope not. But it isn't right. I don't want to be in debt to anyone. You've done so much for us already, and I'm grateful, but we can't ask for more.'

'I don't think my husband sees it as a favour,' explained Mrs Anderton. 'From what he's said to me about it, he thinks that Agnes has a good idea and that it's a good investment of his money.'

144

'Investment?' asked Kitty. 'I don't understand what you mean.'

'Well, he thinks it will benefit him.'

'In what way?' Kitty asked, puzzled.

'Well, when he lends money he gets interest,' explained Mrs Anderton. 'The people he lends to pay him back a little extra as a thank you.'

Kitty stared at the woman. It was even worse than she'd thought.

'So she's paying back even more than she borrows? That can't be right.'

'It's how business is done,' explained Mrs Anderton.

'It's got to stop!' said Kitty, even more afraid of the consequences now. 'Agnes can't do that. She'll have us in the poor house. We'll end up on a boat back to Ireland.' Kitty felt her emotions overwhelm her and by the time Dorothy came back with the tray of tea she was sobbing uncontrollably. She knew she was making a complete fool of herself in front of the calm young woman and her maid, but they would never understand how deeply this affair was distressing her.

Mrs Anderton put a cup of tea on the side table near Kitty's chair. 'Drink that,' she advised. 'It'll help you feel better.'

'I'm sorry,' said Kitty after she'd wiped her eyes and picked up the cup. Her hands were trembling and she worried that she might drop the fragile china, so she took a quick sip and set it back down on its saucer.

'I can see how worried you are,' said Mrs Anderton.

'I think you should speak to my husband about it. I'm sure he will reassure you that there's nothing to worry about.'

'Can you not speak to him for me?' asked Kitty. She didn't like to confess that she was slightly afraid of Mr Anderton – as she'd become afraid of all the men who had the power to disrupt her life. It was all very well Aileen saying that he wasn't gentry, but he was her landlord, and she knew how the landlord in Ireland had treated them.

'It would be better if he explained it to you directly,' said Mrs Anderton. 'He can tell you why he thinks Agnes's idea is a good one.'

'But it isn't,' Kitty protested. 'I don't want her doing it. She's supposed to be getting married.'

'Is she? That's lovely news!' replied Mrs Anderton. 'Who is she marrying?'

'He's called Patrick Ryan; he comes to our church. He works at the Pearson Street Mill as a winder. It's a good job.'

As she spoke, Kitty heard Dorothy answer the door and a moment later Mr Anderton appeared in the doorway.

'Hello,' he said, looking at her curiously.

'Mrs Cavanah has come to talk about Agnes,' said his wife. 'There's fresh tea if you'd like some,' she added. 'I'll just go and fetch another cup and saucer.' On her way out, she passed her husband in the doorway and spoke to him in a low voice. Kitty couldn't hear what she said, but she saw the puzzled look clouding Mr Anderton's face as he came to sit down in the chair his wife had vacated.

'I hear you're worried about Agnes borrowing the money,' he said.

'I am,' Kitty admitted. 'I don't like being in debt.'

'Have you spoken to your daughter about it?' he asked.

'I have,' Kitty told him, although she didn't say that the subject always ended in an argument.

'And what did Agnes say?' he asked.

'She says she can pay you back, but I'm worried that she might not be able to. It all seems such a precarious idea. If she can't sell the cheese and it goes off she'll not have the money – and I can't pay it,' Kitty explained.

'I wouldn't expect you to pay it,' said Mr Anderton. 'The arrangement is between me and Agnes.'

'But what if she can't pay?'

'I'd lose out,' Mr Anderton told her. 'That's the risk I'm taking because she has no securities – nothing of value,' he went on when he saw that Kitty didn't understand.

'But you wouldn't just let it rest if she owed you so much,' said Kitty. 'You'd want it back.'

'Well, I'd like to get it back,' he agreed, 'but sometimes when you do business you have to take a risk, a calculated risk,' he added. 'You have to judge what ideas are likely to make a profit and which are non-starters. Now take Agnes's idea – I believe she can make a profit from it. I wouldn't have lent her the money if I didn't.'

'But she's just a girl. What does she know?'

'Yes, she's young and she has a lot to learn,' he agreed. 'But she's sensible and she's shrewd. I think she deserves a chance.'

Kitty was at a loss to know how to respond. She felt bewildered by Mr Anderton's calm explanation that Agnes had a good idea. She was sure it was just frivolous, a fancy that her daughter had that could amount to nothing.

'But she can't be getting into business now,' she said after a moment, hoping to make Mr Anderton understand the situation. 'She's going to be married.'

'Well, I don't see it's a problem, unless her future husband forbids it. Does he?' he asked.

'I don't know. He doesn't know about it.'

Mr Anderton frowned. 'Who is this person she's set on marrying?' he asked.

Kitty explained and he listened carefully, rubbing a finger across his mouth.

'How does this Patrick Ryan not know what Agnes is doing?' he asked, genuinely puzzled.

'They . . . they haven't spent a lot of time together yet,' Kitty admitted.

'Is it an arranged marriage?' asked Mr Anderton as if he suddenly saw the situation clearly.

'I suppose it is . . . in a way.'

'And Agnes is happy for it to go ahead?'

'Of course she is.' Kitty knew that she didn't sound convincing and she could see that Mr Anderton wasn't convinced by it either. 'So she has to stop this cheese selling,' she added. She wanted to tell Mr Anderton that he must stop lending money to Agnes, but she didn't dare. It felt too much like a criticism.

'I'm sorry you feel like that,' said Mr Anderton. 'But I'm glad you've spoken to me about it.'

'Well, as long as you understand,' she said. 'I'll not take up any more of your time.'

Kitty got up from the chair, eager to leave. The encounter had not gone as she'd planned. She could only hope that Mr Anderton would take heed of her words and refuse Agnes the next time she came.

'She might go elsewhere if she doesn't borrow from me,' he said as he watched Kitty gather her shawl around her shoulders.

It was a thought that hadn't occurred to Kitty, although now that she considered it she recalled that Agnes had borrowed sixpence from Mr Reynolds against her wages.

'There are others who might not be quite so honest,' Mr Anderton warned her. 'Some charge a very high rate of interest and your daughter would quickly fall into a lot of debt if she went to them.'

'She wouldn't do that.'

'Don't be so certain. She's a determined girl. It would be better for her to deal with me than a money lender,' he warned.

As she was walking back to Butcher's Court to collect her younger children, Kitty thought about what

Mr Anderton had told her. She must have very stern words with Agnes, she decided. She must make it clear that her borrowing money had to stop before she brought any more trouble on them.

'I've heard of the money lenders,' Aileen told her when she'd recounted her conversation with Mr Anderton. 'There's one who has the shop on Shorrock Fold – the one with the three brass balls above the door. He's a pawnbroker by trade, but I've heard he'll lend money to anyone, but at a rate of going on for a hundred per cent for a short-term loan. Most people who fall foul of him end their days in the debtors' prison.'

The words sent a shock through Kitty. She must do everything she could to prevent Agnes being sent to prison, and the only thing she could think of now was to go and see the Ryans again and get the arrangements for the wedding under way.

## 15

By the time Agnes left the warehouse she had sold almost all the cheese. There wasn't much left to go door to door with and she hoped her regular customers wouldn't be too disappointed if they missed out. When she went to pay Mr Anderton she must ask him if he would be willing to lend her enough to buy two wheels of cheese for next week. She didn't want to let people down and send them back to the cheese stall on the market.

She wheeled the barrow home, hungry for her tea and feeling pleased with herself. As soon as she'd eaten she would go down the street with what she had left, and the next evening she could go to King Street to repay Mr Anderton. And she must keep a portion back for Dorothy, she thought. Of course, the biggest dilemma would be whether to go to the front door or the back. She would go to the back door, she decided. She was more afraid of Dorothy than she was of Mr Anderton, and Agnes was sure he would still meet her even if she did come up his back stairs.

She took the cheese inside. Timothy had been coming up the street behind her and she'd called to him to bring in the barrow for her. She could take the remainder out in the basket and her mother could use the barrow the next morning.

Her mother was busy with the food when Agnes went in and only replied quietly to her eager greeting.

'I did well today!' Agnes told her. 'It's nearly all gone. I'm going to get two wheels next week.'

'No, you won't!' Agnes was taken aback at her mother's emphatic answer. 'You won't be buying any more,' she told her. 'I've been to speak to Mr Anderton and I've told him he's not to lend you another penny.'

'You've done what?' Agnes could barely believe what her mother was saying. She knew that she'd been worried about her buying the cheese, but until a moment ago she'd felt so happy that she could reassure her that the business was going well and she was making money from it. Now, the idea that her mother had gone so far as to interfere with the arrangements she'd made with Mr Anderton first shocked and then infuriated her. What would he think of her now, knowing that she was subject to her mother's wishes rather than being a grown-up with the perfect right to make her own decisions?

'Pay him what you owe him and thank him, then let that be the last of it,' said her mother as she dished out the food. 'You can walk out with Patrick Ryan this coming Sunday and come to an agreement with him. Then I'll speak to his parents about making a date for the wedding.'

It was Agnes's turn to utter a heartfelt 'no', but the words wouldn't come. Her mouth was dry and she was close to tears. Why was her mother so set against her idea when all she wanted to do was help? She sat down on a chair without a word and kept her head down so that her mother wouldn't see she was crying.

Agnes said nothing throughout the meal, although the others chatted as if nothing had changed. But for her everything had changed. All that she desired in life was in danger of being snatched from her.

After they'd finished eating and Agnes had forced down the food she could barely stomach, not wanting to be accused of wasting it, she took the basket and went down the street to sell the last of her cheese. All the pleasure had been leached from it and she could barely raise a smile for the neighbours as they greeted her warmly and produced the pennies from their purses to pay her. When she came home she set her earnings on the table and reckoned them up.

'Have you enough to pay Mr Anderton?' asked her mother as she watched her tumble the coins into the cloth bag.

'Yes, of course I have. There's the full sixteen shillings in there,' replied Agnes as she secured the bag. 'The rest is mine,' she added as she put the remaining money into her purse. She'd been planning to go to the hardware shop the next day to ask the price of some scales, but there seemed no point now. She couldn't afford to buy more cheese without a loan. And the worst of it was that if she couldn't go to the farm again, she wouldn't see Jonas.

With her happy mood ruined, Agnes went to bed and

lay awake next to her sister, wondering what she should do next. There was one thing that she was certain about. She had no intention of marrying Patrick Ryan.

The next evening, Agnes walked to the Andertons' house with the bag of money clutched tightly in her hand. She was anxious as she turned into the backs. There were no street lamps here, only the light that spilled from the back windows of the house. It wasn't much and Agnes worried that someone could be waiting to rob her. It would be a disaster if she lost the money when it wasn't even hers but belonged to Mr Anderton.

She moved the bag beneath her shawl to keep it concealed and walked as quickly as she dared in the darkness until she came to the steps that led down to the Andertons' kitchen door. She could see Dorothy moving about inside, washing up the pots and pans from the evening meal, and she waved as the maid glanced up on hearing her footsteps.

'I saved some cheese for you,' she told Dorothy once she was inside the warm room. 'It's only half a pound. I didn't manage to buy so much this week.'

'How much is tha charging?'

'Thruppence,' said Agnes, relieved that Dorothy hadn't thought it was a gift. 'And I've brought the money for Mr Anderton,' she went on, putting the cloth bag down on the table to transfer Dorothy's payment to her own purse. 'Is he in?'

'Aye. I'll go up and tell him tha's here,' she said. 'I was

about to take a pot of tea up to him and Mrs Anderton. I'll put an extra cup and saucer on the tray, and maybe a slice of fruit cake?' she offered, picking up a knife to take off some slices.

'Do you happen to have a cheese wire?' asked Agnes as she looked at all the implements lined up on the kitchen shelves.

'I think I do, somewhere. I don't really use it,' said Dorothy.

'Do you know how much they cost?'

'I couldn't say. Was tha thinking of getting one?'

'I did think about it, and some weighing scales,' Agnes told her. 'But I'm not sure I'll need them now,' she admitted although she didn't say why.

She watched as Dorothy went to the stairs with the tray, unsure whether or not to follow her. The maid saw her hesitation.

'Tha might as well come up with me,' she said. 'I doubt Mr Anderton will refuse to see thee.'

Agnes followed her but waited at the parlour door whilst Dorothy went in with the tea. She came back a moment later. 'In tha goes,' she said, holding the door wide.

Inside, Agnes saw Mr and Mrs Anderton sitting on either side of the fireplace.

'Draw up a chair,' invited Mr Anderton.

'I've brought your money,' said Agnes, handing him the bag before she sat down. 'The full sixteen shillings and a penny. You can count it.'

'I'll count it in a bit,' he said. 'First, drink some tea and eat some cake. I think we have important matters to speak of.'

'I know my mother came to see you,' Agnes told him, feeling self-conscious. 'I didn't know she was planning to.'

'She was very upset,' Mrs Anderton told her as she handed her a cup and saucer. 'We tried to reassure her, but I don't think we managed it. She's very worried about you borrowing money.'

'I know,' Agnes said. 'She told me she'd asked you not to lend me any more.'

'She told us you were getting married.'

'I'm not!' Agnes replied. 'Not if I can help it.' She saw Mrs Anderton exchange a glance with her husband.

'So it is an arranged marriage,' she remarked before she turned her attention back to Agnes. 'You don't have to go through with it if you don't want to.'

'It's what my mother wants.'

'But it's not what you want?'

Agnes shook her head. 'No,' she replied. 'It isn't.'

'What do you want?' asked Mrs Anderton gently. 'Have you met someone else?'

'Maybe. I'm not sure.'

'And how well do you know the boy your mother wants you to marry?' asked Mrs Anderton.

'He comes to our church. We went to tea at his house.'

'Do you like him?'

'He's all right, I suppose. But I'm too young to be thinking of marriage! I'm not eighteen yet.'

She watched as Mr and Mrs Anderton exchanged a smile. 'You won't even think of your age when you meet the right person,' Mrs Anderton told her. 'I was younger than you are now when I was married, but I knew that Mr Anderton was the right man for me.' She smiled at her husband again. 'Don't let your mother force you into something you don't want,' she advised.

Agnes took a drink of her tea. This was not the conversation she had envisaged, but it was still a difficult one. She realized that the Andertons were trying to help her, but it was strange for them to advise her to ignore her mother's wishes. It wasn't what people were supposed to do. Back home in Ireland, family was everything and children were expected to do as their parents told them, and the whole community said the same thing. She couldn't imagine Aileen and Michael Walsh, for instance, telling her to rebel against her mother, yet it seemed to be the message that she was being given here.

'What about your cheese selling business?' asked Mr Anderton. 'Do you want to continue with it?'

'Of course I do. But I don't see how I can if I can't borrow the money to buy from the farm.'

'Don't go to one of the money lenders in the town,' warned Mr Anderton. 'Do you remember what I told you about interest? They charge a lot of interest. Besides, I doubt they'd give you anything without a security.'

'I suppose I could ask Mr Reynolds.'

'You could, but there really is no need,' said Mr Anderton. 'Just because your mother is concerned about me lending to you doesn't mean I won't. I made her no promise.'

'Is that wise?' asked his wife, looking concerned. 'I know we were worried about her being married against her will, but . . .'

'But you don't want me to come between mother and daughter,' he finished for her. 'You're right, of course you are, but Agnes has a good business proposition and I believe she deserves a chance to make something of it.' He turned back to Agnes. 'I tried to explain to your mother that I wouldn't have lent you the money in the first place if I'd thought you couldn't pay it back.' He paused as he rubbed a hand over his mouth and chin. 'I hate to see you diminished like this,' he admitted. 'Forced into a marriage and told to give up your business. It's such a shame, and a waste of your talent.'

Although Mr Anderton looked defeated by the situation, Agnes began to see a glimmer of hope. Perhaps it would be possible for her to continue after all. But it would mean defying her mother and that made her feel sad and afraid.

## 16

When Agnes arrived back home, her mother was banking up what remained of the fire ready to go up to bed.

'You're late,' she said.

'I'm sorry. I hope you weren't worried.'

'There's no hot water for tea.'

'I had some at the Andertons' house.'

'They offered you tea?' Her mother sounded amazed. 'Have you been there all this time?'

'Yes.' Agnes nodded. 'We've been talking.'

'What about?' asked her mother, becoming suspicious. 'I thought you'd just gone to pay them the money.'

'I did.'

'But you haven't borrowed any more?' asked her mother. She sounded frantic.

'I have,' Agnes admitted. She placed the bag of money on the table for her mother to see. In the end, she and the Andertons had agreed that they would continue to finance her business on the condition that she was honest with her mother about it.

'If she's still worried tell her she can come and speak to me anytime,' Mr Anderton had said as he'd added another four shillings to the bag Agnes had brought to him and handed it back to her. With that much she would be able to buy two wheels of cheese and Mrs Anderton had suggested that she could use their kitchen to cut and weigh it.

'Dorothy won't mind,' she'd told Agnes.

'I told him not to lend to you again, so I did!' Agnes's mother burst out, shocked that the Andertons had ignored her wishes.

'He said he made no promise,' Agnes told her.

'He knew I was against it.' Her mother seemed bewildered.

'He said that you can talk to him about it again. He said he tried to reassure you.'

Her mother was twisting a cloth around her fingers as she spoke. 'We should have gone to Stockport, like I planned,' she said. 'I shouldn't have allowed the Andertons to bring us back here. I shouldn't have accepted this house. They think they have power over us now. They do have power over us! They're just using you as a plaything, Agnes! It's for their own amusement. And when we owe them enough they'll turn us out. We'll be sent back to Ireland. And it'll be your fault!' she accused her daughter. 'I don't know why you won't listen to me. They've turned your head, so they have.' She sat down on a chair and continued to thread the cloth through her fingers. 'Perhaps we should leave,' she said after a moment. 'Maybe we should go to Stockport after all and find work there.'

Agnes could barely believe what her mother was saying.

'But what if we can't find that family we walked from

Liverpool with? What if they don't remember us? What if there is no work and nowhere to live?' The thought of living on the streets again as they had when they'd first arrived in England frightened her. It had been hard and cold. They'd been uncomfortable and hungry and some nights she'd been very afraid. It would be stupid to risk that happening again.

Her mother was shaking her head. 'I don't know what to do,' she admitted.

'You could try trusting me,' suggested Agnes. 'I know I can make something of this business if only you'll let me. I can help us have a better life.'

Agnes's mother said nothing more. She seemed to accept it was an argument she couldn't win and she watched in silence as Agnes hid the money away after they'd locked up for the night and then went to bed.


On the next Sunday, Agnes told her mother that she wasn't going to church and that, instead, she planned to walk down to the farm at Samlesbury Bottoms and then spend the afternoon cutting up cheese in the Andertons' kitchen.

'Father Kaye will ask where you are,' her mother argued.

'Make an excuse.'

'And the Ryans are expecting us for tea again. They're keen to set a date.'

'Tell them I have a better offer!' snapped Agnes.

'They'll find another girl if you keep letting them down. Then you'll be sorry.'

'I won't. I don't want to marry Patrick.'

'What if no one else will have you? You don't want to end up an old maid!'

Agnes was about to reply that she didn't care. But it wasn't true. She did care. No woman wanted to be left unmarried, to be jeered at in the street and accused of being a witch or simply too ugly for any man to want them. She knew she did want to be married. It was just that she didn't want to be married to Patrick Ryan. Not when so many of her waking thoughts and night-time dreams were about Jonas Marsden. She wanted to see Jonas again and she hoped he would be at the farm. She shivered at the thought of it. Patrick Ryan was nothing by comparison and she would make sure that she stayed in the Andertons' kitchen long enough to avoid the awfulness of taking tea with him and his family again.

She felt tired as she set off with the barrow on her long walk. She hadn't slept well. The disagreements made her feel unhappy and she knew her mother thought she was being deliberately difficult and contrary when all she wanted to do was improve their situation.

It was a miserable morning too. The weather had taken a turn for the worse after the promise of spring and the fierce wind was blowing clouds in from the west that carried sleet and even a flake or two of snow over the tops of the hills. Agnes wrapped her shawl over the patched but serviceable gown that she wore for work. She hadn't had time to wash it and she knew that it stank of the warehouse, but she hoped that the fresh air would whisk away the worst of the smell before she reached Goosefoot Farm.

She was cold and hungry by the time she reached the lane that led up to the farm. She'd come out without any breakfast because she didn't want to linger under her mother's disapproving eye for a moment longer than necessary. The dog barked as she approached and she waited at the gate for someone to come out, rubbing her arms to try to warm herself.

Agnes felt the now familiar lurch of pleasure when she saw Jonas come out of the farmhouse door and walk across the yard towards her. He smiled a warm greeting.

'You're early,' he said.

'I know. I decided to miss church.'

'That's where my parents are,' he told her as he struggled to unfasten the tight knots in the rope that held the gate closed. 'Across at St Leonard's.'

'Do you not go?' she asked him as the gate swung open for her to go in and Jonas grasped the barking dog by its collar, telling it sternly to be quiet.

'I usually do, but I claimed a stomach ache,' he confessed.

Agnes returned his conspiratorial smile and wondered if he'd really stayed behind in the hope that she might come.

'I've come for more cheese,' she said, not knowing what else to say. 'Is there some?'

He nodded. 'I think there might only be one wheel,' he admitted. 'We went to the market at Preston yesterday and trade was brisk.'

Agnes felt disappointed that she couldn't buy the two wheels she had the money for.

'How much?' she asked.

'You'll have to wait for my mother,' he said. 'She's in charge of it.'

Agnes frowned, but she didn't want to insist and cause him to get into trouble, so she prepared herself to wait.

'They shouldn't be long,' he went on. 'Would you like to wait inside? It's very cold out here.'

Agnes left her barrow by the front door and followed Jonas in. The farmhouse was large, much larger than their tiny cottage on Mary Ellen Street. A long passageway with a flagged stone floor led into a kitchen at the back where there was another dog stretched out in front of the fire and a tabby cat nursing three kittens in a box by the hearth. She thought that another box also contained a dog but when she heard it bleat she realized it was a lamb.

'She wants feeding,' said Jonas. 'She always wants feeding.'

'What's she doing inside?' asked Agnes curiously as Jonas took a bottle filled with milk and offered it to the animal which tugged at it excitedly as its tail wagged with pleasure.

'The mother rejected her. She wouldn't let her feed,

so we're rearing her by hand,' he explained. 'She'll go out in the field as soon as she can eat grass or if we can persuade another ewe to adopt her.'

He grasped the bottle more tightly as the lamb almost pulled it from his hands.

'She's very hungry,' Agnes observed as she felt her own stomach growl. There was bread and butter on the table and she was longing for something to eat.

'Sit down,' Jonas invited, and Agnes settled herself on a chair to watch him tend to the animal. He looked almost serene as he fed her and spoke to her in a calm voice, reassuring her. He made Agnes feel safe.

'I'll make some tea,' he said when the lamb was satisfied. 'They'll be back soon.' He glanced at the tall clock that stood against the wall, ticking sombrely. The fingers pointed almost to midday and Agnes wished that time would stand still so she could relish these moments alone with Jonas in the warm and cosy kitchen.

The tea was still brewing when they heard footsteps and Agnes stood up as Mr and Mrs Marsden came in. They paused, surprised, when they saw her and glanced from her to Jonas and back again.

'What's going on?' asked Mr Marsden as if he suspected some foul play.

'I've come to buy cheese again. I came last week,' Agnes reminded him.

'Aye, I remember.' He put down his hat on the table and untied his cravat as if it had been choking him. 'You're not a churchgoer then? To be here at this time?'

'I usually go to mass,' Agnes told him. 'But not today.'

'Mass, is it?' he replied with a look of disapproval. 'I should have known.'

Agnes knew he meant that it was because she was Irish.

'Do you have any cheese for sale?' she asked Mrs Marsden, trying to defuse the awkward moment. She realized she wasn't welcome in their kitchen now and half wished that Jonas had never invited her in.

Mrs Marsden nodded. 'I have a wheel,' she said. 'Come out to the cold room.'

Agnes was glad to follow the woman across the yard where she opened the door of the same building as last week.

'Don't mind my husband,' she said when they were inside. 'He doesn't mean to be rude. It's just his manner.'

Agnes nodded, not sure what to make of this family. It was clear that Mr Marsden could be a difficult man, but rather than putting her off, it made her feel sorry for Jonas and she wanted to reassure him that she didn't think badly of him because of it.

'How much?' she asked, pointing to the cheese.

'Same as last week?'

Agnes agreed and paid Mrs Marsden ten shillings.

'I'll get the change,' she said, although she didn't invite Agnes back into the kitchen.

Whilst she waited, Agnes wheeled the barrow across to the cold room and loaded the cheese. As she wrapped a cloth around her purchase she wondered if there were any other farms hereabouts where she could buy another wheel.

'Do you know anywhere I could buy more?' she asked Mrs Marsden when she returned with her penny ha'penny. 'I had hoped to get two.'

'There's the Fishes,' she said. 'You could try them.'

'Where will I find them?'

'Old College Farm. If you go back to the main road and take the turn towards Mellor Brook, then it's down there on the left. I don't know if they'll have any, though. It depends so much on milk yield, and the weather's taken a turn for the worse this past week.'

'I'll try them,' said Agnes. She realized it was time for her to leave, but there was no sign of Jonas. She'd hoped he would come out to say goodbye to her at least, and at best that he would offer to push the barrow up the lane for her. She hoped he wasn't avoiding her because of what his father had said. 'Can I come again next week?' she asked Mrs Marsden. 'Will you save a wheel or two for me to buy?'

'I can't promise,' she replied. 'It depends if my husband prefers to go to the market with it, and on how much milk there is. Did you say you'd come from Blackburn way?' she asked.

'That's right,' said Agnes. She couldn't remember mentioning it and wondered if Jonas had told his mother.

'I daresay you could buy from a farm nearer to you,' she said.

'I bought yours at the market,' Agnes explained. 'It was good and my customers enjoyed it so I thought it best to get the same again.'

Mrs Marsden nodded. 'It's a long walk,' she observed. 'But I'll do business with you again if you're willing to come all this way.'

Agnes was thankful for the encouragement.

'I'll call our Jonas to give you a hand getting that heavy barrow back up the lane,' she added, with a smile.

Agnes waited by the gate for Jonas to come. The minutes ticked by and the church clock down by the river struck half past the hour as she wondered if his father had refused to let him out. But then she heard the door slam and saw him hurrying across the yard to where she was waiting. She noticed that he was dressed in the smart clothes he'd been wearing the previous Sunday afternoon.

'My father says I'm to go to the Sunday school once I've helped you up the lane,' he told her. 'He says it's obvious my stomach ache is better. Here.' He reached inside his jacket and took out a round of the fresh bread and butter she'd seen on the table. It had a slice of ham squeezed between it. 'My mother was worried that you were hungry.'

Agnes accepted it eagerly and bit into it. 'Tell your mother thank you,' she said with her mouth full as Jonas closed the gate and took the handles of her barrow.

'Don't mind my father,' he said as she walked beside

him. 'He's a morose old bugger sometimes, but there's no real harm in him.'

'I shouldn't have mentioned going to mass,' said Agnes. 'I don't think he liked it.'

'That's hardly your fault,' Jonas told her, but Agnes worried that it might have changed things between them. She knew how strongly people felt about their religious differences.

When they reached the road, Jonas rested the barrow on its legs and blew on his hands.

'I should have worn gloves,' he said. He glanced at her hands which were also bare. 'You should have worn yours as well.'

Agnes agreed. She didn't tell him that she didn't own any gloves.

'Well, thank you for helping me,' she said.

'Can you manage from here?'

'Yes. I'm sure I can. I managed last week.'

'Are you going straight back?'

'I might try to buy another wheel. Your mother suggested Old College Farm. She said it was down a lane to the left.'

'It is. But you'll never find it on your own,' he told her. 'I could show you the way, if you like?'

'What about your Sunday school?' she asked.

'They'll not miss me.' He grinned and picked up the handles of the barrow again.

## 17

Agnes realized that she would never have found this place on her own and would probably have become totally lost in the countryside if she hadn't had Jonas to guide her.

As she stood beside him in the muddy yard, she heard a cow calling plaintively from one of the sheds, and more of the black and white beasts were gathering near a gate, watching them curiously with their ears flickering back and forth.

'It must be getting near their milking time,' Jonas told her. 'They like to come in because they get a handful of hay whilst they're being milked.'

'Jonas! What brings you this afternoon?' called a man in fustian britches and high boots, who Agnes took to be Farmer Fish. He came across to let them in through the five-barred gate and looked at Agnes as curiously as the cows had.

'We've come to see if you've any cheese for sale,' Jonas told him.

'Hast tha not got enough of thine own?' The farmer laughed.

'It's not for me. It's for Agnes here.'

'What does she want it for?' asked Mr Fish, continuing to address Jonas.

'She's selling it locally,' he explained. 'She's bought one from my mother but she wanted another and we sold most of ours at Preston.'

'She's only a lass. Does she know what she's about? We usually only deal with the market traders.'

'I have the money to pay you,' interjected Agnes, beginning to feel annoyed that the man was not speaking directly to her.

'Well, I think we have some spare. I'll fetch the wife,' he said, as if he wanted no part in the deal.

They stood waiting whilst Mr Fish went back to the farmhouse, whistling to his dogs to accompany him. Agnes wondered whether to tell Jonas that she thought the man was rude, but she kept silent. If she was going to make a success of her business, she would need to learn how to deal with these farmers who found it odd that she was asking to buy directly from them.

It wasn't long before Mrs Fish came out, with a faded shawl clutched around her head, and led them to her dairy.

'We've a few in here,' she said as she pushed open a wooden door that had swelled in the damp weather and was sticking to the uneven stone floor. 'How many are you after?'

'Just one, please,' Agnes told her. 'How much do you charge?'

'Agnes agreed fourpence three farthings a pound with my mother,' interrupted Jonas. Agnes wished he would be quiet and allow her to negotiate for herself.

'All right. Tha can have this at the same price.' Mrs Fish lifted a wheel down from the stone slab and handed it to Jonas who carried it out and settled it into Agnes's barrow. The farmer's wife watched him as if she was expecting him to come back and pay her and seemed surprised when Agnes got out her purse and counted out ten shillings.

'Have you got change?' asked Agnes.

'Aye,' said the woman, looking at her properly for the first time. 'I'll just go and get it. Are you selling it yourself?' she asked.

'Yes. I go door to door with it.'

'First time I've heard of that,' she replied. 'Do folk buy it from you?'

'Yes,' Agnes told her.

'Oh,' the woman replied as if she thought it was a strange thing to do.

As they walked back to the main road, with Jonas pushing the heavy barrow, Agnes wondered if the Fishes would have sold to her if she had gone to their farm alone. Both they and the Marsdens seemed puzzled by the idea of her business. As far as they knew, cheese was sold on stalls at the markets that were held in the surrounding towns. That was how it was done, and doing it differently seemed to baffle them for some reason.

'Are you sure you can push this all the way?' asked Jonas when they reached the road. 'I could come part-way with you, if you like?'

He looked hesitant, as if he wasn't entirely sure if he

would be welcome. Agnes was about to remind him that he was supposed to be on his way to Sunday school, but she didn't want him to think that she was sending him away.

'I'd like that,' she said. 'If it's not too much trouble.'

'No trouble,' he smiled as he picked up the handles of the barrow again and they started off up the hill in the direction of Blackburn.

Agnes walked beside him, enjoying the warmth from the sun that had broken through the clouds and the close proximity of Jonas.

'I hope you won't get into trouble for not going to your lessons,' she said at last to break the silence. She sensed that he wanted to talk but was unsure what to say. His shyness endeared him to her. He was unlike the brash lads that Mr Reynolds employed in the warehouse who gave her cheek every day.

'It doesn't matter,' he assured her.

'My brother Timothy goes to a Sunday school. He works at the post office as a delivery boy.' She didn't say she wished she could go too. 'I can write my name,' she went on, 'and I can do the sums in my head.'

Jonas nodded. 'You surprised me by how quickly you could do calculations.'

'Mr Reynolds at the warehouse says I have a head for business. I really want to make a success of this cheese selling,' she told him.

'So will you be coming for more next week?' he asked, glancing at her. She thought he looked hopeful.

'Of course I will!'

'I could help you again. If you'd like me to,' he offered.

'I would like that,' she replied. 'Your lessons are important though,' she added after a moment. 'It's good to get an education.'

'I know,' he said. 'But given a choice I'd rather be in your company.'

Agnes felt herself blush. It was the first time he'd admitted that he liked being with her, and when she looked at him he seemed embarrassed and unsure what her response would be.

'I enjoy being with you as well,' she told him. He smiled at her then and it was if the air had cleared between them now that they were both sure of the other's feelings.

In the end, Jonas walked all the way back to Blackburn with her and by mid-afternoon he was helping her carry the cheeses down the back steps of the Andertons' house and into Dorothy's kitchen.

'That thy young man, all done up in his Sunday best?' asked Dorothy after Jonas had tipped his hat to her, smiled warmly at Agnes and said that he was looking forward to seeing her the next week, then gone on his way.

'No!' she protested, hoping that Jonas wouldn't be mistaken for Patrick Ryan. 'He's from Goosefoot Farm. He was just helping me with the cheese.'

'Aye,' remarked Dorothy with a knowing look. 'Just helping,' she repeated. 'That'll be it.'

Agnes didn't reply, but the maid's words made her smile. If the attraction that she and Jonas had for one another was so obvious that even Dorothy could see it, then it must be strong.

She hung her shawl over the back of a chair, poured some hot water to wash her hands and set about her task of cutting up the cheese. The wire that Dorothy had found at the back of one of her shelves made the job so much easier, and as Agnes weighed each piece and re-adjusted her estimates of where to cut, she found that she became more accurate as the afternoon wore on and darkness began to fall.

Dorothy provided her with tea and cake and chatted amiably as she sat by the fire. Mrs Anderton came down to see how she was getting on and stayed a while, watching the process, then bought a pound and paid Agnes herself.

Slicing up the two cheeses took longer than Agnes had anticipated and she knew that she was going to be late for her tea. She hoped that her mother wouldn't be too cross with her. She reckoned that if she ate quickly there would still be time for her to go around her usual customers before bedtime, no matter that it was Sunday.

When the portions of cheese had been loaded back into the barrow, Dorothy helped her to carry it up the steps and Agnes set off for home as the lighters were going around the main streets with their flames and ladders, lighting the gas lamps.

Worshippers were making their way to evening service as she passed the parish church and Agnes felt a twinge of guilt about her own non-attendance at St Alban's that morning. Father Kaye would not be pleased with her.

She hurried as she turned into Mary Ellen Street, hoping that Timothy would be at home and would help her get the cheese and the barrow through the door. She pushed it open and called out: 'It's only me! Come and give me a hand!' But the figure that rose from the chair beside the hearth and stood staring at her was not her brother, but Patrick Ryan.

'I've been waiting for you,' he said.

Behind him, Agnes could see her mother, with a face like a thunderstorm.

'We expected you for your tea an hour ago,' she said.

'I know. I'm sorry. I've been at the Andertons' doing the cheese. Can you help me to bring it in?' she asked, not wanting to leave the barrow unattended in the street.

Patrick came to the door and lifted a corner of the cloth that covered the cheese. He looked astonished by the amount she had.

'There's pounds and pounds of it!' he exclaimed.

'Two full wheels,' Agnes told him.

'Your mam said you'd gone to buy some cheese, but I never thought you'd come back with all this. What are you going to do with it?' he asked.

'Sell it,' she told him. 'I've started a cheese business.'

Patrick helped her to bring the barrow inside and watched as Agnes stacked the portions of cheese on the cold stone slab under the kitchen window. She was aware of her mother watching in dismay, and although the last person she'd expected to find in her home was Patrick, she was at least grateful that his presence was preventing her mother from complaining about how much she'd bought.

'Patrick has been waiting for you for hours,' her mother told her. 'When I went to the Ryans' house to explain that you couldn't go for tea because you'd had to go on an urgent errand he said he would eat here with you when you got back. He's been very patient,' she added.

'Have you had anything to eat?' Agnes asked Patrick, feeling guilty that he might have gone hungry on her account whilst she'd been kept replenished by Dorothy's delicious madeira cake.

'We were waiting for you,' he said.

Agnes looked at the table. There were mounds of food covered by a cloth and when she lifted the edge she saw a pile of ham sandwiches, a pile of jam sandwiches and their best tea service. It wasn't much compared to what the Ryans had provided, but she knew that her mother must have used the food that was meant to last them all week to impress Patrick.

'Shall we sit down now?' she asked. 'Where are the others?' She'd been so busy sorting out the cheese that she'd only just realized her brothers and sister were missing.

'Maria took Peter to visit the Walshes,' replied her

mother. 'Timothy was going to call there on his way home from the Sunday school.'

Agnes understood that she'd sent them away so they wouldn't eat everything and also because she wanted to give her and Patrick time alone together. 'Sit down,' she went on. 'Offer Patrick the sandwiches and I'll brew the tea.'

Agnes pulled out a chair for Patrick at the table then sat down opposite him. The air was thick with tension as he accepted a ham sandwich and put it on his plate, then waited as her mother came to the table with the teapot.

'Let it brew a while,' she instructed as she reached for her shawl. 'I'll go to fetch the others.'

Agnes listened to her mother's footsteps as she went down the street.

'Tea?' she asked Patrick as she lifted the lid of the pot and gave it a stir.

He nodded and Agnes added a dash of milk to the cup first to prevent it cracking when the hot liquid was poured in.

She picked up one of the sandwiches herself although she only nibbled at the edges. Her appetite had deserted her. She knew what was coming and she was unsure how to deal with it.

'When your mother said you'd gone on an errand I didn't know you were buying cheese,' said Patrick as his glance strayed to the neat piles that Agnes had stacked up.

'If I buy it cheaply enough from the farm I can sell it on at a profit,' she explained.

He nodded. 'I wondered why you wouldn't agree to walk out with me,' he said.

'It's something I want to do – the cheese business, I mean,' Agnes explained. 'My mother has so little. I want to help her by earning some extra money.'

'I know you're poor,' said Patrick. 'I know your mother finds it hard to manage. But I have a job that pays fairly well. I could help you.'

'There's no need for you to do that.'

'No. I mean that if we were married you wouldn't need to do this.' He waved his hand towards the cheese. 'You wouldn't need to work on a Sunday,' he said, and Agnes could see that he disapproved of it. 'It should be a day to rest. In fact, if we were married you probably wouldn't need to work at all.'

'But I want to work. I want to make a success of this business,' she told him.

He seemed puzzled. 'But you can't enjoy it,' he said, 'pushing all that heavy cheese about and knocking on strangers' doors.'

'I do enjoy it,' she told him, although she didn't mention how much she'd hated being on the receiving end of abuse from some people. 'I want to make a success of it. Mr Anderton thinks I can. And Mr Reynolds says I have a flair for business dealings.'

'But you wouldn't need to if you were my wife,' Patrick persisted. 'My wage would be enough to keep us.'

'But what if I wanted to? You wouldn't stop me, would you?' she challenged him.

Patrick looked uncomfortable. 'I wouldn't want people to think that I couldn't support you,' he mumbled.

Agnes put down her half-eaten sandwich and wished that her mother would come back to save her from having to pursue this conversation.

'I don't think that us getting married is such a good idea,' she said after a few moments of awkward silence.

He looked directly at her, seemingly bewildered.

'I thought it was what you wanted.'

'No.' Agnes was shaking her head and wishing that she didn't have to disappoint him like this. He was a nice enough lad and she hated to hurt his feelings, but being sorry for someone wasn't reason enough to marry them. Besides, as her mother had so rightly pointed out, there were plenty of other girls who would be glad to have him.

'But I thought it was all arranged?' he protested.

'It's what my mother wants,' admitted Agnes, 'and your parents too.'

'It's what I want,' he told her, reaching out across the table to grasp her hand. Agnes pulled away and as she did so she knocked over her teacup so that the brown liquid ran in a rivulet across her mother's best tablecloth. She jumped up to fetch the dishcloth to try to mop it up. It would stain and her mother would be upset, and Agnes felt so guilty about the whole thing.

She was letting so many people down and she knew it would be easier to simply agree and let the wedding go ahead. But she couldn't. There was her business, and there was Jonas. She couldn't just forget Jonas, because she thought she was falling in love with him, and she hoped that he was with her as well.

# 18

Kitty walked slowly down to Butcher's Court. She wanted to give Agnes and Patrick enough time alone to agree that they would be married. She'd been angry with Agnes when she'd gone out with the barrow that morning instead of attending mass, and she'd been embarrassed when she'd had to explain to the Ryans that they couldn't come for tea because her daughter had gone out on an errand.

Bridie had obviously been put out and Kitty was terrified that she might begin having second thoughts about the wedding. If Agnes lost this chance, she might never have such a good one again, and Kitty wished that she could make her daughter realize that. If only her father were here. He would have been able to make her see sense. She'd made the mistake of relying too heavily on her daughter and making a friend of her. It made it much harder to talk to her as a parent.

In the end she'd compromised by asking Patrick to call to take his tea with them, saying that she was sure Agnes wouldn't be late home. But she'd waited and waited, making small talk with her prospective son-in-law until she was at a loss to know what else to say. And Patrick was no conversationalist. He'd sat in the best chair by the fire and looked awkward and ill-at-ease until Kitty had been reduced to praying silently that Agnes would come. Then, when she did, she'd brought all that cheese and Kitty had been forced to pretend that it was a normal thing to do and that she didn't mind when she wasn't sure who she was the most annoyed with – Agnes for buying it, or Mr Anderton for lending her the money when she'd expressly begged him not to.

'Everything all right?' Aileen asked her when she arrived at the Walshes' home.

'I hope so,' she replied. 'I've left them to it,' she told her friend, 'and I pray to God that they'll have agreed it between themselves by the time I get back.'

'I'm sure they will have,' Aileen reassured her. 'I've fed the little ones. Timothy wouldn't have anything.'

'Oh, thank you,' said Kitty. 'You didn't need to do that.' She knew that the Walshes had no more to spare than she had, and she thought guiltily of all the sandwiches that she'd made – more than she could really afford because she didn't want Patrick to think she was ungenerous or grudging in her invitation. She would send Timothy back with some of them later, she decided.

As they walked home, the church bells fell silent as the evening services began and the streets were quiet for once. Kitty relished the unusual silence. She often found herself longing for the peace of the rolling hillsides in the land of her birth, but she knew that she would never see it again, and tears threatened at the unbidden loss.

She shushed the children as they reached the door on Mary Ellen Street.

'We have a visitor,' she warned them before they went in.

She went in first, pushing open the door cautiously, not wanting to embarrass the happy couple if they were kissing, but when she looked around there was no sign of Patrick, and Agnes was loading pieces of her cheese into the basket.

'Where's Patrick?'

'He's gone home.'

'I expected him to stay longer – to tell me the good news.'

'There is no good news,' her daughter replied. 'I told him I didn't want to marry him and he went.'

'Went?' Kitty found that she was staring around the kitchen as if she would suddenly see him there. This couldn't be true. It made no sense. She couldn't believe that Agnes had thrown away such a good chance at happiness and security and that she didn't even seem to care.

'What are you doing?' she asked.

'I'm going out to sell some of this cheese before it gets too late,' Agnes replied, as if the answer was obvious.

Kitty watched as her daughter put on her shawl, picked up the basket and walked past her. She had no words. No words at all. Just despair and disbelief that everything she had hoped for was being thrown away.

# 19

Agnes hurried out on to the street. She knocked on Wilf and Edna's door and sold them a pound of cheese, then worked her way down the street, visiting her usual customers until her basket was empty and her purse was beginning to fill. She contemplated going round some other streets, but it was growing late so she walked home slowly, putting off the inevitable row with her mother.

She went in, locking and barring the door behind her, and put the basket on the shelf. She would fill it again the next morning and go to work early to sell cheese to the warehouse workers. Her mother and Timothy were still up, but when he saw her, Timothy gave a protracted yawn and said that he was tired and was going to bed.

Agnes sat down opposite her mother and listened to his footsteps climbing to the bedroom above.

'I'm sorry you're disappointed . . . about Patrick,' she ventured when she couldn't take the strained silence a moment longer.

Her mother shook her head. 'I can't force you,' she admitted.

Her mother's weary resignation made Agnes feel worse than the recriminations that she'd been expecting.

'I don't want to think about marriage yet,' she told her mother.

'He'll be wed to some other girl before the summer's out,' her mother predicted. 'I hope you won't regret it then.'

'I won't.'

'You say that now,' her mother persisted, 'but when the day comes you may think differently. It was a good chance for you. He liked you. And I don't know what the Ryans will think of us now,' she admitted. 'I was so pleased when they agreed to it.'

It would be awkward, thought Agnes, seeing the Ryans at church. She wouldn't know what to say to Patrick the next time she saw him. She would prefer to avoid him and it might be best if she kept away from St Alban's for a while at least, although she knew that would hurt her mother even more.

'I can make money from the cheese business,' she told her, in an attempt to reassure her mother that she knew what she was doing. 'I'm doing it to help you.'

'I know you mean well, Agnes,' her mother replied with a sigh, 'but these ventures aren't easy to make a success of. There's every chance you'll lose more money than you make. It isn't worth it when you could have had a husband and a home of your own. You've thrown so much away and I don't think you even realize it.'

Agnes watched as her mother stood up and began to bank up the fire for the night. The table had been cleared, she saw. The best pots washed and put away, the remains of the sandwiches wrapped up for tomorrow.

'I'll go up then,' she said, lighting a candle to guide her way. 'I've locked the door.'

She would normally have wished her mother a good night and kissed her, but instead Agnes turned away and went up the steep steps. She put the candle on the little table by the bed, quickly undressed and got under the covers. It was imperative now that her business did succeed, or she would never hear the last of her failures and her mother would never forgive her.

Next morning, Agnes was up first. She'd been restless all night, switching between wakefulness and dreams that left her feeling anxious and unsettled. She went down to the kitchen and filled her basket, took one of the ham sandwiches to eat later and let herself out into the street.

At the warehouse she waited for what seemed ages until Mr Reynolds came, but at least she was out of the house. As the other workers arrived she offered them cheese and was pleased with the steady stream of customers she attracted until it was time to begin her work.

She felt tired after her long walk the day before and her disturbed night, but she put the feeling aside and stifled her yawns. She didn't want Mr Reynolds to think that she was neglecting her warehouse duties.

When dinnertime came she walked down to the market square with her basket, offering cheese for sale. A few businessmen glared at her as they passed by, but most looked at her curiously, although she made no sales to them. It was their wives and maids who were in charge of any food purchases.

Not many people were out shopping as it wasn't a market day, but a few came by and bought from her.

'You were here last week,' said one.

'I'll be here every week,' said Agnes, hoping that word would get around. Whilst there was no competition from the market trader, anyone who wanted fresh cheese had to come to her, and by the end of an hour her basket was empty. She walked back to Clifton Street feeling pleased with herself.

That evening, she went out again, around the courts and streets where the Irish lived. Some bought from her, but others hung back even though their faces were eager.

'How much?' asked one woman with a cluster of scrawny, malnourished children hanging on to her ragged skirts.

'Thruppence a half-pound,' said Agnes.

The woman stared at the cheese then shook her head.

'I can't afford that,' she admitted as she reluctantly closed the door of her cellar dwelling and Agnes heard the pathetic crying of her children who looked as if they hadn't eaten for days.

Agnes could see that they were desperately hungry and she was tempted to give some of the cheese away. But she knew she must harden her heart. If she gave to one family then they would all expect it and it would be the ruin of her.

Next, she went along the backs of the better houses on

Richmond Terrace and then down to King Street. She saw Dorothy in her kitchen and waved as she went past.

'Is tha not calling here?' Dorothy called after her from the open door.

Agnes walked back to speak to her.

'Mrs Anderton bought a pound on Sunday,' she reminded her.

'That's all gone. I'll take another pound.'

Agnes went down the steps and waited for Dorothy to bring her the money.

'Will tha take a cup of tea?' she asked.

Agnes knew she should refuse. She wanted to visit as many houses as she could so that she would return home with an empty basket, but she was so tired and cold that the temptation was too much for her and she sank into the cushions of Dorothy's fireside chair and closed her eyes for a moment whilst the maid brought a cup and saucer.

'Tha looks all in,' observed Dorothy as she handed her the drink. 'Tha wants to be careful that tha's not doing too much. It'll do thee no good to exhaust thyself.'

'I'm all right,' said Agnes, sipping the hot, sweet tea and struggling to keep her eyes open in the warmth of the comfortable kitchen. She wasn't going to admit it, but she was tired out. Doing a full week's work and then working all day Sunday and every evening was demanding, and she wished that there were more hours in the day. But the tea refreshed her and before long she roused herself to carry on.

'Tell Mr Anderton I'll call with his money before the

end of the week,' she said to Dorothy as she left. Her purse was already bulging and Agnes was confident that she could pay her debt by then.

She decided to try some streets she hadn't been down before. She felt anxious because she hated knocking on strangers' doors, but she knew she must be brave if she was to sell the two full wheels of cheese before the end of the week.

As she turned into Heaton Street, she saw a man on the other side of the road. At first she thought he was going to approach her and she held out the basket ready to offer him a portion, but when he realized that she'd seen him, he pulled down his hat, turned up the collar on his jacket and strode away with his hands deep in his pockets.

Agnes thought no more about him but knocked on the first door, and when it was opened she made her little speech about her wares.

'Only thruppence for half a pound,' she added. 'You'll not get it that cheap on the market.'

The woman shook her head and closed the door. Agnes tried not to fret. She'd learnt that she would never make a sale at every house and that it was no use feeling as if she'd failed when a door was shut in her face. She must move on and keep knocking. If she sold cheese at every fifth door, she thought she was doing well, and even every tenth door would mean her basket would be empty before bedtime.

It was always harder when she was selling to new customers. On other streets she was beginning to know her regulars who welcomed her with a smile and fetched their money eagerly. But each successful transaction added a boost to her step and helped her to forget how weary she was.

When she turned the corner into Clayton Street, she heard footsteps behind her and, turning quickly, she thought that she saw the man she'd noticed before. But when she looked again there was no sign of him and Agnes thought that she must have imagined it.

She reached the third door down before she made a successful sale. The woman bought a full pound from her and recommended her neighbour where Agnes knocked with enthusiasm.

'I have cheese for sale – fresh Lancashire cheese, straight from the farm. It's only thruppence a half-pound.' Agnes saw that the woman was about to close the door. 'Your neighbour's just bought a full pound from me,' she told her.

The woman hesitated. 'Really?' she asked.

'You can ask her yourself. She said you enjoy a bit of good cheese.'

'All right,' agreed the woman. 'I'll take a half-pound.'

Agnes made steady sales all down the street. Her basket became lighter and her purse heavier until she came to a space between two rows of terraces where a narrow ginnel led to the backs of the houses. The light of the street lamps didn't reach this far and by the time she saw the man lunge out at her it was too late to avoid him. Agnes swung the basket at him, but its wickerwork bounced easily off his shoulder without deterring him and he pushed it aside, knocking it from her grip. Agnes watched as the remaining cheese portions spilled out on to the dirty cobbles. They would all be spoiled. Even if she took them home and wiped off the mud they wouldn't be fit to be sold. Angrily, she turned on the man to berate him for his clumsiness, but rather than the apology she expected from him she felt his hand grasp her arm and the ground rushed up towards her face. Agnes didn't have time to put out a hand to save herself and she felt the stones smash into her cheek. Stunned, she lay still for a moment trying to make sense of what had just happened. Then she felt someone tugging at her clothing and before she could even call out, she saw the man running away down the street, his boots thumping on the flagged pavement and something clutched in his hand.

It took Agnes a moment to register that he had stolen her purse. He must have had a knife, she realized when the remains of the ribbon that had tied it around her waist dropped to her feet as she struggled up.

'Stop!' she cried out as he turned the corner and disappeared. She ran after him, but by the time she reached the end of the street he'd disappeared into the night.

Agnes wiped the tears that were streaming down her face, and as she glanced at her hand in the light of a gas lamp she saw that her fingers were smeared in blood, either from her nose or a cut to her head. She didn't know which.

Curtains were twitching as people came to their windows to see what all the commotion was about, and as Agnes limped back to where her basket and her cheeses were strewn in the gutter she saw the woman she'd sold the full pound to hurrying towards her.

'What happened?' she asked, staring at Agnes, who wiped her face again and realized that it was her nose that was bleeding profusely. She picked up the cloth that had covered her basket and almost wiped her face with it, until it occurred to her how cross her mother would be if she stained it with blood. Instead she lifted the edge of her shawl and held it to her face to staunch the flow.

'I was robbed,' she told the woman.

'You'd best step inside for a moment.'

'I'm all right,' Agnes protested. She reached down to pick up the cheese, but as she did so the world swirled about her and she sat down hurriedly before she fell.

'You're not all right,' the woman told her, putting an arm around her and helping her to her feet again. 'You've had a shock. Come inside for a moment until you've gathered your wits.'

Agnes allowed the woman to help her into the house and to her kitchen where she brought a chair for her to sit on and hurried to rinse a cloth in a bucket of cold water and hand it to Agnes to hold to her face.

Someone else came in with the spoiled cheese put back in the basket and placed it beside her.

'Tha'll not be able to sell that now. What a shame,' they said.

'What did he take?' asked the first woman.

'My purse,' sobbed Agnes as the full impact of what had occurred took hold of her and she began to tremble. 'All my takings.' She tried to reckon how much she'd lost, but she felt confused and nothing made much sense.

'Do you think she needs a doctor?' someone said. Agnes could sense the women crowding in around her, but she couldn't focus on any of them.

'I don't know. Do you think we should send for a constable?' asked another.

'No. Not a constable!' exclaimed Agnes. Her mother would never forgive her if she involved the police.

'Did tha see who the man was?' asked another.

Agnes tried to describe him, but it might have been anyone. He was just a man in dark clothing. There was no chance that she could identify him, and the women agreed that it was unlikely the local constable would find him anyway.

'Probably from out of town,' said one.

'Probably Irish,' said another, and the comment hurt Agnes more keenly than the blow. Irish stealing from Irish didn't concern anyone and she knew she would never see her money again.

A while later, when her nose had stopped bleeding and she'd drunk the cup of tea her rescuer had made, Agnes thanked the woman for her help and walked slowly home. She was dreading telling her mother what had happened. She didn't want to admit that she had lost so much of her money, and she felt a failure for allowing it to happen when she knew she ought to have been more careful.

She pushed open the door and turned to lock it behind her, hoping she didn't look too much of a mess. She'd been able to wash her hands and face, but the way the woman who'd taken her in had kept glancing at her face she knew it wasn't a pretty sight.

'Agnes! What happened?'

The alarm on her mother's face was clear as she leapt up from her chair.

'I'm all right. I took a tumble, that's all,' Agnes replied. She'd been thinking about what she should say as she walked home and had decided that it would be better if her mother didn't know about the robbery and thought that she'd just had an accident. She didn't want to worry her or give her a reason to try to stop her selling the cheese.

She put the basket on the table because she knew she couldn't hide the spoiled contents.

'Sit down,' said her mother. 'You look as white as a ghost.'

'I'm all right,' Agnes insisted. 'A lady took me in and helped me clean up the worst of it. I had a bit of a nosebleed, that's all.'

'Oh, Agnes.' She felt herself folded into her mother's embrace and it made her cry again. It seemed so long since her mother had held her and rocked her like this whilst kissing her head and promising that she would make it better. It transported Agnes back to the time when she was a child in Ireland and every bump and scrape could be cured with her mother's touch. It made her feel safe, but also guilty that she wasn't telling her mother what had really happened. But she wasn't a child any longer, she reminded herself. She was a grown-up now and it was her turn to protect her mother from the worst of the truth. She didn't want to tell her about the lost money because she knew how much it would worry her.

Her mother helped her take off her shawl and brought a cloth and warm water to bathe her face and hands again.

'I knew no good would come of this walking about in the dark,' she said as she carefully wiped Agnes's face.

'I know,' replied Agnes, as she flinched from the touch. She ought to have realized sooner that a young woman walking the streets alone, after dark, was sure to attract the wrong sort of attention. She should have seen the danger sooner. She'd been foolish and now she'd landed herself into just the sort of trouble her mother was worried about. She had half a basket of cheese that she couldn't sell and all the money she'd taken that night was gone. She didn't know if she would be able to pay Mr Anderton back – and even if she could, it would mean using all the profit she'd made so far. She wondered if she should give it all up and agree to marry Patrick Ryan after all. It suddenly seemed the sensible thing to do.

## 20

When Agnes got up the next morning and looked in the small mirror that they kept on the windowsill by the sink, she was horrified by her reflection. With the swelling and bruising around both her eyes, she barely recognized herself.

She splashed her face with cold water, but it made the cuts sting and did nothing to improve her looks. She wished that she didn't have to go to work, but her wages were even more important now that she'd lost the cheese money, so she gently brushed her hair, pulled on a cap and set off for the warehouse.

'What on earth happened to thee?' gasped Mr Reynolds as soon as he saw her. 'Tha looks a right mess!'

'I tripped and fell,' she told him. Every time she repeated the story it felt more like the truth.

He shook his head as he looked at her. 'Tha'd best not be seen in t' shop today,' he said. 'Tha'll frighten t' customers away. Best come across to the warehouse and I'll send young Freddy to mind things here until tha's fit to be seen again.'

It seemed like a demotion to Agnes as she tied a coarse apron around herself and began work at one of the sorting tables. As the other women came in they all asked her how she'd been hurt. Agnes repeated her story and they expressed sympathy and told her not to worry. The bruises would fade, they said. Agnes wished that it was that simple, but she said nothing and smiled as best she could, even though it hurt to move her face.

At dinnertime she walked home. There was some cheese left on the slab but she couldn't bring herself to take it to the market square today. She chewed painfully on some bread and dripping, drank tea and then went back to her work, knowing that before long she must count up her money to see if she could repay Mr Anderton.

She worked mechanically all afternoon, trying to remain cheerful and ignore her pain.

'Chin up!' the other workers told her, trying to make her feel better, but their words plunged Agnes into deeper despair. The more she thought about her situation, the more depressed she felt. And what about Jonas? she asked herself over and over again. She couldn't bear the thought of him seeing her face like this.

That evening she brought down the money that she'd put away in her drawer upstairs and began to count it at the kitchen table. There was eleven shillings and six-pence and she owed Mr Anderton a pound and a penny. There were twelve portions of clean cheese left on the slab and if she managed to sell them all she would have another three shillings, but that still wasn't enough to repay the debt. She'd lost almost three shillings in the robbery and over two shillings' worth of cheese had been spoiled. Even if she added in all her profit from the previous weeks, she would still only have seventeen shillings. Agnes knew that she had no choice but to go to King Street the next day and admit that she had failed.

'Is there enough?' asked her mother anxiously as she watched Agnes count the coins yet again.

'I need to sell what's left of the cheese.'

'You're not going out in the dark again!' her mother told her.

'I won't,' she agreed. 'Maybe I'll take it to the market square tomorrow.'

'But it's market day,' her mother reminded her. 'The cheesemonger will be there.'

'I know. But I can walk around with the basket. If I'm selling it cheaper than he is I'm almost bound to get some custom.'

'You'll only have an hour. You can't miss your work. If Mr Reynolds were to lay you off I don't know what we'd do.'

'I'll not lose my job,' Agnes reassured her.

The next day she took what cheese she had left with her to the warehouse. The swelling on her face had reduced, but the bruises were turning shades of purple and green and Mr Reynolds still didn't want her to be seen in the shop, so there was no opportunity to put her basket on the counter there in the hope of a few extra sales.

When dinnertime came she hurried to the market

square, eating some oatcakes she'd brought from home as she walked. The market was busy and she knew that she would need to do something to mark herself out as a seller rather than a buyer. Agnes hated to draw attention to herself, but she knew that Jonas had failed to make sales by not calling out his wares and that she mustn't make the same mistake.

'I have cheese for sale,' she began to say to the women who pushed past her. 'Lancashire cheese. Fresh from the farm. Only thruppence for a half-pound.'

If anyone showed interest, she lifted the corner of the clean cloth she'd taken from her mother's drawer to show them that they were getting a bargain.

She walked about near to the cheese stall. She reckoned it was where she would find customers who were out to purchase cheese, and she hoped that when they heard her price they would buy from her.

As she sold to one woman, she noticed the cheese-monger was watching her. He must have seen what she was doing and she hoped he wasn't going to reduce his price to compete with hers or even undercut it as he had done with Jonas. Agnes could see him speaking urgently to his wife who also glanced in her direction and shook her head. They were obviously rattled by her presence, but it was a free world, thought Agnes. She could sell her cheese wherever she wanted to.

She continued to walk around in the vicinity of the stall, offering her wares, whilst keeping an eye on the market house clock. The time ball on top of the clock tower would be raised as it approached one o'clock and at one it would drop and the gun would be fired. Agnes knew that she must run back to the warehouse for her afternoon shift as soon as that happened.

Several portions of the cheese had been sold and Agnes was hoping that they might all go when she suddenly felt a heavy hand on her shoulder. She turned abruptly, thinking how ill-mannered the person was when she was just finishing a sale to someone else.

'You can't sell here!' the man barked at her. Agnes stared at him. He was a squat little man with bushy whiskers, a dark hat and a blue coat. He seemed familiar but she couldn't place him.

Agnes took a step away and put a protective hand over her purse. Surely this man wasn't about to rob her in broad daylight with so many people around? She looked about desperately for someone who might help her.

'Get away from me!' she shouted at him, hoping that someone in the crowd might stop to assist her.

A few people did look in her direction, but none of them seemed unduly concerned as the man took hold of her again.

'You can't sell here!' he said.

'I can sell if I want to,' Agnes protested.

'Not on the market square, you can't,' replied the man. 'Not without paying for a pitch.'

Agnes suddenly remembered where she'd seen him before. He was the market superintendent who'd been waiting to lock up the market house the night she'd returned to buy from Jonas.

'I've a good mind to send for a constable,' he told her sternly.

'I didn't know I was doing anything wrong,' Agnes insisted. Clearly, she'd made a huge mistake. It had been no problem when it wasn't market day, but now she realized that the cheesemonger must have complained about her because she was taking his trade. 'I'll go,' she told the market superintendent, trying to wriggle free from his tight grasp. 'I won't come again on market day. Please,' she added. 'I'm sorry.'

The superintendent looked doubtful. 'You lot are all the same,' he muttered. 'You think the law doesn't apply to you.'

'I honestly didn't know I was doing anything wrong,' pleaded Agnes. All she wanted to do was get away from him. She didn't want to get on the wrong side of the law. And she didn't want to be late back to the warehouse.

'I have to go,' she told him. 'I have work at the rag warehouse. I was only doing this in my dinnertime.'

The man looked as if he might relent and his grip on her eased.

'Who did that to your face?' he asked.

'I fell,' said Agnes, but it was obvious he didn't believe her. She'd been getting stares and glances ever since she'd arrived, and from what she'd heard people say, when they thought they were out of her hearing, it was clear the consensus was that she'd been beaten, probably by a husband or father.

'Aye,' said the man, continuing to soften. 'I'll tell you what. You clear off to wherever you've come from. And don't let me see you around here again,' he warned, 'or I will bring a constable.'

Agnes pulled her arm away and turned to go before he changed his mind. It would save him a lot of bother just to let her off with a warning, she thought. As she hurried back to the warehouse, she heard the one o'clock gun and she began to run. The last of the cheese jiggled in the basket and she hoped that it wouldn't break into pieces. She would have to risk going out again that evening to sell it, no matter how afraid she was. She would stick to well-lit streets, she decided, and she would make an excuse to her mother. But she needed every penny she could make if she was to stand any chance of repaying Mr Anderton.

'I'm going to the Andertons' house with the money,' she told her mother later, after she'd eaten her tea.

As she stepped out on to the street, she looked both ways to check there was no one hanging about. If her mother had known the truth of what had really happened to her, she would never have allowed her to leave in the dark, especially with so much money on her.

She had intended to go down the alley behind the King Street houses and try to sell what she had left at the kitchen doors, but when she reached the ginnel she was shaking and couldn't bring herself to step into the gloom, so she retreated and went to the Andertons' front door instead, hoping that Mr Anderton wouldn't be too angry when she explained to him that she couldn't repay all of his money.

Dorothy looked surprised when she answered the door and saw Agnes on the front steps. For a moment Agnes thought that the maid was going to send her around the back, but she invited her into the hallway, her expression changing to shock when she saw Agnes's face in the lamplight.

'What happened to thee?' she gasped.

'I fell,' Agnes told her.

'What? Flat on your face?'

'I tripped up. Is Mr Anderton in?' she asked, trying to change the subject.

'I thought I heard voices,' Mr Anderton said as he came out of the parlour door. 'Oh my goodness!' he exclaimed when he saw at Agnes. 'What happened to you?'

'She says she fell,' Dorothy answered for her in a tone that made it clear she didn't believe a word of it.

'Well, you've certainly made a mess of your pretty face. Come in,' he invited, holding the door open. 'Fetch up some tea and a slice or two of your cake,' he instructed Dorothy. 'Miss Cavanah sure looks as if she could do with it.'

'Give me thy shawl and basket,' said Dorothy holding out her hand. 'And I'll have another pound of the cheese,' she added. Agnes mentally added sixpence to the offering in her purse.

'Have you seen this girl's face?' Mr Anderton asked his wife as Agnes followed him towards the fireplace, feeling self-conscious about her bruises.

'Oh, that looks sore!' Mrs Anderton put her sewing on a side table. 'Come and sit down,' she invited, patting a cushion on the sofa next to her. 'Let me get a proper look at you. You could do with some arnica ointment to help that bruising,' she said after a moment. 'I'm sure I have some upstairs. Let me fetch it.'

Mr Anderton waited until his wife had closed the door before he turned back to Agnes.

'What really happened?' he asked. 'I hope it wasn't this boy that your mother is set on you marrying.'

'No!' Agnes was shocked that anyone might think Patrick Ryan had hit her. 'No. I was robbed in the street as I was selling cheese,' she confessed. 'He took my money and some of the cheese fell out of the basket when it happened. It was spoiled.' She took out the cloth bag and put it on the table. 'I'm sorry, but the money's a bit short. There's seventeen shillings and ninepence there,' she told him. 'And another sixpence if Dorothy buys a pound from the basket. That's eighteen and thruppence. So I still owe you one shilling and tenpence. But I'll give it to you on Saturday when I get paid.'

It would be all her wages. But Agnes had decided that she must hand over everything, even though she would be left with nothing to give to her mother and they would go hungry.

Mr Anderton looked at the bag but made no attempt to count it.

'Oh Agnes. I'm so sorry.'

The sympathy in his voice completely undid her and she began to cry.

'Please don't tell my mother,' she begged. 'I don't want her to worry. And I didn't want her stop me going out,' she gulped, accepting the linen handkerchief that he handed to her to wipe her eyes.

At that moment the door opened and Dorothy came in with tea and cake and Mrs Anderton followed her.

'Agnes was attacked and robbed in the street,' said Mr Anderton. 'That's why her face is such a mess.'

'I knew there was something amiss!' declared Dorothy as she put the tray down on the table. 'I knew there was a reason she didn't come around to the back.'

'It's not surprising you were afraid of the back alley,' Mrs Anderton said. 'The streets aren't safe for a lass alone in the dark,' she said to her husband. 'We should never have encouraged her to sell door to door on her own. We ought to have known it would end badly.'

'It's a damned shame a girl can't walk the streets in safety!' he replied. 'Do you think we should get one of the constables involved? I thought it was their job to keep folk safe?'

'Please, don't involve the law,' pleaded Agnes, wishing

that she'd never told him the truth. 'I'll get you the money I owe,' she promised.

'It's not about the money,' Mr Anderton said. 'You can't allow whoever did this to you to get away with it. He must be brought to justice.'

'The constables are there to help,' Mrs Anderton told her. 'I really think we should report this to them. They may be able to get the money back.'

'No,' Agnes said desperately. 'I don't want to speak to a constable. My mother said we mustn't have anything to do them. They'll send us back to Ireland.'

'What nonsense!' Mr Anderton burst out. He reached out a hand and put it on Agnes's. 'I know how you feel,' he told her. 'Believe me, I really do. But no constable has the power to send you away unless you're a vagrant. I'll come with you if you're afraid of going alone. It isn't far. I think there should be someone there at this time,' he added, taking out his watch from his waistcoat pocket to check the time.

'No,' said Agnes, wishing she'd said nothing about her ordeal. 'I don't want to.'

'Let her drink some tea first,' suggested Mrs Anderton. 'Dorothy,' she said to the maid who'd remained in the room. 'Cut Agnes some of the sponge cake. Be generous with it.'

A moment later a plate with a huge slice of cake was thrust into Agnes's hand and a cup of tea was placed on the table beside her. Upset though she was, she bit eagerly into the sponge, which was sandwiched with a generous filling of jam and dusted with sugar. It was delicious.

'I do think you should report this attack,' Mrs Anderton told her. 'The same man might be stealing from other girls, and he needs to be stopped.'

Agnes knew she was being put under pressure to do the right thing, but she still shuddered at the prospect, especially after her earlier run-in with the market superintendent. Her mother had told her so often to keep away from anyone in authority that she felt as if she was betraying her trust over and over again.

'Does my mother need to know?' she asked after she'd swallowed the cake.

'I think she deserves to know what happened,' Mrs Anderton said. 'I'm sure she wouldn't like you to keep it secret from her.'

'I don't want to worry her.'

'I understand that. But you shouldn't have to deal with this alone, Agnes. Here,' she said, picking up the cup and saucer from the table. 'Drink your tea and then Mr Anderton will go with you to the police station. He won't let any harm come to you.'

## 21

The police station was housed in a building that had once been a warehouse, not far from Mr Reynolds's premises. Mr Anderton took her through a courtyard further down King Street and they soon came to a door that was standing ajar with the flickering light of a gas mantle spilling out on to the cobbles.

Mr Anderton pushed the door open and stood aside for Agnes to go in before him. She found herself in a small hallway with a heavy oak desk on which there was an inkwell, some pens and a pile of paper and a bell. Mr Anderton picked it up and rang it confidently. A moment later a door opened and a man in a dark blue coat with a high collar came out and looked from her to Mr Anderton with an expression of distrust. If she'd been alone, Agnes would have turned and run. The bunch of keys jangling at the man's wide leather belt made her think she was going to be locked up immediately and charged with some crime that would see her on a boat home by the next day.

'Joshua Anderton,' said her companion, reaching out a hand to introduce himself to the policeman, who ignored it and ran a finger around the inside of his collar as if it was too tight for him. Then his gaze returned to the bruises on Agnes's face.

'What happened to her?' he asked as if he suspected that Mr Anderton had had a hand in it.

'She was robbed in the street, and as you can see, viciously attacked.'

'Sit down,' said the constable wearily, pointing at the two wooden chairs in front of the desk. Having unfastened the lowest two of the shining brass buttons that fastened up his coat, he sat down himself, behind the desk. He pulled a sheet of paper towards him and dipped a pen into the ink.

'Name?' he asked.

'Joshua Anderton.'

'Her name?' asked the constable with an audible sigh.

'Agnes Cavanah,' replied Mr Anderton.

'Can she not speak, then? What's your name?' he repeated, looking directly at Agnes.

'Agnes Cavanah,' she told him.

'Irish,' he said. It wasn't a question. 'Where do you live?' he went on. Agnes told him.

'She works at the rag and bottle shop. She's no burden on the parish,' Mr Anderton interrupted. 'In fact, she's a businesswoman. She sells cheese and was out making her rounds when she was attacked and her takings stolen.'

'This true?' the constable asked Agnes.

She nodded. 'Yes,' she said. 'That's what happened.'

They sat in silence, except for the scratching sound of the nib on the paper as the constable wrote it down.

'What did this man look like?' he asked.

Agnes did her best to describe him but admitted that it had been dark and he'd had a scarf pulled over his face, and she didn't get a good look at him.

'So would you recognize him if you saw him again?'

'I'm not sure,' Agnes said. She shivered as she relived the memory of the assault. She hoped she would never come face to face with her assailant again.

The constable made copious notes and then said he would see what they could do, but he couldn't make any promises. Mr Anderton thanked him and they walked back to the King Street house. To Agnes, it all seemed like a waste of time.

Inside the house, Mr Anderton checked the money she'd brought and told her that he would wait for what she owed him and that she wasn't to worry about it. It was the nature of their agreement that he was taking a risk, he assured her. He only had himself to blame if he lost out.

'So? Do you need another loan?' he asked when the coins had been counted into neat piles.

Agnes was surprised that he was offering. She'd never expected him to give her more money when she couldn't pay back what she already owed.

For a moment she was tempted to say yes, but then she shook her head.

'I'm not going to do it any more,' she told him.

'Why not?' he asked. 'Surely you're not giving up at your first setback?'

'It wasn't a good idea.'

'Of course it was a good idea. You were turning a profit.'

'No. Mrs Anderton was right when she said it's too risky going door to door after dark and carrying money about.'

He leaned back on his chair and rubbed his chin as he thought about it.

'What about selling on a market stall?' he asked.

'I can't without paying for a pitch,' she told him and recounted her troubles with the market superintendent. 'Besides, the cheesemonger who already sells there will put me out of business, like he did with Jonas.'

At the thought of Jonas she felt tears threatening. She would never see him again now, and it was almost too much to bear. She would have to relent and allow her mother to speak to the Ryans again about her marriage to Patrick. She could see no other alternative.

'A shop would be the ideal solution,' mused Mr Anderton.

Agnes didn't reply. It was like the suggestion that she get a pony to carry the cheese. It was so far beyond what she could afford that it wasn't worth considering. How could she find a shop to rent and then buy enough cheese to stock it every day? It would cost much more than the pound Mr Anderton had been willing to lend her, and she would have to give up her job at the rag and bottle shop. No. It just wasn't possible.

'Think about it,' Mr Anderton told her. 'You know I'm willing to help you, so don't dismiss the idea out of hand.'

'I think I ought to listen to my mother,' Agnes replied. 'She's right when she says I should marry and be content to raise a family.'

'Well, if that's what you really want . . .'

'It is,' said Agnes, although this was a lie. The idea of a cheese shop might be a dream that could never come true, but how she would love it. She allowed herself to daydream for just a moment, seeing herself behind a shining marble counter, dressed in a pristine white apron, her hands spotless as she reached for the cheese wire to serve a customer. But then she shook the vision from her head and told Mr Anderton that she must go home.

'I'll pay you the one shilling and tenpence when I get my wages,' she promised before going down to the kitchen to retrieve her shawl and basket from Dorothy. The cheese she had left would have to feed her and her family until the end of the following week when she was paid again. It would be hard, but they'd been hungry before and Agnes hoped it would be the last time. She would marry Patrick because that was what her mother wanted. She'd learned the hard way that she ought to have listened to her before and not been led astray by notions that she could achieve things that were far beyond her capabilities.

When she reached home she put the cheese on the slab and the basket on the shelf. She'd already decided not to tell her mother that Mr Anderton had taken her to the police. The less she knew about that the better, and Agnes doubted that anything would come of it anyway.

## 22

Kitty was sorting through her morning's finds, ready to take them to the warehouse, when she was disturbed by confident knocking on her front door. Wondering who it could be, she debated with herself whether or not to answer it.

'There's someone at the door,' said Maria.

'I know,' she replied. 'But I don't know who it is.'

'Shall I open it?' offered her daughter.

'No! I will.' Kitty glanced at the sharp knife she kept in the kitchen, the one Agnes had used to cut up cheese, but she decided not to pick it up. It was the middle of the day, she reminded herself. There couldn't be any danger.

When she cautiously pulled open the door, her worst fears were revealed. She heard herself gasp and she tried to close it again, but the constable standing there reached out a hand to prevent it.

'What do you want?' asked Kitty. She heard her voice trembling, and she was afraid that her fear would mark her as guilty before she was even accused of anything. Perhaps it was about some item she'd picked up that morning, although there'd been nothing of especial value amongst her finds. Or maybe someone had reported her or complained about her, when all she'd been doing was trying to earn an honest living.

'My name's Constable Westwell,' he said. 'I'm looking for a Miss Agnes Cavanah. I believe she lives here?'

So it was Agnes who was in trouble!

'She's not here,' said Kitty.

'Do you know where I might find her?'

'I've no idea,' Kitty told the constable. She wasn't going to reveal Agnes's whereabouts to him. But as soon as he'd gone she would have to run down to the warehouse and warn her daughter.

'Are you Mrs Cavanah?'

Kitty nodded, reluctant to admit to anything.

'It's about the robbery,' the policeman went on.

'Robbery!' exclaimed Kitty, feeling herself fill with a cold dread. Was Agnes being accused of robbing someone? She knew there were harsh penalties for such a crime.

'Yes. Are you feeling unwell? Perhaps if you'd like to invite me in you could sit down.' The man sounded genuinely concerned and under his tall hat his brown eyes looked kind, but Kitty wasn't going to be fooled. She knew that anyone in authority was her enemy. And how could she trust a man who was accusing Agnes of being a thief?

'I'm feeling quite well,' she assured him, even though she felt faint and was leaning on the doorframe to steady herself.

'Well, perhaps I can call back later? What time will your daughter be at home? We're holding a man who we think might be her assailant and we'd like her to come to the station and see if she can identify him.'

'Assailant?' gasped Kitty.

'The man who attacked your daughter and stole her money. I think we've caught him,' the constable explained. 'Though he no longer has the money he took from her.'

Kitty stared at the man, hardly comprehending what he was saying.

'I really think you need to sit down, Mrs Cavanah,' he added. 'You look very pale.'

'I didn't know,' replied Kitty, feeling foolish. She ought to have seen the truth of it, she told herself. Agnes's face. The spoiled cheese. But why on earth had her daughter not told her the truth?

'May I call again this evening? To speak to Miss Cavanah?' persisted the constable.

Kitty reluctantly agreed. She didn't want the man to come back. Heaven alone knew what the neighbours must be thinking. But she would be glad to be rid of him for now, and after she'd taken a moment to recover her senses, she must go down to the warehouse and demand the truth from Agnes about what had happened to her.

Agnes could see that her mother was agitated and was looking around the warehouse for her. She left her work at the sorting table and went across to speak to her, anxious about what might be wrong.

'Agnes! I've had a constable at the door asking for you!'

Agnes's heart sank. 'What did he want?' she asked, trying not to show how horrified she was. She'd been so sure that nothing would come of her visit to the police station. The constable who'd taken her details hadn't seemed very interested, and although she'd had to give him her address it had never crossed her mind that he might go and knock on the door of Mary Ellen Street.

'He said you'd been attacked in the street. Why didn't you tell me? Why make up some story about a fall?'

'I didn't want to worry you.'

'But I'm your mother! You should have told me! I should have known a fall wouldn't have made such a mess of your face.'

Mr Reynolds came across before Agnes could answer her mother.

'What's the matter?' he asked.

'It's nothing,' Agnes reassured him.

'Did you know she was attacked?' demanded her mother.

'Attacked? No. Is this true?' he asked Agnes.

'I've had a constable at the door,' her mother whispered to Mr Reynolds.

'What did he say?' Agnes interrupted. 'The constable?'

'He wants you to go to the police station because they've caught the man. He wants you to identify him. Don't go, Agnes,' she begged. 'They'll want you to go before the magistrate. No good will come from it.'

'But if they've caught the man, he can't be allowed to get away with it,' Mr Reynolds objected. 'And she might not have to go to court. The police might just use her evidence without her having to say anything.'

'Why did you go to the police?' Agnes's mother asked her. 'I've told you time and again to stay away from those people!'

'Mr Anderton took me. I had to tell him the truth about why I couldn't pay him.'

'But you wouldn't tell the truth to your own mother!'

'I didn't want you to worry.'

'I was already worried,' her mother told her. 'I told you to stop buying that cheese. I knew no good would come of it.'

'How much did this assailant steal from thee?' Mr Reynolds asked Agnes.

'Nearly three shillings,' she admitted. 'And some of the cheese was spoiled as well, when I dropped it.'

'Dost tha need an advance on thy wages to pay Mr Anderton?' offered Mr Reynolds.

'I promised to pay him at the weekend.'

'I'll lend thee a bit extra to tide thee over,' he said.

'She doesn't want to be getting into more debt!' her mother protested.

'Be that as it may, I'll not see these young uns go without a meal,' Mr Reynolds told her, waving a hand towards Maria and Peter who were standing, wide-eyed as they listened to the grown-ups.

'Don't worry, Mam,' said Agnes. 'I'll go to the police station when I've finished work. I'll make sure they don't come to the house again. And if they have caught that man . . .' She shuddered as she thought of him. 'Maybe they found the money as well,' she said hopefully.

'The constable told me they hadn't. So there's no need for you to go. Best not to get involved with them.'

Agnes nodded. She could see how frightened her mother had been by the encounter. 'Let's weigh in your finds,' she suggested, wishing that she'd never gone near the cheese stall on the market. If she'd never been tempted to buy cheap cheese, none of this would ever have happened.

'Go to the police station,' Mr Reynolds told her as she was putting on her shawl to leave. 'They need to get this man, whoever he is, locked up. Here.' He thrust two silver sixpences at her. 'Call it an advance on your wages. You can pay me back at thruppence a week.'

Agnes accepted the money gratefully, although she quickly decided not to tell her mother about this new debt. Neither did she intend to follow Mr Reynolds's advice and go to the police station. But when she walked past the street that would take her to its door, she changed her mind. If she didn't go, the constable might come knocking at Mary Ellen Street again, and it would be better to spare her mother that.

Agnes was trembling when she went into the hallway of the building. She waited for someone to come – it seemed too forward to ring the bell to summon them. After a while the inner door opened, but it wasn't the same man she'd seen before. This one was younger and taller, and he smiled when he saw her.

'I'm Constable Westwell,' he said. 'How can I help you?' He sounded kind and his manner reassured her.

'I'm Agnes Cavanah,' she told him.

'Sit down,' he invited. 'We've caught the man we think did this to you, but we need you to identify him – to say that you recognize him,' he explained. 'Do you think you can do that?'

'I . . . I think so,' said Agnes. 'But I didn't get a good look at him. It was dark.'

'We caught this man in the act of robbing another lass,' the constable told her. 'We just need more evidence against him. I'm sure you can provide that. In a moment I'm going to take you through to another room. The man will be there, but you don't need to worry. He'll be handcuffed and he won't be able to hurt you. All you have to do is nod if you recognize him. Can you manage that?'

'Yes,' Agnes agreed. This constable was very different from the one she'd seen before. He seemed nice and she was surprised.

'Wait there for a moment,' he said. 'I'll come back for you.'

He disappeared through the door and Agnes was tempted to flee whilst she had the chance. But she stayed, hoping it wouldn't be too much of an ordeal and wondering whether she really ought to tell her mother what she'd done when she got home. She supposed that she better had. There had been too many secrets already, and she vowed that she would be honest with her mother in the future.

Her stomach lurched when the constable came back, but he smiled encouragingly.

'Are you ready?' he asked.

Agnes nodded and followed him through the door to a small room containing two desks. For the moment it was empty, but then a far door opened and a dishevelled man with his hands fastened behind his back was brought in by another constable. The man kept his face down and his eyes averted from Agnes.

The first constable glanced at her and Agnes nodded quickly. He looked a lot like the man who had attacked her and she was keen to leave and go home.

Her ordeal wasn't over, though. When the man was taken away, the constable made her sit down and wait whilst he took a statement from her and then read it back to her to check it was correct.

'Can you write?' he asked when it was finished and blotted.

'I can manage my name,' she said, as she took the pen that was offered and carefully signed her name at the bottom of the sheet of paper, even though her fingers were shaking.

'Will I have to go before the magistrate?' she asked.

'No. This will be enough. You can go now,' said the constable. He held the outer door open for her. 'Thank you for coming – you've been very brave. I know some people are afraid, but we're here to help those who are honest.'

Agnes nodded and hurried away. She would try to reassure her mother about what had happened.

## 23

On the Sunday morning, Agnes sat beside her mother in St Alban's Church and tried not to think about Jonas Marsden. She failed. She kept picturing him watching out for her coming down the lane with her barrow to buy cheese. And she imagined how disappointed he would be as time passed and she didn't arrive. At least she hoped he would be disappointed.

She glanced across to where Patrick was sitting. The Ryans had already been in their places when she and her family arrived, so there'd been no chance to speak to them yet. When Agnes had told her mother that she'd changed her mind and would marry Patrick, the joy and relief on her mother's face had almost made the sacrifice worthwhile, but the prospect of spending the afternoon walking out with him and then going to the Ryans' for tea did nothing for her sombre mood.

She wondered what Jonas was doing now. Was he at the gate watching for her? Was he walking up the lane, hoping to meet her, hoping she would come whilst his parents were still in church so that they could drink tea together in the farmhouse kitchen? Or maybe he was in church too. Listening to an interminable sermon and fretting that she was waiting for him in the farmyard.

At least he would be able to go to his class this afternoon, she thought. She'd been uncomfortable at the thought of depriving him of his education, although she'd been incapable of sending him away rather than enjoying his company as he'd pushed the barrow back to Blackburn for her.

After the service was finished, Agnes walked reluctantly to the church door, knowing that she was about to seal her fate for the rest of her life. She would soon be a weaver's wife, married to a man she didn't love and the cheese business nothing but a memory of a young woman's foolish fantasy.

Her mother hurried ahead of her, keen to speak with the Ryans, but when Agnes reached the door, she saw her mother standing as if turned to stone, staring at something. Agnes followed her gaze and saw the Ryans in conversation with another family called the Kellys. They had a daughter, Hanora, who was a little older than Agnes. She was a tall, thin girl who worked as a winder at the Brookhouse Mill. People whispered that she was a bit simple, although Agnes had always thought that was cruel. She spoke with a lisp and was so conscious of it that she tried to avoid conversation with people, but she seemed nice enough, even if she had never responded to Agnes's offers of friendship.

Agnes watched as the two families spoke warmly. Patrick looked across at her, but quickly turned his attention back to Hanora. She wondered if the possibility of a marriage between them was being discussed.

'No!' Agnes's mother sounded as if she was in physical pain. 'Not her,' she muttered as if she couldn't believe what was happening. She moved forward and then stepped back, unsure whether she should go and interrupt the conversation. Agnes hoped she wouldn't. But then her mother turned to her and put a hand on the small of her back to push her forwards.

'You must go and speak to Patrick,' she said. 'You're going to lose out to that other girl if you don't do something quickly!'

'I can't!' Agnes protested.

'You can't lose out to her!' her mother replied. 'Go and speak to him!'

Slowly, Agnes walked towards the group. Patrick noticed her but turned away to speak to Hanora who was smiling almost radiantly at his attention. Let her have him, thought Agnes. It was obvious that she wanted him.

'Hello,' she said when she reached them, feeling self-conscious and silly. It was clear they didn't want to talk to her.

'Hello,' replied Hanora. There was so much pleasure radiating from her, along with a new-found confidence, that she looked beautiful. As Agnes watched, Hanora slipped her arm through Patrick's and held on to him as if he were a great prize that she would never let go. He seemed awkward and merely gave Agnes a nod in greeting, but allowed Hanora to keep his arm in her grasp.

Mrs Ryan noticed them and she frowned. She stepped between Agnes and the couple as if to physically block any contact they might make.

'Good morning, Mrs Ryan,' said Agnes politely, but the woman who had fussed and fawned over her before now pretended not to hear her greeting.

'We'll expect you for tea at four o'clock,' she said, a little too loudly, to Mr and Mrs Kelly. They nodded enthusiastically and Bridie Ryan put out an arm to move her son and Hanora away from Agnes. 'Patrick will call for you at two,' she told the girl and Hanora beamed at her with all the esteem of a future daughter-in-law.

Agnes was left standing alone as the two families moved away as one. The insult to her was clear.

Her mother came up behind her. 'What did you say?' she asked.

'Nothing. They just ignored me.'

Her mother shook her head and looked close to tears of frustration. 'If only you'd walked out with him last week,' she said with a sigh. 'I knew someone else would snap him up if you weren't quick. What a chance you've lost,' she lamented. 'You'll never get another one as good.'

Her mother grieved the loss of Patrick Ryan all the way home, wondering out loud if it was indeed too late or if Agnes could win him back if she tried really hard. Agnes tried not to listen. She had no intention of pursuing Patrick and the whole affair felt like a reprieve for her. She wondered if she ate her dinner quickly she might have time to go and look for Jonas before he gave up on her and went to his class. But as soon as she'd washed up the pots her mother insisted that she sit down and help Maria with the mending.

'You've no excuse not to,' she told her. 'It isn't fair to leave it all to your sister again.'

So Agnes was forced to sit by the hearth and sew whilst Timothy went to school. She had no way of getting a message to Jonas. But she wasn't going to give up on him. She'd been stupid to think that she could forget him so easily.

Later that evening, not wanting her mother's company for a moment longer, Agnes took the extra shilling that Mr Reynolds had given her, along with tenpence from her wages, and went to pay Mr Anderton.

When she arrived on King Street she went to the back door. Although she felt afraid, she reminded herself that the man who had attacked her was locked up in the police station and could do her no harm. Even so, Agnes shuddered as she remembered the way he'd glared at her when she identified him, and she hoped he wouldn't come looking for her when he got out of prison to pay her back.

Dorothy let her in with a smile.

'Not got your young man with you tonight?' she asked.

'No. I'm not sure if I'll be seeing him again. I've no reason to now that I'm not going for cheese,' Agnes said gloomily.

'That's a shame. He seemed nice,' said Dorothy.

'He is,' Agnes agreed, wishing that her mother could be charmed by Jonas as easily as the maid was. 'I've just called to pay Mr Anderton what I owe him,' she explained.

'It's a shame about the cheese as well,' Dorothy told her. 'It was very tasty. I would have bought more from you, and one or two of the neighbours were saying it was much nicer than what they can get on the market. Cheaper too. That cheesemonger on the market, I don't like him,' she went on as she brewed tea in her big pot. 'He's sly,' she added. 'I don't like to do business with sly folk.'

Agnes, remembering how the man had cheated Jonas and had her thrown off the market square, tended to agree.

'You should go for the cheese again,' Dorothy advised. 'Ask thy brother to walk the streets with thee if tha's still afraid. I'm sure he would.'

'He walks them all day long,' said Agnes. 'I can't ask him to come out again with me in the evenings.'

'Shame,' repeated Dorothy as she loaded teacups on to a tray. 'Come on up,' she said when she was ready. 'I know Mr and Mrs Anderton are always pleased to see thee.'

Upstairs, in the Andertons' warm parlour, Mr Anderton counted her money and nodded.

'I expected to wait longer for this,' he told her.

'Mr Reynolds gave me an advance on my wages,' she explained.

'He had no need.'

'My mother's afraid you might put us out of the house.'

'I'd never do that!' he protested.

'I know. But she can't forget what happened to us in Ireland,' said Agnes.

Mr Anderton nodded. 'I understand what it's like to leave the land of your birth,' he told her. 'It seems unfair, I know.'

Agnes saw Mrs Anderton reach out a hand to comfort her husband.

'My husband had to leave America so that he could be safe,' she explained to Agnes. 'He knows it isn't easy to be a stranger in a new land.'

'I've done all right, thanks to your father,' Mr Anderton told his wife. 'And most folks here have welcomed me – although there will always be some who cling to their prejudices. They're mostly the same ones who don't welcome the Irish, but don't let their words hurt you,' he advised Agnes. 'Work hard and rise above them, that's what I say. And you could do so much better for yourself than working in that warehouse,' he added. 'Tell me you'll think again about the cheese business. I'm more than willing to lend to you if you change your mind.'

'I'll think about it,' Agnes promised, wondering if, in fact, her decision to give it up had been too hasty. Perhaps she should talk to her mother again. Now that marriage to Patrick Ryan was no longer an option, perhaps she would be more amenable to the idea.

# 24

When she got home, Agnes broached the subject of buying cheese again, but her mother wouldn't hear of it.

'No!' she said. 'It's far too dangerous. I'd never have a moment's peace worrying about you walking the streets with all that money in your purse. You don't want to be attacked again, do you? No,' she answered for her. 'You must concentrate on getting Patrick Ryan back. It isn't too late and I'm sure he would never choose Hanora Kelly over you. You must make him realize he's made a mistake. You must tell him you're sorry and that you want to marry him. Go round to the Ryans' house tomorrow after work and beg them to forgive you.'

Agnes had no intention of doing any such thing. But whether she dared to defy her mother and buy cheese again was another matter. It was true that the streets were more dangerous than she had realized, but surely there was another solution?

The following week passed slowly with nothing for Agnes to look forward to. They couldn't afford to buy much food, and because Agnes thought it was all her fault that money was short, she went without eating most days rather than see her younger brothers and sister go hungry.

When Mr Reynolds paid her on Saturday evening she gave him thruppence back and took the rest of the money home to give to her mother. She avoided the market, as she had all week. The temptation would have been too much.

After their tea was finished and they were clearing away the pots, the front door was pushed open and a voice called out.

'Hello!'

'Come in, Edna!' called Agnes's mother.

'Is there any cheese this week?' their neighbour asked. 'I was going to buy some from the market, but that man is more expensive and I'll swear his half-pounds look nothing like enough.'

'She's not doing it any more,' replied her mother before Agnes could explain. 'Have you not seen her face? She was attacked in the street.'

'What? Whilst she was out selling cheese?'

'Yes. And all her money stolen. It's not safe. It's not like it was in the old country. Folk would look out for one another there, but it's different here. It's dangerous.'

'Well, I'm right sorry to hear that. There's bad folk everywhere,' replied Edna. 'But I'm sure she'd be safe enough if she just stuck to the neighbouring streets. It was good cheese,' she went on.

'I'm sorry,' Agnes apologized. 'I'd like to get you some more. Maybe if I get just enough for the neighbours?' she suggested to her mother, suddenly hopeful that she would have an excuse to go to Goosefoot Farm the next day.

'No.' Agnes's mother was shaking her head.

'Wilf will be disappointed too,' said Edna. 'It was quality cheese.'

'I know. I'm sorry,' said Agnes again, feeling as if she was letting people down.

'Well. If you do get some, you can bring me round a half-pound,' said Edna. 'I'll see myself out.'

'I'm sure if I did what Edna says and stick to the streets we know, I'd be all right,' said Agnes when she'd gone. 'It was going down the other streets that was the trouble.'

'I'm surprised you'd even consider it, after what happened to you,' her mother said.

'That man's locked up now.'

'But there are other bad people. Edna's right about that.'

Agnes said nothing more, but she still hoped she could find a way to carry on with her idea.

The next morning she went to church. The weather had turned, quite suddenly, from chilly days with an overnight frost to a welcome warmth, and Agnes decided that it was a morning to cast off her shawl now that the hawthorn blossom on the hedges was bursting into flower. Still, she couldn't help but shiver when she went inside St Alban's, although the cold was not as chilling as the way the Ryan family turned their backs on her.

Agnes knew it hurt her mother more deeply than herself. This community was the only form of friendship she had, and it was being split into two between those who sided with the Ryans and thought that Agnes was a very foolish girl, and the ones who offered more sympathy and said the lass should be allowed to marry whomever she chose.

After the service, Patrick Ryan flaunted his relationship with Hanora Kelly in the churchyard. It seemed that they were engaged to be married now and that in a few short weeks they would be man and wife. They would have their own house too, and Hanora was to begin work in the Pearson Street Mill, beside her husband and his family.

'It could have been you,' her mother told her as they walked home. 'You'd never have needed to go hungry again.'

After Timothy had gone to his class, Agnes picked up the basket with the mending and threaded her needle. There was always something fraying at the seams or coming in holes and the weekly task seemed neverending. She sometimes wondered how many more times she could stitch things together before they fell apart completely, but it would have to be done because there was no spare money to buy more clothes.

She wondered if she should try to sell the barrow. It ought to bring in a few shillings, but it would mean depriving her mother of it on weekdays and she was worried that Michael Walsh would think she was making a profit at his expense seeing that he hadn't charged her for the repairs.

Agnes was still wearing her Sunday gown despite her mother having urged her to change out of it when they arrived home from church.

'I might go for a walk later, when the mending's done,' she said, knowing that her footsteps would take her towards Goosefoot Farm.

Agnes paired the last of the darned socks and put away the thick bodkin with the other needles. She stood up to stretch her aching back and wondered if she could slip out without anyone seeing her go. The sun was shining outside and the bruises on her face had faded to a greenish yellow that were only visible if she looked at herself closely in the mirror. With her hat on she thought no one would notice them.

The tentative knock on the door made her turn and her mother dropped her scissors. They clattered to the floor but she made no move to retrieve them.

'I hope that's not the police again,' her mother whispered. The colour had drained from her face.

'They wouldn't come on a Sunday, would they?' asked Agnes, hoping that Constable Westwell hadn't come to tell her that she must speak up before the magistrate after all.

The knocking came again and Agnes went to open the door. She had readied herself to see the tall policeman in his dark uniform, so the sight of Jonas standing on the step left her momentarily speechless.

'Agnes,' he said, pulling off his cap and twisting it awkwardly in his hands.

'What are you doing here?' she asked.

'I came to see if you were all right. I've been worried.'

'Who is it?' she heard her mother ask from behind her in an anxious voice.

'It isn't the police,' she reassured her. 'Just someone else come about cheese.' She didn't want her mother to know it was Jonas. Agnes was worried about what she might say to him and she didn't want him to be sent away. 'Wait here,' she told him. 'I'll just get my hat and then I'll walk with you. I'll explain,' she promised before she ran upstairs to the bedroom, pinned her hat firmly over her thick hair and then ran back down, thankful that she hadn't heeded her mother and changed into something shabby.

'I'm sorry I didn't come last week,' she told him as they turned the corner of Mary Ellen Street, out of sight of her mother and sister.

'Are you buying from someone else?' he asked. He sounded part hurt and part accusatory.

'No!' she burst out, appalled that he might think such a thing. 'I haven't bought any. I haven't had the money.'

'Will that man . . . Mr Anderton, was it? Will he not lend to you any more?' Jonas asked.

'It's complicated,' Agnes told him.

'Well, explain it to me,' he said.

They walked up towards the Preston Road. It was partly because that was the way Jonas needed to go to take his long walk back home again. But it was also because Agnes knew that Patrick Ryan and Hanora Kelly would be parading there along with all the other young couples showing off in their Sunday best – and she had an overwhelming urge to let them see her arm in arm with Jonas Marsden just so that they would know she had no regrets and had turned Patrick down for a much handsomer boy.

'I had some trouble,' she admitted to Jonas. 'I lost some money and so it took a while to pay Mr Anderton back.'

'But you will be coming again, won't you?' he asked.

She wanted to reassure him that she would. She didn't want him to think she didn't want to see him again, but he noticed her hesitation.

'It doesn't matter,' he said. 'You don't have to come for cheese, but I'd like it if you came anyway. Or I could come here again?'

They'd reached the top of the hill and Agnes slipped her hand under his elbow. He smiled at her.

'I thought you'd had second thoughts, after what my father said,' he told her. 'I haven't been able to think about anything else.'

'I don't care about what your father said,' replied Agnes, although she did really because she knew it was another stumbling block they would have to surmount if they were to have a future together.

'What's wrong?' asked Jonas as she glanced about, looking for Patrick and Hanora. 'You seem different.'

'It's nothing,' she said, turning her face away so that he couldn't get too close a look at her. 'It's just that my mother's being difficult about the cheese. I need to talk her round.'

'My mother saved a wheel in case you came,' he told her. 'I kept telling her you would come, so she didn't send it to market, and now she's cross because she says it could have been sold rather than sitting on the cold room slab.'

'I'm sorry.'

'You could come now,' he suggested. 'There's still time.'

'I don't have the money.'

'Then next week? Shall I ask her to save some for you next week?'

'I don't think I can do it again,' Agnes confessed.

'But you were so keen. And you were making money.' He sounded puzzled and then his face darkened. 'It's not that cheesemonger on the market, is it?' he asked. 'He's not making it difficult for you?'

Agnes didn't reply and Jonas stopped walking and turned her to him.

'What's happened?' he asked, looking directly at her, and as the sun illuminated her face she saw the shock register in his eyes. 'Who did this to you?' he demanded as he reached out his fingers and gently traced the bruises on her face.

Agnes winced and moved back. 'I fell.'

'Agnes. Tell me the truth.'

She hesitated and then admitted what had really happened.

'Who was he? This man?' asked Jonas as if he suspected it might not have been a random attack.

'I don't know. It was pitch black. But the police have caught him and he's locked up.'

'And was it the right man?'

'I think so,' she said, although the truth was that she hadn't been completely certain when she identified him. She'd never even considered that the cheesemonger on the market might have something to do with it until Jonas had mentioned him. But now she was beginning to wonder.

'Perhaps this selling door to door isn't such a good idea,' said Jonas. 'Especially going out alone in the dark. Once people know you're carrying money there'll always be someone looking to take it from you. You need someone to walk with you.' He was silent for a moment. 'I'd do it, if I didn't live so far away.'

'Would you?' said Agnes, although she knew it would be impossible for him to walk all the way to Blackburn most evenings to spend an hour or two with her and then walk all the way back to Samlesbury Bottoms again. If only he lived in town, she thought, it would be an ideal solution.

'So will you come next week?' Jonas asked hopefully.

'Yes,' Agnes agreed and was rewarded by a broad smile. 'Tell your mother to save a wheel of cheese,' she told him. 'I'll go and ask Mr Anderton for the money and I'll just sell it amongst the neighbours. They say it's better than the cheese they get on the market and cheaper too.'

'Good! But you won't go selling door to door on your own?'

'No,' she reassured him. 'I'll just sell to people I know.'

She would only make a small profit, she knew, but a few pennies was better than nothing and meant that she would be able to pay back Mr Reynolds without them going short of food.

Kitty had known when her daughter went off without a word that it would concern some boy – and when she'd gone to the door, her fears had been confirmed as she saw them disappear around the street corner. It was the boy who'd wheeled cheese in his squeaky barrow, and Kitty worried for the rest of the afternoon that Agnes would come back with more, despite everything that had happened.

If only she hadn't been so stubborn about Patrick Ryan, the arrangements for a wedding could have been well in hand by now. The other boys in their small community were much younger, and unless one of the older men had the misfortune of becoming a widower, then Kitty could think of no one else who might be a suitable husband for Agnes. The prospect of her daughter spending her life struggling alone with no man to support her concerned Kitty. She knew how hard it was, and even though she tried to conceal the worst of her struggles from the younger children, she'd tried to explain it to Agnes to make her understand how important the offer from the Ryans had been. But all she'd been interested in was selling her cheese. And now there was this fresh problem to contend with. She needed to make it clear to her daughter that she mustn't encourage this boy, whoever he was. She doubted he was a Catholic, so he could never marry her, and the danger was that Agnes might fall for his charm and find herself left with a child. Then what would happen? Apart from the shame of it they would struggle to feed and raise another little one.

Kitty knew she needed to speak frankly with Agnes when she came back, but she dreaded a confrontation. She'd been on such good terms with her daughter up until now and she hated the thought of spoiling their friendship, but things would have to be said, for Agnes's own sake.

Agnes walked partway to Samlesbury with Jonas, but when they reached the Halfway House, he insisted that she turn back.

'I'll see you next week,' he reminded her. 'You will come?'

'I will,' she replied to alleviate his doubts. 'I promise I will.'

'Even if you don't come to buy cheese?' he asked.

'I'll come anyway,' she reassured him.

He smiled then and after an awkward moment in

which they simply looked at one another he leaned in and quickly kissed her.

'Till next week,' he grinned and they reluctantly parted, turning and looking back every few steps and waving until the brow of the hill hid them from each other's sight.

When she got home, her mother was sitting alone by a small fire. It was late and the others had gone up to bed.

'Where have you been?' she asked Agnes.

'Walking.'

'Who with? That farmer's boy?'

'He came to see if I was all right.'

'It can never be,' her mother told her. 'Don't get your hopes up, Agnes. He's not one of us.'

Agnes was too tired to argue.

'I'm going to bed,' she told her mother. She didn't want a discussion about it tonight. She wanted to hold on to the pleasure that being with Jonas had given her – his voice, his smile, his expressive eyes, his concern that she'd been attacked, the gentle softness of his lips when he'd kissed her. What she and Jonas felt for one another was genuine. It was real. It wasn't like the fantasy that the adults had concocted for her and Patrick. And why did she have to marry someone from the Irish community? Why couldn't she fall in love with someone who wasn't Irish, who wasn't even a Catholic? Why did it matter so much?

# 25

'Who was that you were walking out with yesterday?' the girls at the warehouse wanted to know the next morning. That and why she had no cheese for sale.

'She's too busy with a lad to be selling cheese,' laughed one.

'We'll be needing to re-trim our bonnets for a wedding then,' said another.

'Aye, but we'll have to go on t' market at dinnertime to get some cheese,' complained a third. 'And his isn't as nice. He underweighs it, too, I'll swear he does.'

'So who is he, then? This lad?' they asked Agnes.

'Just a friend,' she said, but she couldn't keep the smile from her face. The thought that Jonas cared enough to walk all the way to Blackburn to find her sent thrills through her. And she was already counting the days until Sunday when she would see him again.

When dinnertime came, she walked across to the market to take another look at the cheesemonger's stall. It was busy as usual and he was calling out his wares with enthusiasm.

'Lancashire! Tasty Lancashire! Sevenpence a pound!'

Agnes knew that she could undercut that price and

she'd also begun to consider what quite a few of her customers had said about the size of his portions.

She watched carefully as the man pulled his wire through the cheese and then put the portion on the scales. It balanced, showing it was a full pound, and Agnes wondered if the Andertons' scales or the ones at the warehouse were faulty. If so, Mr Reynolds was overpaying everyone who brought goods in. She thought she'd better mention it to him when she got back.

Mr Reynolds looked doubtful when she told him of her suspicions about the scales.

'That's not possible,' he explained. 'Look.' He picked up the pound weight that was by the side of the scales and turned it over to show her the base. 'You see these marks?' he asked. 'They mean that the weight is genuine. This one shows who made it and this one shows it's been tested and is true. If you used this to weigh your cheese then you can be certain that it was accurate.'

With her concerns allayed, Agnes went back to her tasks in the rag and bottle shop. She was relieved that she wasn't overweighing her portions because her slim profits were too important for her to be giving it away, but it did make her wonder how honest the cheesemonger on the market was.

That evening she went to see Mr Anderton. Her mother tried to persuade her not to, but Agnes had argued that many of their neighbours and the workers at the warehouse had been disappointed that there was no cheese this week, and that she wouldn't come to any harm if she bought just enough to share amongst the people she knew, rather than trying to sell to strangers on the street.

In the end, she went without her mother's blessing, but short of trying to physically restrain her, Agnes knew that there was nothing her mother could do. And even though she hated the disagreements that were growing between them, she was sure that her mother would come round in the end when she saw her being successful and making money from her enterprise.

'So! You're back in business!' replied Mr Anderton when she explained that she'd come to ask for another loan. He looked so pleased that she was forced to respond to his enthusiasm.

'Just for friends and workmates,' she told him. 'I'm not risking walking the streets again.'

'It's a start,' he told her. 'We'll have you in a cheese shop before long.'

Agnes smiled. She knew it was an impossible dream. Nevertheless, she accepted a sovereign, thinking that she might buy two wheels after all, and promised she would pay it back the next week.

When Sunday came, Agnes put on her best gown. She knew her mother was hoping she would go to church with them, but Agnes had no intention of attending. Instead, she manoeuvred the barrow out of the front door and set off briskly towards the end of the street. She knew she was hurting her mother and it made her feel terribly guilty, but she also knew that what she was trying to do would benefit them all in the long run.

The morning was bright and the well-oiled wheels of the barrow made it easy enough to push whilst it was empty. Agnes was wearing some gloves she had bought cheaply from the rag and bottle shop. She didn't want any more blisters on her hands.

She walked along, enjoying the sight of the trees laden with blossom and listening to the bleating of the lambs in the fields. Soon, she would see Jonas. Her eagerness made the miles seem like mere yards and before long the road dipped down towards Samlesbury.

Agnes turned into the track that led to Goosefoot Farm and felt the barrow bouncing over the rough ground, sending jolts through her arms, but nothing could quell her anticipation – not even the farm dog that came barking and snarling to the gate as soon as it saw her.

She rested the barrow on its legs and looked around. There was no point calling out. The dog would have alerted anyone who was in the house to her presence and she was confident that Jonas would come out at any moment to greet her and quieten the dog. Perhaps he was brushing his hair, or straightening his jacket, she thought with a smile. She waited, tucking escaped strands of her own hair under her hat and shaking dirt from her skirts. She hoped that his parents were out and that he would offer her tea in the farmhouse kitchen – just the two of them.

After minutes had passed with no sign of anyone, and even the dog's barking had become less insistent, it became increasingly clear to Agnes that there was nobody at home. She looked at the farmhouse. There was a trickle of smoke from the chimney, so someone had lit a fire that morning, but the door remained stubbornly closed, and although Agnes doubted it was locked, she was too afraid of the dog to try to climb the gate and go in.

Maybe Jonas's parents had insisted that he attend their church with them this morning. Agnes knew how difficult it would be for him to refuse.

She looked back up the track, wondering what to do. The church clock chimed noon. Surely they would all be home soon. The best thing to do was wait.

Agnes tipped the barrow over to make a seat and rest her legs after the long walk. The dog seemed to have lost interest in her and had wandered off towards its kennel where it lay down and rested its nose on its paws. It still watched her, though, and Agnes knew that it would bark again if she moved.

She watched the track. A couple of times she thought she saw someone coming, but it was just the shadows of branches moving in the wind. She waited and waited, until she began to wonder how much longer it was going to be before they arrived. If they'd been to church they should have been home by now. It wasn't that far off. Agnes began to fear that something was wrong.

In the end, she decided to leave the barrow where it

was and walk back up the track and down to the church. She would probably meet the Marsdens as she walked, she reasoned, and her fears would have been for nothing. At the top of the track she turned left and walked until she saw the lane that led down to the church by the river. She walked towards it, hoping that she wouldn't have to go inside. She doubted that she would be welcome even if she dared to enter.

As she neared the churchyard, surrounded by a stone wall and an ivy-clad lychgate, she saw a few people were gathered by the door. One wore white flowing robes, similar to Father Kaye's surplice, and she guessed he was the vicar. Agnes hesitated at the bottom of the path, watching, until the vicar came down the path and greeted her with a smile.

'Are you looking for someone?' he asked curiously. 'Have you come to visit a grave?'

'I'm looking for the Marsden family,' she told him.

'Oh.' His face took on a serious expression. 'Are you a relative?'

'No.' Agnes shook her head. 'I came to buy cheese.'

'Then you haven't heard.' It was a statement.

'Heard what?' Agnes saw from his expression that he was about to give her some bad news. Her heart thumped in terror that something awful had happened to Jonas.

'Mr Marsden has had an accident,' he said, and Agnes quickly suppressed her relief, feeling guilty that she'd only focussed on Jonas being hurt.

'What happened?' she asked.

'It was one of his cows that had a young calf. It tossed him and trampled him as well by all accounts. Happened yesterday afternoon. They put him in a cart and took him to the workhouse hospital, but he was badly hurt. We've offered prayers for him.'

So Jonas and Mrs Marsden must have stayed with him, thought Agnes. He must be very ill. She longed to go and find them so that she could be with Jonas and support him, but she didn't know where the Preston workhouse was or if she would be welcome.

She thanked the vicar and turned away, wondering what to do. It was clear she wasn't going to be able to buy any of the Marsdens' cheese today, and although she was worried by the news she'd been given, she felt frustrated and disappointed too. She walked back to Goosefoot Farm to collect the barrow, wondering if she should call at Old College Farm on her way home. If they had a wheel or two for sale it would mean she didn't have to walk back empty-handed with nothing to sell.

As Agnes came down the track to the farm, she saw that someone was in the yard. She slowed her pace, wondering who it could be, but when the figure turned around she was relieved to see that it was Jonas. She waved to him, and with her skirts in her hands to keep them clear of the mud she began to run until she met him at the gate.

'I've just heard about your father!' she gasped. 'How is he?'

Jonas looked troubled. 'He's badly hurt,' he told her. 'I wanted to stay with him, but my mother sent me back to feed the animals.'

'What happened?' asked Agnes as he let her in through the gate. 'I went down to the church to see if you were there and the vicar told me he'd been trampled by a cow.'

'That's right,' Jonas replied. 'The doctors think he's been injured inside.'

Agnes reached out a hand to comfort him as Jonas clasped a hand to his own stomach and tears threatened to overwhelm him.

'I'm sorry,' she said, realizing how serious the matter was. He looked bereft and Agnes could see that it had been a shock for him.

'Do you want the cheese?' he asked her. 'I was waiting to see if you would come. We have two you can choose from.'

'I'll take them both. I have enough money.' Agnes reached a hand into her pocket to retrieve her purse. She knew that the Marsdens wouldn't be able to get to market this week and she still felt guilty about Mrs Marsden keeping back a wheel that she hadn't come for.

'Bring your barrow into the yard and I'll fetch them,' said Jonas.

She watched as he opened the door to the cold house and brought out the cheeses and loaded them into her barrow.

'Will you be all right getting home with these?' he asked. 'I'd offer to walk with you, but . . .'

'No. You must go back to your father,' she told him. She'd been looking forward to him walking into Blackburn again with her, but she could see that he needed to be with his family.

'Well, I'll push it up the track for you at least,' he said, grasping the barrow handles.

Agnes followed him. They walked in silence until they came to the road where he put the barrow down.

'I must go,' he told her.

'Of course you must. I hope your father will be better soon.'

Jonas shook his head. 'It's bad,' he told her and Agnes realized that the man might not live.

'Go to him,' she said, grasping Jonas's hand for a moment before letting him go.

He nodded and turned away down the lane. He walked for a few yards, his pace quickening, and by the time he rounded the bend he was running. Agnes felt the tears well up in her own eyes. Jonas's sadness had been profound and she felt helpless that there was nothing she could do to take the burden from him.

It was only when she'd pushed the heavy barrow up to the Halfway House and paused to recover her breath that she remembered Jonas hadn't given her the change for the money she'd paid him. Never mind, she thought. He'd had so much on his mind and he would probably straighten it out with her the next week.

Agnes took the cheese back to the Andertons' house so that she could slice it up.

'All alone?' asked Dorothy when she answered the back door. 'Tha's not fallen out with thy chap, has tha?'

'No, nothing like that. But his father's had an accident.' She explained what had happened to Mr Marsden and Dorothy looked suitably shocked.

'A cow, tha says? I thought it were only bulls that did that sort of thing.'

'It was a cow,' confirmed Agnes. 'And it's hurt him very badly.'

'I don't like the countryside,' Dorothy told her. 'Nasty place on the whole. I'd rather stick to the towns where tha knows what's what.'

As she sliced the cheese, Agnes fretted about Jonas. She'd hated to see him so upset and unhappy and she prayed that his father would recover. If he didn't, she wondered what would happen. Would Jonas and his mother be forced to move from the farm? Or would Jonas have to take it on himself? She didn't know and it made her own problems seem insignificant.

The next morning she got up early and took a basket of the cheese to the warehouse with her. She would sell what she could before work and then go around the streets in her dinner hour. Surely she would be safe there in broad daylight, she reasoned, and as it wasn't market day she would have no competition.

Agnes was pleased that before the market house clock reached the hour, her basket was empty and her purse was growing full. That evening she went down Mary Ellen Street to sell to her neighbours and they all seemed eager to buy. She arrived home feeling pleased with herself. The robbery had just been a setback, she thought. There was every chance that she would make a profit again this week and she was glad that she hadn't given up.

She sold more the following day, and when Wednesday came she decided that she would walk around the streets near to the market square but not risk the wrath of the market superintendent or the other cheesemonger by going on the actual market. Agnes doubted that she would make many sales but was surprised when she did quite well.

'This is much nicer cheese than what I normally get from the stall,' one woman told her. 'And the portions are generous too.'

'They're all full pounds and half-pounds. They've been weighed!' she assured her customer.

'Well, I'm not complaining,' the woman replied. 'I wouldn't be buying from you if I thought you were cheating me!'

Agnes walked up and down King William Street and circled past the new town hall and back towards Darwen Street, making sales as she did so whilst keeping an eye open for the market superintendent, but she didn't see him and even if she had there was little he could do if she didn't stray on to the square where the stalls were.

Just as she was thinking that she needed to get back

to the warehouse, she saw someone watching her from a distance and recognized the woman as the cheese-monger's wife. They must have realized that they had competition again, Agnes thought, but even if they began to cut their own prices now it was too late. Her basket was almost empty and she'd finished for the day.

She went back to the warehouse and began to weigh in the finds that the gatherers were bringing in. Later, she would go back to the rag and bottle shop and put her basket on the counter. She was making quite a few sales there now that word was getting round, and Mr Reynolds seemed happy enough for her to sell her cheese without asking for a cut of the profits. Without him and Mr Anderton, she could never have got her business up and running. All she had to do now was make a success of it and prove to her mother that she could improve their lives.

# 26

The next Sunday, Agnes set off once more for Goose-foot Farm. She was thankful to see smoke rising lazily from the chimney as she approached the farmhouse, and pleased that when the dog barked, it was Jonas who called out for it to be quiet.

He came to open the gate for her.

'Your father?'

'He lives,' Jonas assured her. 'He's still in the hospital, but the doctors hope he will recover.'

'Thank goodness!'

'But I'm sorry, there's no cheese,' he told her.

'I'm not surprised your mother hasn't had time to make any,' Agnes replied. She ought to have known Mrs Marsden would be too busy at the hospital with her husband.

'Oh, she made it all right,' Jonas replied. 'But it spoiled. The curds wouldn't set and it all had to be thrown away. She blames Buttercup – the cow that hurt my father. She said her milk was soured by her bad temper and that's what caused it. She wants to get rid of her, and the rest of our herd. She won't go near them, not even to do the milking. I've been having to do it all myself.'

He looked despondent and Agnes wasn't sure how to reply.

'If you get rid of the cows, there'll never be any cheese,' she said at last, aware, as she spoke, that her words sounded selfish.

'It may be for the best,' said Jonas. 'My father won't be able to do much when he comes home, probably not for a long time – if ever,' he said sadly. 'If my mother won't milk the cows then everything will fall to me, and I don't think I can cope alone.'

Agnes watched as he turned away from her, not wanting her to witness his overwhelming emotions.

She reached out and touched his arm. 'You have to do what's right for you,' she told him, feeling guilty that her first thoughts had been about her own needs.

'There'll be no reason for you to come if we have no cheese,' he said, turning to her with immense sadness in his eyes. He looked so bereft, yet Agnes felt pleasure that he wanted to see her.

'I would come to see you,' she told him.

He shook his head. 'My father warned me against it,' he said.

'Why?' asked Agnes.

'Because you're not one of us. He says I should take up with a local girl. Someone who comes to our church.'

It sounded depressingly familiar to Agnes.

As she and Jonas stood and looked at one another,

neither of them sure what to do or say next, Agnes heard the farmhouse door open and his mother came out, pulling a shawl around her shoulders.

'There's no cheese,' she told Agnes. 'I'm sorry. It wouldn't set.'

'I know. Jonas told me.'

'Perhaps you could buy elsewhere,' she suggested. 'Somewhere nearer Blackburn. I don't know why you keep walking out all this way.'

'My customers like your cheese,' Agnes told her. 'They say it's the best they've tasted.' She saw that the praise pleased Mrs Marsden. 'It would be a shame not to make it any more.'

'We're getting rid of the cows. The ones we have will go to the butcher and that'll be the end of it. Dangerous creatures! I'll not have them near my family.' Mrs Marsden glanced at Jonas and Agnes saw that she feared for him too.

'Buttercup was only defending her calf,' Jonas protested. 'She knew my father would take it away and she tried to stop him. You can't blame the cow.'

'I do blame her!' his mother said. 'Your father'll never be the same. He's lucky to be alive. Black and blue, he is, all over,' she told Agnes. 'Bloodied and bruised inside and out.'

'I'm sorry to hear it,' she replied.

'Perhaps you could try Old College Farm again?' Jonas suggested. 'I'll walk over with you, if you like?'

'No,' his mother said. 'I want you here. There's a lot

to be done now your father's in the hospital. I'm sure she can manage by herself.'

'I can manage,' said Agnes. Although she wanted nothing more than to spend some more time with Jonas, it was clear that his mother needed him. She went to retrieve her barrow and as she walked up the track she resisted the temptation to look back because she didn't want him to see that she was crying.

Agnes was tempted to go straight home, but when she reached the turning for Old College Farm she hesitated. She had money in her purse and she needed cheese, so why not walk down and ask?

The yard was as muddy as Agnes remembered and she knew her best gown was going to get filthy, but she didn't expect the big dog to come rushing at her and plant its paws firmly on her skirts as soon as she set the barrow down.

'Get away!' she cried out, catching sight of the creature's sharp white teeth as its tongue lolled out. She would have pushed it off if she hadn't been afraid that it would snap at her.

She heard a man laugh.

'He'll not harm thee. He's friendly enough,' Mr Fish told her as he whistled to the animal to come away. It retreated and sat at his feet, but kept its dark brown eyes fixed firmly on Agnes. She was unsure about it. She didn't have much experience of dogs and was wary of them.

'He's a sheep dog, not a guard dog,' Mr Fish reassured

her as he fondled the animal's ears. 'He'd not hurt a fly. Stay!' he told the animal firmly as he walked towards her. 'You came t' other week with the Marsdens' lad,' he said.

'I came to buy cheese. I was wondering if you had any for sale today? I usually buy from Mrs Marsden, but she's none this week. Her husband was in an accident.'

'Aye. I've heard about it. Sounds nasty. But I can't help thee, I'm afraid. It all went to market.'

Agnes thanked him anyway. She wasn't certain that she believed him and wondered if he would have produced a wheel if Jonas had been with her, but there was nothing more she could do. It wasn't as if she could force the man to sell his cheese to her.

She wheeled her barrow back to the road where she stopped and tried to wipe the mud from her gown, but only made it look worse. Then she turned for home, wondering what she could do next. If Mrs Marsden really did stop making cheese and Mr Fish was reluctant to sell to her, it meant she would need to source it from elsewhere. There were plenty of farms, she told herself as she walked along. Surely some of them would be willing to do business with her.

A farm nearer to Blackburn would make more sense. It was a long walk all the way to Samlesbury Bottoms to make her purchases, and if it hadn't been for Jonas she would never have contemplated it.

As she neared the town, she paused at a track that led down to a farm at Yew Tree. Perhaps she should she go and enquire there. It wouldn't do any harm to ask.

The lane that led down to the farm was shaded by the large trees it was named for, but when Agnes heard the familiar sound of a dog barking she hesitated. The worst part of approaching farms was the dogs, she thought, fearing that she would be bitten by one that was fierce.

As she approached the yard warily, she was relieved to see that the dog was tied to the end of a long chain and she waited out of its reach, hoping that someone would come out from the house to ask what she wanted.

Before long she saw the door open and the farmer called to the dog to be quiet and lie down. He came across to Agnes, looking puzzled to see her there.

'What dost tha want?' he asked brusquely. His hair was sticking up and he smoothed it down with a hand and stifled a yawn. It seemed that Agnes had woken him from a nap and he didn't look particularly pleased about it.

'I was wondering if you had any cheese for sale,' she said.

The man looked her up and down.

'Tha's Irish,' he said.

'I am,' Agnes agreed.

'I don't deal with Irish,' he told her.

'I have the money. I can pay,' she said, pulling out her purse and tipping some of the shining coins into her hand.

'Where's tha got all that from?' he asked suspiciously.

'I'm in business, selling cheese.'

'That's a likely tale,' he responded. 'Folk don't do business on a Sunday.'

He glanced up the lane behind her as if he expected her to have accomplices who were concealed there.

'Best get on thy way afore I set the dog loose,' he warned.

The threat sent a shiver of fear through Agnes, but the man had made her angry with his prejudice and she stood her ground determinedly.

'All I want is to buy a wheel of your cheese, if you have one. I'll pay a fair price.'

'Nay. I'll not defile the Lord's Day with buying and selling,' he told her. 'And neither should thee – though I wouldn't expect thee to know any better. Best get on thy way,' he said again before he turned to untie the dog.

Agnes quickly picked up the handles of the barrow and almost ran down the lane, glancing back as she did, expecting to see the snarling beast closing in on her heels. But all she heard was the farmer laughing as he watched her hurry away.

She was crying again and breathless by the time she reached the safety of the main road. The farmer had frightened her, and he'd made her feel worthless too. She hated the way that some people thought she was bound to be a thief as soon as they heard her voice. It wasn't as if all these English people were angels. Take the man who'd robbed her in the street. He certainly hadn't been from the old country. In fact, she didn't know anyone who was who would do such a thing. All the people who lived in their community were honest and kind and trying hard to make a living for themselves in a hostile world. Not for the first time, Agnes wanted to weep for the life she could have had. Even though her family had been forced to leave their home, they should have been in America by now. It would have been different there, she thought as she pushed the empty barrow towards Blackburn. And her father would have been with them to protect them. He would never have allowed anyone to speak to her in the way that horrible farmer just had.

## 27

'I was expecting thee last night to cut up thy cheese,' said Dorothy as soon as she saw Agnes the following evening.

'There was none,' Agnes told her. 'Mrs Marsden made it, but it curdled. She says she's not going to make more.'

Dorothy looked disappointed.

'Will you tell Mr Anderton I'm here?' asked Agnes. She was keen to give him his money back and go. It had become clear to her that it would be impossible to buy any more cheese to sell, and she didn't want to keep explaining it to people. Last night a few neighbours had come to the door and she'd had to send them away, and the women at the warehouse had been disappointed again too. Agnes hated to let them down, but when she'd tried to explain why she had no cheese it had all sounded such a poor excuse.

Upstairs she had to tell her story again. She hoped this would be the last time.

'So I brought your money back,' she ended, putting the bag of coins down on the side table.

'You're giving up?' asked Mr Anderton.

'What else can I do?' she asked. 'I can't force Mrs Marsden to produce cheese. And I can't make the other farmers sell to me if they don't want to.' She shrugged. Her tears were always near to the surface these days and she felt a complete failure.

Mr Anderton didn't pick up the coins.

'No one said it would be easy. Business never is,' he told her.

'But what can I do?' she asked.

'Go to other farms,' he replied. 'Go to every farm you can find. If they all refuse to do business with you, then you can say you've failed. But until then there are still opportunities.'

'But I only have Sundays free. What if none of them will do business on a Sunday?'

'They'll do business if it's in their interests,' said Mr Anderton. 'Or what about going one evening now that the days are becoming longer?'

'I don't know,' said Agnes. 'It would have to be some-where nearby.'

'There are farms nearby,' he said. 'You don't have to walk all the way to Samlesbury Bottoms.'

'I know,' Agnes said. She was thinking of Jonas. She wanted to see him again, and if she gave up the cheese business it would mean she would be free on Sundays. She could attend church with her mother in the morning and then go down to Goosefoot Farm in the afternoon. She hoped he would be there waiting for her, rather than going to his classes. In fact, she doubted he would have time for classes now that he had to take on more of the farm work. It wasn't a job where he could rest all day on a Sunday – not when there were cows to be fed and milked. Unless they had already gone to the butcher. The thought made Agnes feel sad. Their milk had made delicious cheese. It seemed such a waste and she hoped he might have persuaded his mother to change her mind.

Mr Anderton picked up the bag of money and moved it closer to her.

'You'll need this,' he said. 'It's too soon to give up.'

Agnes looked at the money. She didn't want to pick it up, but Mr Anderton was watching her and she didn't want to let him down. Maybe she should give it one more try. If she didn't get cheese the next weekend, then she would come again and insist that he kept it.

Reluctantly, she reached for the money.

'Good!' he said when she picked it up. 'And now, a cup of hot chocolate and a slice of Miss Dorothy's sponge cake!'

On Wednesday, when it was market day, the sight of the wheels of cheese piled high on the cheesemonger's stall made Agnes feel jealous.

She kept to the back of the throng of shoppers as she watched the man and his wife serving their customers. Each piece was sliced and weighed, and every time the scales balanced, but Agnes could see that the portions he was selling did look smaller than the ones she weighed out.

Just before one o'clock she walked back to her work, lost in thought. How was it possible to sell underweight cheese when the scales balanced? Mr Reynolds had explained to her about the accuracy of the iron weights that counterbalanced the pounds and ounces of the cheese. It made no sense to her. Perhaps she and the other women were mistaken. Maybe his cheese was more solid so it weighed heavier than the ones that the Marsdens made. Still, the only thing that was certain was that the stall had been doing a brisk trade and she saw many of her regular customers there, turning back to a source that was steady and reliable rather than waiting to see if Agnes had cheese or not.

If she was to carry on, Agnes knew that she must find a supplier who would promise to sell to her every week. She knew it wouldn't be easy. But maybe Mr Anderton was right when he said that she'd given in too soon. And Mr Reynolds had said much the same when she'd told him what had happened.

'Business ain't for them that's easily defeated,' he'd told her. 'The difference between them as succeeds and them as doesn't is that the successful ones were too stubborn to give up.'

When the weekend came Agnes had a dilemma. She wanted to go down to Goosefoot Farm to see Jonas again, but she knew that if his mother had been as good as her word and not made any cheese then it would be another week with nothing to sell to her customers. And she knew that if she was to make a success of her business then she must find a reliable supplier.

So she missed church again, to the growing consternation of her mother, and, dressed in workaday clothes, she wheeled out the barrow and went to visit as many local farmers as she possibly could between the hours of dawn and dusk.

There was, in fact, no shortage of small farms on the hillsides all around Blackburn and she'd made a plan to walk in a circular route beyond the confines of the terraced streets and try her luck at every one.

First she tried the farms nearest to the town, but at every one she was met with suspicion or excuses. One had none to spare. One claimed they didn't even make cheese even though the herd of cows in their field was plain to see. And at a third, the farmer swore at her for being a tinker.

Knowing she must try further afield, Agnes pushed the barrow up the steep hill that they called Shear Brow, thankful that it was empty and that a return journey, even with a full barrow, would be easier. At the summit of the hill she reached a farm they called Oozebooth. The farmhouse was an imposing two-storey structure, built from local stone with long, narrow windows. An inevitable dog began to bark as Agnes approached and she braced herself in case it came running at her. But the animal was on a short chain and she waited until the farmer came out and opened the yard gate.

'I'm hoping to buy cheese,' she told him. 'A full wheel or even two.'

His mystified expression was one that Agnes was becoming used to.

'I'll fetch the wife,' he replied after a moment.

When the farmer's wife came out she seemed pleased to see Agnes. Mrs Robinson, as she introduced herself, took Agnes to her dairy at the back of the house.

'I have some here,' she said, pushing open a battered wooden door, and when Agnes followed her into the gloomy interior, the pungent and now familiar aroma of cheese filled the air.

The wheels were similar in size to the ones she'd bought from the Marsdens. Twenty-five pounds each, Agnes reckoned, wondering how cheaply she could buy them. She'd already decided to offer only fourpence a pound to enable her to haggle, but knew she couldn't go as high as fivepence if she was to afford two wheels.

But the offer of fourpence was obviously an insult to the farmer's wife.

'No!' she responded and Agnes worried that she had misjudged the deal.

'Fourpence ha'penny then,' she said quickly.

Mrs Robinson paused for thought.

'You'll take both?' she asked.

'I will,' Agnes replied eagerly. 'And I'd like to come again next week.'

'Come into the house then and we'll settle up,' agreed Mrs Robinson.

Agnes followed her across the yard bursting with delight. After her poor start to the day she'd expected to be turned away at every farm, and this easy purchase had boosted her confidence and proved that both Mr Reynolds and Mr Anderton were right. Sometimes it paid to be tenacious.

When the money had been counted out and Agnes had the change safely stowed away in her purse, she stood up to load the cheeses into her barrow and leave, glad that she could spend the afternoon weighing out the portions.

'Nay, lass,' said Mr Robinson. 'Tha can't go yet. We haven't raised a toast.'

'No. It's all right,' replied Agnes, anxious to be on her way.

'Nay,' protested Mr Robinson. 'Tha can't do a deal without a toast,' he insisted as he brought a bottle from the sideboard and set it on the kitchen tale. 'Fetch the glasses,' he instructed his wife as he took off the top.

Agnes watched as he poured a generous amount into each glass and passed her one.

'To business!' declared Mr Robinson as he raised his glass in the air. Mrs Robinson picked hers up too and seeing that she was expected to do the same, Agnes reached for hers and closed her fingers around it.

'To business,' she repeated and saw Mr Robinson lean to clink his glass against hers and then tip the contents down his throat.

'Drink up!' he encouraged her.

Agnes raised the glass to her lips. It smelt odd, but she took a sip of it. The liquid ran down her throat with a burning sensation that made her gasp and then cough. She coughed uncontrollably until she took another sip to relieve it. But it made matters worse. Her throat felt as if someone had set it on fire and she wondered if she would ever be able to breathe properly again.

'It's good stuff!' said Mr Robinson, grinning as he watched her. 'Here, take some more.'

Agnes tried to refuse when he picked up the bottle again, but her voice was lost and nothing came out but a squeak of protest. She shook her head and tried to move the glass away, but Mr Robinson grasped it and refilled it.

'Get it down,' he told her. 'Do thee a power of good!'

Not wanting to make matters worse, but not knowing how to refuse without seeming rude, Agnes took another sip. The heat had passed down through her chest now and reached her stomach. Her legs felt odd and her head was wobbly.

Somehow she managed to empty the glass again and then decided that she must leave before Mr Robinson poured from his bottle a third time. She stood up, but the stone floor beneath her feet seemed to have lost its stability and it felt like she was walking across a peat bog as she made her way towards the door. She tried to thank the Robinsons but the thoughts wouldn't articulate themselves into the words she intended to say, and after muttering something about wheeling cheese she managed to reach the door where she steadied herself against the frame before stepping out into the fresh air.

The cold wind rushed around her head, but she felt so hot that she was tempted to throw off her shawl. She grasped hold of the barrow and tried to turn it, but it seemed to have developed a mind of its own and it took several attempts to line it up with the farm track. After giving a brief wave to the Robinsons, Agnes pushed the barrow forwards. It refused to go in a straight line, but with a determined struggle she kept it moving until she reached the road into Blackburn.

At times the way was so steep that the barrow threatened to get away from her. Agnes had to break into a run to keep up with it and the sensation made her giggle as she chased her load along. She could see that people were watching her and she wanted to laugh and call out to them, but most turned away as she approached. For once, Agnes found that she didn't care.

The cheeses bounced in the barrow as she steered it at speed across the cobbles of the market square. At one point she almost lost one into the gutter and had to reach out a hand to save it. Her legs still felt strange, as if they didn't quite belong to her, as she approached the back alley of the King Street houses. Agnes rested the barrow on its legs and stumbled down the steps to knock loudly on the kitchen door.

The expression of horror and disbelief on Dorothy's face when she opened it, made Agnes laugh out loud.

'Come inside!' Dorothy told her, grasping her arm

and pulling her into the kitchen whilst she glanced up and down the back alley.

'My cheese!' Agnes giggled as she tripped on a flagstone and only saved herself by reaching out a hand to the table and then collapsing on to one of the wooden chairs.

'I'll fetch it in,' replied Dorothy sternly.

Agnes watched as the maid carried first one of the wheels and then the second into the kitchen and put them on the table before bringing the barrow down the steps and propping it against the wall.

'Where hast tha been?' she asked when she'd closed the door.

'Buying cheese,' replied Agnes, thinking that it was a ridiculous question.

'Where?'

'Oozebooth Farm. It's a very silly name, isn't it? Ooze. Booth!'

'Did they give thee summat to drink?'

'Oh yes! Mr Rob . . . Rob . . . Robinson had a big bottle and he poured and then poured some more to *seal the deal*, he said.' Agnes laughed again at the thought of it. 'It made my throat burn like fire!'

She heard Dorothy sigh but didn't understand why.

'Sit there,' the maid told her when Agnes tried to stand up.

'But I've got the cheese to cut.'

'Tha's in no fit state to be cutting owt,' Dorothy told her as she filled her kettle with water. 'I'll make thee a drink that'll happen sober thee up a bit.'

'Sober?' Agnes repeated, trying not to laugh again, but failing. 'I'm not drunk!' she protested. The idea was unthinkable and she felt insulted that the maid should have suggested it. Drunks were the men and women who came reeling out of the inns and beerhouses late at night into the streets, shouting and singing. She wasn't one of those.

'Just sit there until tha feels better,' Dorothy told her. 'Tha can't go home to thy mother like that.'

'I'm all right,' Agnes insisted, although she wasn't entirely sure that she was.

'Here,' said Dorothy as she poured a dark brown liquid into a cup and added just a dash of milk and a spoonful of sugar. 'Drink that,' she added as she put it on the table next to Agnes.

Agnes picked up the cup, expecting it to be chocolate, but the drink tasted strong and bitter.

'Ugh! What is it?' she asked, wondering if Dorothy was trying to drug her, or even poison her.

'It's coffee. Drink it!'

Agnes did as she was told. The hot liquid soothed her sore throat and when Dorothy put down a plate of bread and butter she took a slice, and when she swallowed it, her stomach felt better than it had since early that morning.

'I don't know what that farmer was thinking of, plying a young lass with drink like that!' Dorothy complained. 'It's the devil's work, it is! And on the Sabbath Day too.'

Agnes watched as the maid lifted down the scales and the cheese wire from the shelf and set about slicing and weighing the cheese herself. She felt guilty for not helping, but every time she tried to stand up, the room felt as if it was moving around her and Dorothy told her to sit down again and poured her another cup of coffee.

After a while, Agnes felt as if things around her were steadier. She hung her shawl over the back of the chair and watched Dorothy silently. None of it seemed particularly amusing any more and she realized that it was whatever Mr Robinson had given her to drink that had made her feel so strange.

'If tha's going to make a habit of going round farms buying cheese, tha needs to learn how to refuse any drink,' Dorothy lectured her as she worked.

'He insisted,' Agnes told her. 'I didn't know how to refuse. I didn't know what it was.'

'It would have been gin, or some such concoction.' Dorothy sniffed her disapproval. 'Tha needs to tell 'em that tha's taken the pledge, that alcohol doesn't pass thy lips, except as a medicine.'

'But what if they refuse to sell to me?'

'They won't. Thy money's as good as anyone's.' Agnes watched as the maid cut another slice and popped it on to the scales. It was an exact pound. It made her think again about the cheesemonger on the market and his portions.

'Do you think some Lancashire cheese weighs heavier than others?' she asked.

Dorothy frowned as she considered the question. 'I wouldn't have thought so,' she said at last. 'Why dost tha ask?'

'It's just that some people say my portions look more generous than the ones the cheesemonger on the market cuts.'

'Happen this cheese is lighter.' Dorothy studied the piece in her hand. 'It seems good and creamy anyway.'

'But not as nice as Mrs Marsden's,' Agnes said sadly, suddenly feeling tearful again when she remembered what was to happen to the Goosefoot Farm cows.

By the time Dorothy had finished and the cheese was loaded into the barrow and covered with a cloth, Agnes felt more like herself.

Dorothy helped her carry the barrow up the steps from the back yard and Agnes set off towards home. She was grateful to the maid and tried to thank her as best she could, but Dorothy flapped a hand at her and said that she'd kept a pound of cheese back for herself and that was payment enough.

By the time Agnes reached Mary Ellen Street, her head was throbbing and each jolt of the barrow over the uneven street made it worse. She knew she only had herself to blame. She should never have accepted the drink from the Robinsons and she must take care not to do it again. It had made her careless as she'd brought the cheese back to Blackburn. She shuddered now as she remembered how she'd bounced it over the cobbles.

Her mother watched as she brought it in and began

to stack up the portions on the cold slab. She seemed resigned to it, but the anxiety on her face still troubled Agnes. She really must make a success of this business, she thought, if only not to let her mother down.

Despite her mother's look of disapproval, Agnes filled a basket and went down the neighbourhood streets before it got too late. She took Maria with her, telling her mother that they would be safe enough if they didn't stray beyond the familiar area.

'Can I come with you to the farm next time?' asked Maria. 'It's not fair that I have to stay at home and do all the mending when you and Timothy both get to go out.'

Guiltily, Agnes agreed that her sister was right. 'It depends what our mam says,' she told her. 'But you can come if she lets you. You can help to push the barrow.'

'And can I take the money tonight?'

'Can I trust you to add it up correctly and give the right change?'

'Of course you can. I'm not stupid!' Maria retorted.

'I'll test you then,' said Agnes as they came to Wilf and Edna's house and knocked at the door.

'Oh, cheese! Good!' exclaimed Edna. 'Step inside a moment.'

'It's from a different farm this time. Though it's just as nice. I've tasted it,' said Agnes.

'I'm sure it's lovely. I'll take a pound.'

Agnes placed the cheese on the outstretched plate that Edna had ready and waiting.

'That'll be sixpence,' she said.

Edna looked in her purse and took out some copper coins.

'Maria's in charge of the money tonight,' said Agnes. 'She's going to count it to make sure it's right.'

She exchanged a smile with Edna as they watched Maria take the coins with a serious face and count them into Agnes's purse.

'That's the right money,' she confirmed.

'We'll make a shopkeeper of her yet.' Edna smiled indulgently and offered Maria a pear drop from a jar on her mantelpiece. Maria's eyes lit up. It was a rare treat.

When the basket was empty they walked home. As they went into the house, Maria was still talking about how good the pear drop had tasted in her mouth.

'Why don't we sell sweets instead of cheese?' she asked. 'I don't like cheese much. Sweets are much nicer.'

'Perhaps you should become a confectioner,' Agnes suggested.

'Don't go filling her head with ideas,' grumbled their mother when Maria had reluctantly climbed the stairs to bed. 'It's bad enough one of you having hare-brained schemes.'

'Is it so bad?' Agnes asked her. 'To try to better ourselves? Do you really want us to spend the rest of our lives scouring the streets for other people's rubbish?'

Agnes had a point, thought Kitty. A few years ago, at home in Ireland, she would have been horrified by the idea of making a living picking through filth on the streets. But so much had changed and she'd become afraid of taking any risks. All she'd ever wanted was some security, and she thought that the best way of providing that for her daughters was to see them married to responsible husbands who would give them the care that she'd once received from her beloved Peter until he'd been lost to the waves on that terrifying sea. She was still furious with Agnes for turning down Patrick Ryan, and now he was to be married to Hanora Kelly the next week. The Kelly family certainly hadn't allowed enough time to pass for the Ryans to change their minds. And Kitty didn't blame them. The whole community had been taken by surprise. Hanora had never been seen as marriageable, but to Kitty it seemed like an insult. Agnes was younger and prettier and she deserved to marry well, if only she could have been persuaded to see reason.

Still, Kitty had to admit that her daughter was making money from her enterprise and she had paid back Mr Anderton every week. But this cheese selling could never be more than something Agnes did in her spare time. She couldn't possibly make a proper business of it because she had her work at the warehouse. And as for Maria wanting a sweet shop – well, that was just the dream of a foolish child. Kitty hoped that in a year or so she might be offered a job at the rag warehouse too.

At least Timothy was bettering himself, she thought with a feeling of pride. How she loved to see him out and about in his uniform delivering letters. He enjoyed it too and never grumbled, not even when he had to give up his Sunday afternoon to go to school. At least she didn't have to lie awake at night worrying about what would become of him, unlike her headstrong daughter Agnes, whom she loved so much, but who was causing her so much concern.

# 28

The next morning, Agnes sold cheese to her workmates and at dinnertime she walked the streets with her basket on her arm and sold more.

On Wednesday, it was market day and she took advantage of the crowds of shoppers on Church Street and King William Street to sell her wares. She emptied her basket long before the market house clock reached one o'clock and she wished that she'd brought more. At thruppence a half-pound the cheese was greeted as a bargain and Agnes enjoyed chatting to the regular customers who had begun to look out for her again.

'I didn't see thee last week,' said one.

'I had a problem with my supplier, but I've a new one. I'll be here every week from now on,' she promised.

'I hope the cheese is as good.'

'It is,' Agnes reassured the woman.

She had sampled the cheese from Oozebooth Farm, and it was good, but she had to admit that it didn't have the special taste of the Marsdens' cheese. Whether it was because of the way it was made or because of the particular pasture that the cows grazed down near the River Ribble, she didn't know. She just hoped that her customers wouldn't mind the difference and that they would come back for more.

Thursday was a quieter day. The shops closed early in the afternoon and there weren't many shoppers out and about, but Agnes made a few sales. Friday was better, with a thriving market in full swing. She tried to catch women before they reached the market square, so that she could sell them her cheese before they reached the cheesemonger's stall.

It was still busy and Agnes was doing well when the firing of the gun on the clock tower alerted her to the time and she reluctantly walked back to Clifton Street, wishing that she had the rest of the afternoon free.

'Tha's late,' grumbled Mr Reynolds when she arrived back at the warehouse. 'There's a queue of folk waiting to weigh stuff in.'

'I'm sorry. I was doing really well with my cheese,' she explained as she tied her apron strings around her waist and then lifted the first batch of rags on to the scales.

'Tha's going to have to choose one of these days,' Mr Reynolds remarked.

'Choose?' she asked, not sure what he meant.

'Aye. Choose to work here. Or choose to sell thy cheese.'

'Why can't I do both?' she asked as she added the weights to balance the scales. Her estimate of the cloth was almost always right and she quickly calculated the price in her head and paid the gatherer.

'I should show thee how to write all these figures down,' mused Mr Reynolds as he watched her.

'I'd like that,' she told him.

He grinned. 'I'm a fool to myself,' he said. 'I'll teach thee and then tha'll be gone, writing down thine own sales.'

'You did encourage me,' Agnes reminded him.

'I did. More fool me.' He laughed. 'I'll be sorry to lose thee when the time comes.'

He walked away and left her to her task, but as Agnes worked she thought about what he'd said. Business had been brisk for her and she wondered if she could have earned more in profit selling cheese all afternoon than Mr Reynolds was paying her for her work here. He seemed to think that it was only a matter of time before she gave up her job with him and worked for herself full-time, but Agnes knew it was a huge decision. It would mean that her income would be dependent on what she bought and sold, and the security of having a regular wage paid to her every week would be gone. Part of her was eager to take the step, but she knew how angry and upset her mother would be if she went home and told her that she'd given up her job.

When the other workers had gone at the end of the day, Agnes lingered, taking time to hang up her apron and tidy the tables.

'Still here?' asked Mr Reynolds when he came out of his office with his keys in his hand, ready to lock up for the night.

'Can I talk to you?' she asked.

'Talk away, lass.'

'I've been thinking about what you said earlier, about me having more time to sell the cheese.'

'Nay, tha's not goin' to tell me tha's leavin' already?' He sounded surprised.

'No,' said Agnes, 'but I wondered if you could do without me some of the time. If I could stay on the street tomorrow afternoon, I'm sure I could clear the cheese I have left.'

'And who'll do thy work here?'

'I could send my little sister, Maria. You've seen her with my mother.'

'How old is she?'

'She's ten, but she knows her coins and she can add up.'

'Nay. She's not old enough,' said Mr Reynolds. 'If she were a year or two older, happen I'd take her on. But ten's too young for this work.'

'Could you not manage without me, just for one afternoon?' pleaded Agnes. 'You did encourage me to get into business,' she reminded him again. 'And Saturday's always a quiet day in the shop.'

'But who can I trust to weigh in and give out the right money?' he asked her. 'I've come to rely on thee.'

Agnes understood his concerns and she tried to think of someone who could take her place, but it was Mr Reynolds who came up with the idea.

'What about thy mother?' he asked. 'She seems a sensible sort.'

'I could ask her,' said Agnes, hoping that she would agree.

'Does she know her money?'

'She knows her coins. And Maria could help her.'

'Well, if she can stand in for thee then tha can take thy cheese to market,' Mr Reynolds told her.

'Thank you,' said Agnes. It seemed an obvious solution because her mother would have finished her gathering by dinnertime. All she had to do was convince her to do it. But she knew it wouldn't be easy.

'No!' said her mother when Agnes reached home and told her what she and Mr Reynolds had agreed.

'Why not?'

'Because it's your job, not mine. And you should be doing it. Besides, who would look after Maria and Peter?'

'Maria can go with you. She could help. She took all the money for me when I went out on Sunday evening.'

'And what about Peter?'

'Can Aileen not have him?' she suggested.

Her mother sighed. 'You can't have everyone just fall into line to suit you, Agnes,' she told her. 'You must go and do your own job.'

'But I can earn more selling cheese. And if Mr Reynolds pays you, we'll be better off.'

'I don't know.' Agnes could see that the prospect of extra money was swaying her mother. Timothy needed some new boots and Peter had suddenly grown out of all his clothes. And whilst Maria wore Agnes's cast-offs, there was such a difference in age between Timothy and Peter that Timothy's clothes wouldn't fit his younger brother for years yet.

'Just this once,' wheedled Agnes. 'Just to see how it goes. If it doesn't work out then you don't need to do it again.'

'I thought it was only once,' her mother replied. 'There's things I need to do on a Saturday afternoon. Shopping for one, or do you think the food sets itself on the shelves?'

Agnes could see that she was softening and would soon give in.

'If you enjoy it, maybe you could take it on instead of gathering,' she suggested. 'Then I could spend all my time selling cheese.'

'You're not to give up that job!' her mother told her. 'We need the money.'

Agnes didn't pursue things. She'd sown a seed, given her mother an idea, and perhaps that would be enough.

She was up early the next morning and packed all the cheese she had into her basket, until it was almost over-flowing. Agnes fastened a cloth over it and left for the warehouse, though not before reminding her mother that she needed to come promptly at one o'clock to do the afternoon shift.

All morning Agnes worried that her mother might change her mind, or that Aileen might not be willing to look after Peter. But just as the workers were beginning to drift off to get their dinners she saw her mother come in through the warehouse door with Maria at her side.

'You know what to do, don't you?' she said as she took off her dirty apron and began to scrub her hands in a basin of water she'd prepared earlier. No one would buy cheese from a costermonger with filthy fingernails. 'You've seen me do it often enough,' she went on. 'Weigh in the whites and the colours separately, then the nails and other metal, and then the bones.'

'I know what to do,' said her mother. She looked nervous, Agnes thought as she fetched her basket of cheese. But Maria would help her. They would be all right.

Agnes burst out of the warehouse into the fresher air and hurried up the street towards the market. Her full basket was heavy and dragged on her arm, but she hoped it would soon become lighter as she made her sales.

'Cheese! Fresh Lancashire cheese!' she began to call out when she reached the junction with Darwen Street. The town was busy and her enthusiasm was high. This was what she loved to do and she felt happy that she'd been granted her freedom from the malodorous confines of the warehouse, even if it was only for one afternoon.

There were people about that she hadn't seen before and her calls of 'Thruppence a half-pound!' generated quite a lot of interest.

'Can I see it?' asked a woman.

'Of course.' Agnes drew back the cloth. 'It's all fresh and locally made up at Oozebooth,' she assured her.

'Then I'll take a piece.'

Agnes walked up and down making a satisfying number of sales. She'd be finished early at this rate, she thought, and could go back to relieve her mother before the warehouse closed. She walked down King William Street, on the edge of the market square, concentrating on selling to the women whose baskets were empty rather than the ones who were leaving the stalls.

She was within sight of the cheesemonger's stall here and she was aware that he had seen her and was watching. Agnes knew that he would begin to reduce his own price when he realized she was selling for thruppence, but if she didn't call out, she wouldn't attract customers.

Her basket was becoming steadily lighter and her purse heavier as she walked and traded, exchanging smiles and pleasantries with her customers. The weather was fine, the sun felt warm on her back and Agnes felt proud of herself. If only the cheese she was selling had come from the Marsdens' farm then her pleasure would have been complete. But every time she thought about Goosefoot Farm and about Jonas a sadness overcame her good mood, like a black cloud obscuring the sun on a summer's day.

'Tuppence three farthings!' shouted the cheesemonger and Agnes saw the women who were queuing to buy from her hesitate and turn away.

'You'll get the full half-pound from me!' she called to them.

'But we only have your word for it,' one pointed out. 'Yours is cut ready into portions but we don't see it on the scales. How do we know we can trust you?'

'It's all weighed out in the kitchen of the Andertons' house on King Street,' she told them.

'Aye, well,' remarked another. 'That's not the same as seeing it cut and weighed in front of us.'

The queue of potential buyers dissipated as the women went off to purchase a bargain at the cheese stall. Agnes felt frustrated, but she could see the women's point of view. She couldn't prove the weight of her cheese unless she brought a table to sell from and put the scales on it.

She was just wondering if Dorothy and the Andertons would be willing to lend her the cheese wire and the scales and contemplating whether she could source a table and find somewhere to set it up without having to pay a fee, when she felt a hand on her arm. She turned to see a dark blue jacket and shiny buttons and when she looked up she met the gaze of Constable Westwell under his tall hat.

'There's been a complaint,' he told her.

Irritably, Agnes shook off the man's arm. 'I've done nothing wrong,' she told him, knowing that it must be the cheesemonger who had made the complaint to try to get rid of her.

'A few women have told me that you're cheating them,' the constable insisted.

'Cheating? *I'm* not cheating anyone,' she replied. 'I think you have the wrong cheese seller.'

For a moment the constable hesitated, but then he told her that she must go with him.

'Go where? To the police station?'

'No. To the superintendent's office.'

'Is he the one who's complained?' asked Agnes. It wouldn't have surprised her. The man was probably in cahoots with the cheesemonger. It was probably him who had made sure Jonas got a stall well away from any prospective customers.

'No. But he has the set of standard weights,' explained the constable. 'I need to check that the portions you say are a half-pound really are a half-pound. Otherwise I'll have to arrest you for cheating,' he warned her.

Although Agnes was confident that her cheese had been honestly portioned, knowing that Dorothy had weighed it out meticulously, she still felt anxious at the prospect of having to prove it. Her mother's fear of getting mixed up with the law still prevailed and she felt guilty even though she knew she'd done nothing wrong. The guilt must have shown in her expression, she thought, as the constable took her arm again.

'This way,' he said, steering her towards the market house building.

Agnes was left with no choice but to comply. It would have looked worse if she'd tried to run away or make a fuss, although she was already aware that her conversation with the constable was attracting a crowd of curious onlookers and that some of her customers were amongst them. Even if any accusation against her was refuted she was worried that it might put them off buying from her again.

The constable took her to a small room just inside the main doors of the market house where the superintendent was waiting. He looked smug and it made Agnes feel angry as well as frustrated by the turn of events.

'Put your basket on the table,' instructed the constable.

With a sigh, she complied. The man had been so kind to her when she'd last seen him, but now his face was stern, as if he was already convinced of her guilt.

'It's not my cheese you should be weighing,' she told the men as the superintendent peered into the basket, looking for a portion that was obviously small. 'That cheesemonger outside sells portions much smaller than mine.'

'So you say,' remarked the superintendent, 'but he has weights and scales on his table so no one can accuse him of cheating.'

'This has all been weighed out at the Andertons' house. You know Mr Anderton,' she told them.

Neither replied and Agnes watched as the superintendent finally selected a piece of cheese and put it on his scales. He added a half-pound weight and Agnes couldn't help but smile at his astonished face when it balanced perfectly, although she restrained herself from saying *I told you so.*

'Well, it seems there's no case to answer,' said the constable. 'I'm satisfied that Miss Cavanah is an honest vendor. And she wasn't actually on the market square, so it's my decision,' he reminded the superintendent.

Agnes was grateful for his decisive words. She'd warmed to the man on their previous meeting and he'd proved himself to be fair with her again.

'Can I go now?' she asked. Even though it was proven that she'd done nothing wrong, she knew that the cheesemonger would be taking full advantage of her absence to make as many sales as he could. 'Maybe you should check the cheesemonger's weights against these weights you have here,' she said as she tidied her basket and covered it with the cloth. 'It would only be fair to make sure he isn't cheating either.'

'The lass has a point,' said Constable Westwell.

'No one has made a complaint about him,' replied the superintendent.

'Plenty of people have remarked to me that his portions look undersized,' Agnes persisted. She was certain now that the complaint against her had been made by the cheesemonger.

'You can't just accuse people!' the superintendent told her, packing his weights away.

'But you took notice when someone accused me!' She felt exasperated that these men in authority were always willing to think the worst of her and her countryfolk, and she was surprised and grateful when the constable took her part.

'Miss Cavanah is right,' said Constable Westwell. 'I think it is only fair that we should check the cheesemonger's weights, if only to prove he is honest and that his complaint was a genuine error.'

So it was him, thought Agnes, even more determined not to allow him to get away with his attempts to put her out of business.

The superintendent seemed doubtful and Agnes turned to the constable for support. Although she was anxious to get back to her sales, she knew that she would never be fully vindicated in the eyes of her customers unless her accuser was found to be the cheat.

'His portions do look smaller than mine,' she repeated.

'Different cheese,' muttered the superintendent. 'It's all to do with density,' he explained to the constable. 'You can't expect a lass like her to understand.'

'Humour me,' said Constable Westwell. 'I'll happily stand corrected if you turn out to be right. Bring the weights,' he instructed.

With a sigh, the superintendent tucked his wooden box under his arm and they waited whilst he locked his office door.

'Complete waste of time,' he was muttering. 'This is going to make you both look foolish,' he warned as they set off across the square towards the cheese stall.

As they approached, Agnes saw the cheesemonger glance at her, walking beside the constable, and he smirked, probably thinking that she was being taken to the police station. She hoped that the smug expression would be quickly wiped from his face when he was found out, but she also prayed that she was right because it would be mortifying to discover that her own accusation had no substance.

The cheesemonger looked astonished when they stopped at his stall and the superintendent put his box of weights down beside the scales.

'This girl claims you're a cheat,' he told him. 'So I'd like to prove her wrong whilst the constable is a witness to her lies.'

He spoke in a loud voice, as if he were making a speech, and the coming spectacle attracted a flurry of interest as shoppers crowded forward to watch what was happening.

The cheesemonger glared at Agnes.

'Why would you take any notice of her? This is absolute nonsense!' he proclaimed.

'Let's just make the checks,' said Constable Westwell as he tried to hold back the gathering crowd of onlookers. He nodded to the superintendent. 'Get out a half-pound weight,' he instructed him.

The man selected the weight from his box and placed it on the scales.

'Now, your cheese,' instructed the constable.

Agnes watched as the cheesemonger turned to a part-cut wheel and sliced a portion with his cheese wire. He placed it on the scales and it balanced perfectly.

'Satisfied?' demanded the cheesemonger.

'He's cut it larger than usual,' protested Agnes. 'That doesn't prove anything. Tell him to put his own weight against yours,' she pleaded with the superintendent.

'Oh, this is ridiculous!' the cheesemonger burst out. 'Take her out of my sight!' he told the constable. 'I've no time for a little Irish colleen like her trying to upset my business!'

'It does look bigger than the pieces he usually cuts,' one woman remarked doubtfully.

The cheesemonger glared at her. 'It's all about the density,' he told her as if she were an imbecile and could never understand.

'I know about weights,' persisted Agnes, plucking at the constable's sleeve. 'I work with them every day. Proper weights have marks on them to show they're genuine.'

'If you wouldn't mind passing me your half-pound weight, sir,' requested Constable Westwell.

Agnes saw a flicker of worry cross the cheesemonger's face. Then he began to bluster.

'I have a business to run here. I haven't time for this,' he complained. 'I've shown my cheese is sold at full weight. Let that be the end of it!'

'If you would just pass me the weight, sir,' the constable insisted.

The crowd had fallen silent now as they watched to see what would happen next. It was the best entertainment many of them had had for a long time, thought

Agnes, thankful that the constable was determined to get to the bottom of the matter.

There was a long pause, until the cheesemonger, with a snort, passed his weight to the constable who balanced it on his palm, assessing it. Then he handed it to the flustered superintendent.

'Weigh that against yours,' he instructed.

The man placed his own weight on one side of the scales and the cheesemonger's on the other. Women were standing on tiptoes to get a better look and Agnes held her breath and barely dared to watch. Suddenly there was an exclamation from the crowd as the superintendent's weight fell and the balance rose.

'There must be some mistake!' cried out the cheesemonger. 'That can't be right!'

The superintendent shuffled the weights, moving them about on the scales and even swapping sides, but he was unable to make the scales balance. It was clear to everyone that the cheesemonger's weight was not the full half-pound.

Agnes felt a rush of elation that she was right. 'See?' she said to Constable Westwell. But the policeman had lost interest in her and his attention was focussed on the scene in front of him.

'I'm afraid you'll have to come with me, sir,' he told the cheesemonger.

'Where? Why? I've done nothing wrong. I bought those weights in good faith. I had no idea they were faulty. I would never knowingly cheat anyone!'

He sounded convincing and many of the crowd began to take his side, calling on the constable to let him be and crying that it was a shame. Others, mostly the women shoppers, began to talk amongst themselves, saying that they'd always known his portions were underweight but that they'd never been able to prove it before and that it served him right for taking advantage of honest hard-working folk.

Someone bumped into Agnes as the crowd surged forward, splitting into two factions. She looked up at Constable Westwell and saw that he was concerned at the turn of events. Even though he was tall and imposing in his police uniform, he was just one man in a seething mass, and Agnes feared that things were about to turn nasty as those who supported the cheesemonger began to point a finger of blame at her.

'There's always trouble where there's Irish!' someone said.

She wondered whether she should try to creep away, but she was trapped against the stall and realized that there was no escape.

The superintendent seemed afraid and the cheesemonger was speaking urgently to his wife, who had begun to pack up their wares.

As Agnes turned to the constable to beg for his help, she saw him draw his truncheon with one hand and reach into a pocket with the other. He withdrew an oblong object with a handle, and once he'd deployed his truncheon to make some space around them, he lifted the rattle into the air and began to swing it around, making an almost deafening sound that carried over the voices of the crowd.

The mob moved back, wary of being struck with the truncheon as the constable wielded it with little mercy for those who tried to come too near.

'Get back! Make way!' he told them.

Agnes waited with trepidation for reinforcements to arrive from the police station, and soon the crowd began to disperse as more policemen came running across the market square with their truncheons drawn to assist Constable Westwell.

'Get hold of that man!' he shouted to one of them as he noticed the cheesemonger trying to make an escape. 'Take him to the lock-up and he'll be up before the magistrate on Monday morning!'

## 29

As soon as she saw her daughter, Kitty could tell that there had been some sort of trouble. Agnes looked dishevelled and Kitty knew she would never have returned so soon, and with cheese still in her basket, if she hadn't been badly frightened. She should never have agreed to let her go. She should have insisted she did her job here where she was safe and her wages were guaranteed.

'Have you been attacked again?' she asked, examining Agnes for any injuries as her heart pounded in her chest and all manner of terrible things flashed through her mind.

'No,' Agnes replied.

It was only then that Kitty saw Constable Westwell in the doorway.

'Is she in trouble?' she gasped, thinking that he must have arrested Agnes for some reason. What would happen now? How would they ever manage if they were sent back to Ireland? Kitty felt tears well in her eyes as she fought to stay calm and try to discover what was amiss.

'No, Mrs Cavanah, your daughter isn't in trouble. In fact, she's been very brave and helped me to uncover some cheating that's been going on at the market for quite a while.'

Kitty met the steady gaze of the policeman. He had kind eyes, she thought, surprised that a policeman might show any kindness.

'I thought I'd walk her back here,' the constable explained. 'Folk are a bit over-excited by the proceedings, but they'll soon settle down.'

'Well, thank you,' said Kitty as the workers began to crowd around to see what all the fuss was about. It brought Mr Reynolds out of his office.

'Agnes Cavanah! I might have known tha'd be the centre of all this attention!' His teasing stopped when he saw the constable. 'She's not in bother, is she?' he asked, looking concerned.

Constable Westwell explained again and then said he would leave them as his colleagues might need his assistance.

Kitty turned back to her daughter. The colour was returning to Agnes's cheeks and she looked quite pleased with herself.

'That cheesemonger *was* cheating people,' Agnes told them. 'His weights were untrue. It was because of what you told me about weights that I got him caught out,' she told Mr Reynolds with a smile. 'He'll not come back to this market again. In fact, he's up before the magistrate on Monday.'

'Well, well. That's a turn up,' said Mr Reynolds. 'I always knew tha were a sharp one. She's a clever one, is this lass of thine,' he told Kitty. 'Tha should be proud of her.'

They were all congratulating Agnes and Kitty knew she ought to feel proud, but she didn't. She still felt afraid for her daughter and for herself. And even when the policeman had gone she still couldn't shake off the feeling that there might be repercussions.

In the end, Mr Reynolds told them all to get back to their work and Agnes helped Kitty with the last of the weighing in. She was good at her job and Kitty wished she could be content with it and that Mr Reynolds and Mr Anderton wouldn't encourage her so much. She doubted any good would come of it and she was determined not to stand in for Agnes again. The girl was much safer here than getting into goodness only knew what danger out at the market.

Agnes had been badly shaken by the encounter. When the crowd had closed in on her she'd been frightened and it was only the presence of the constable that had reassured her. She thought he'd been magnificent when he wielded his truncheon and his rattle, and the way all the other constables had come running to break up the crowd and arrest the cheesemonger had been wonderful.

Once the fuss had died down, she'd wanted to stay and sell the rest of her cheese, but Constable Westwood had been insistent that he walk her back to the warehouse to find her mother. She'd been grateful to him, but she hadn't wanted to cower away from those who were accusing her of having tricked the cheesemonger in some way. Many were convinced that he was an honest man and that she must be at fault, simply because she was Irish. It was so hard to fight back against the prejudice, so very hard, but Agnes was determined to prove them wrong. She would never cheat anyone.

Still, when she looked into her basket at the end of the afternoon, she saw that her sales had been good, and when she added up her takings on the kitchen table back on Mary Ellen Street, as her mother cooked some potatoes for their supper, she was pleased that she had more than enough to pay her debt to Mr Anderton.

'I hope you learned your lesson this afternoon,' said her mother when she'd put the money away. 'The market is too dangerous a place to be selling on your own. Anything could have happened to you.'

'I was perfectly safe,' Agnes told her.

'Well, you'll not be doing it again. I'll not take your place in the warehouse and worry myself sick about what's happening to you on the streets.'

'Nothing was happening to me. I was doing well until that cheesemonger tried to have me arrested. But it did him no good. It's him in the lock-up.'

'Maybe he didn't know his weights were faulty,' said her mother as she put the meal out into dishes. 'Maybe he was the one who was cheated.'

'That's for the magistrate to decide,' replied Agnes, although a shiver of fear ran through her that the magistrate might agree with her mother and let the man go. If he came back to the market he would never be content until he put her out of business.

Her mother refusing to do her Saturday afternoon shift was a disappointment too. Her only other option was to give up her warehouse job completely and she wasn't sure she was ready to do that yet.

After they'd eaten she decided to get out of the house and away from her mother's lectures about giving up her selling and finding a nice boy to settle down with – one of whom she approved and not Jonas Marden who was already halfway to hell in her estimation simply by being a Protestant.

'It's such a shame you let Patrick Ryan slip through your fingers,' her mother was saying yet again when Agnes announced she was going to take Mr Anderton his money. She knew her mother would approve of that at least.

The streets were still busy as she walked to King Street. Some of the stallholders were still trading on the market and Agnes regretted leaving her basket at home. She was sure she could have sold up if she'd brought it with her. Still, she'd wrapped a pound of cheese for Dorothy and she went around to the back door with it.

'I hear there was a bit of a commotion on the market earlier,' said Dorothy as she put the cheese away on the cold slab. 'Something about the cheesemonger getting arrested?'

'It's true. He was cheating people with untrue weights. I told you his portions were smaller than mine.'

Agnes grinned with satisfaction. The fear she'd felt earlier was gone now and she felt proud of the part she'd played in bringing the man to justice.

Upstairs she repeated the story again for Mr and Mrs Anderton. With every telling she made her own part seem more heroic and she was enjoying the admiration she received for what she'd done.

'It's amazing that he's got away with it for so long,' said Mrs Anderton. 'You certainly are a force to be reckoned with, Agnes.'

'And you've rid yourself of competition,' Mr Anderton told her. 'It was a smart move. You should make the most of it.'

'What do you think I should do?' Agnes asked, eager for advice from someone who supported her.

'Well, you could take a stall on the market yourself,' he said. 'You'd have to pay the rent, but you wouldn't have anyone undercutting your price.'

Agnes could see the sense in it.

'I'd have to set up properly with scales and a cheese wire. It wouldn't be like selling from a basket. It would be more expense.'

'That's true,' replied Mr Anderton, 'but it would be worth the investment. If you don't have enough saved, I'm sure we can come to some arrangement.'

Agnes received his words eagerly. 'You know I would pay back any loan, with interest,' she added.

He smiled, looking indulgent. 'I was thinking that you could borrow the scales from the kitchen for a small fee.'

'What about Dorothy?' asked his wife. 'She might need those scales.'

'Have you ever seen her use them?' asked Mr Anderton. 'She measures out with a spoon and her cooking is always perfection. But if she complains I'll gladly buy her a new set.'

'It would mean spending a full three days on the market,' said Agnes, pointing out the pitfalls in the plan, 'and I don't think Mr Reynolds would let me work part-time.'

'Maybe the day has come for you to make that final step and give up the warehouse job?' suggested Mr Anderton.

'I don't know.' Agnes could hear her mother's furious voice in her head. She would be so angry. 'What about the days when the market isn't on?' She knew she could go around from door to door on those days, but she doubted it would bring in enough to compensate her for giving up her job.

'There are other markets,' said Mr Anderton. 'Other towns hold their markets on different days. Darwen, Accrington, Preston. Preston is a huge market. You could sell there.'

'But how would I get there?'

'You could walk.'

Agnes gave the suggestion some serious consideration

as she drank the tea that Dorothy had brought and accepted the huge slice of fruit cake that Mrs Anderton offered her even though she was still satiated from her potato stew. She would have to get up very early, she thought. Preston was further on than Samlesbury and without a cart or a pony it would take her a few hours to walk there. But it wasn't impossible. The barrow would be heavy and there was a steep hill up from the river into Preston, but, as Mr Reynolds had told her, she wouldn't be successful without huge effort on her own part.

The next morning, Agnes walked up to Oozebooth Farm to buy more cheese. All the way there she was dreading Mr Robinson bringing out his bottle again, but thankfully he didn't and there was no need for her to pretend that she'd taken the pledge. She still missed going down to Goosefoot and seeing Jonas, but buying her cheese was more important. Besides, he could have come to look for her like he had done before but he'd stayed away, and she'd begun to wonder if he really did care.

She spent the afternoon in Dorothy's kitchen weighing out portions from one wheel. The other she left intact, knowing that customers on the market liked to see their portions cut and weighed in front of them.

'Mr Anderton says tha's to take the scales and cutter with thee,' Dorothy told her.

'Only if it's all right with you,' replied Agnes, not wanting to offend the maid.

Dorothy shrugged her shoulders. 'Makes no difference to me. I don't often use 'em,' she admitted.

So, with her friend's blessing, Agnes put the scales, weights and cheese cutter into the barrow with the cheese. Dorothy helped her up the back steps with it and she bumped it all home along the cobbled streets. Next, she would have to have two difficult conversations, neither of which would be easy. She would have to face her mother and tell her what she'd decided to do, and she would have to explain to Mr Reynolds that she was leaving the warehouse.

As she expected, her mother was upset. She cried and she pleaded with Agnes to think again and not take such a rash step.

'But we'll be better off,' she insisted.

'We'll be ruined, so we will,' her mother wept, wiping her eyes on the corner of her apron and making Agnes feel wretched. But she refused to be talked out of it. Mr Anderton was certain she would be successful and he knew much more about business than her mother did. She had to trust his advice, work hard and pray that it all turned out well.

'I've decided to give you my notice,' Agnes told Mr Reynolds when she arrived early at the warehouse next morning. 'I can work today and tomorrow,' she went on. 'But on Wednesday I'm taking a stall on the market.'

'I knew this would happen,' he complained, shaking his head. 'Will thy mother be replacing thee? She was doing well on Saturday. She's far more capable than she gives herself credit for. I can see where tha gets thy brains from.'

'I did ask her,' Agnes told him. 'But she's not speaking to me. She thinks I'll bring us all to ruin.'

'I'll set her right, if she'll hear me out,' he replied. 'Go and set out thy stall,' he advised Agnes. 'I've only myself to blame. I knew when I spoke to thee about business it would come to this. Tha's got a gleam in thine eye that I rarely see from the lasses hereabouts. Tha'll do all right, mark my words.'

Agnes wanted to kiss him. She didn't, but she smiled so much she could feel her face aching. She was sure she could make a success of this business and she was determined not to let anyone down – especially her mother.

'I have another favour to ask,' she admitted.

'Go on then,' he said.

'Can I borrow a table?' she asked with a cheeky smile.

He sighed theatrically. 'Tha'll be the ruin of me,' he complained, but Agnes could tell that he was secretly pleased with her for listening to his advice and trying to better herself. 'See what tha can find in yon shop,' he told her. 'Tha can pay me for it when tha's made thy fortune.'

# 30

The market superintendent seemed doubtful when she went to his office very early on Wednesday morning and told him that she would like to set up a stall.

'Are you sure?' he asked.

'Yes,' Agnes replied. 'It's only a small one, but I want a good position – on the outdoor square.'

'You have to pay more for a better position.'

Agnes knew that wasn't true. Mr Anderton had told her that she should pay no more than sixpence a day for a stall outside. He had offered to negotiate for her if she came up against difficulty. Agnes didn't want to accept his help because she didn't want the superintendent to think she was weak, but it was reassuring to know she could call her adviser in if it became necessary.

'There's space where the previous cheesemonger used to stand,' she remarked. Agnes thought she would be better off setting up her table as near as possible to where the original cheese stall had been, because that was where customers would head to. The superintendent frowned. It seemed a sore point with him and Agnes decided not to antagonize him more than was necessary. 'Or somewhere thereabouts,' she conceded.

'All right,' he agreed grudgingly. 'You can set up on that row.'

Agnes wheeled her precariously laden barrow to the spot between the butcher and the fruit stall where the cheesemonger had always stood. The table she'd brought from the rag shop was a trestle, no more than a wooden board with a pair of A-frame legs placed under it. The top was balanced across the barrow with the legs and the cheese underneath it. It had been a struggle to bring the whole load down from Mary Ellen Street, and as Agnes lifted the board on to its legs she knew that it wouldn't be possible for her to wheel the whole contraption to the market at Preston. She would need to take the ready cut cheese there and pop each portion on to her scales as she sold it to reassure her customers.

The stallholders on either side watched her curiously as she covered the trestle with a clean white cloth and set out her weights and scales, the cut cheese and her full wheel. It all looked professional and appealing, she thought as she stood back to admire her work, ready to begin selling in her clean white apron.

'So tha thinks tha can take Old Haworth's place,' remarked the butcher as Agnes went to stand behind her stall. 'It's a pity tha didn't think to bring butter and eggs as well. They always sold well.'

'I just sell cheese,' Agnes told him.

'Aye. So I see.'

He didn't seem impressed and Agnes began to worry

that he might have a point. She'd seen that the butter and eggs had been popular and she wondered whether she ought to have bought some from Oozebooth Farm. But she would scarcely have had room on her barrow and the eggs would surely have been cracked or broken as she struggled across the uneven streets. What she really needed was a horse and cart, but she was still a long way from even considering that sort of expense.

At seven o'clock the bell rang to mark the start of trading and butterflies filled Agnes's stomach with a mixture of excitement and anxiety. She knew that she needed to call out her wares, but her mouth was dry and the vendor on the fruit stall was yelling so loudly about his apples and pears that Agnes was convinced nobody would ever hear her.

Trade was slow at first, but people on their way to work stopped to see if there was anything to buy for their breakfast or dinner. She saw that the stalls selling freshly baked muffins and pies were doing well at this time and was reassured that a few customers came to get a couple of ounces of cheese to put on a sandwich for later. Things picked up later in the morning when the housewives and the cooks from the bigger houses came along with their baskets. Her price of thruppence a half-pound was popular and soon she was busily cutting and weighing portions for a short queue.

A few customers enquired after butter and eggs.

'Not today,' Agnes told them. 'But I may bring some next week if there's enough demand.'

By dinnertime she was hungry and she was glad when her mother came by with Maria and Peter to see how she was doing.

'Mind the stall for a minute,' she said. 'I'll go and get one of those fresh loaves and we can have cheese sandwiches.'

'It's no good us eating your profit,' her mother pointed out.

'We have to eat something. And I've done all right.' She paused to show her mother the purse where she was keeping her takings.

'Hide that away!' exclaimed her mother in alarm. 'You don't want to be robbed again!'

Agnes did as she was told, laughing off the suggestion, but it was an aspect of standing out in the open that worried her. She thought she was safe here, but there had been some rough lads who'd come past earlier, already looking the worse for drink.

'At least it's a nice day,' remarked her mother as they stood eating their dinner. 'It'll not be so good in the rain though.'

Agnes almost sighed. Her mother always pointed out the pitfalls in any plan.

'I could get a tarpaulin,' she replied. She'd already noticed that some of the other sellers had set up shelters over their produce. The trouble was that it would be even more to bring down on the barrow and she doubted she could manage. She would just have to hope for a good summer and protect her cheese from either rain or sun the best she could.

'Could you not have gone inside the market house?' asked her mother.

Agnes shook her head. 'They charge more,' she told her. 'Besides, no one goes in there for cheese. This is where they look.'

As she spoke she pictured the abandoned stall where she'd first seen Jonas. He was never far from her thoughts and she longed to see him, to know how he was coping after his father's accident and to check whether they really had got rid of the cows. If his mother had relented and was making cheese again, Agnes would have been willing to walk out to Samlesbury every Sunday to buy from them, but as it was, she couldn't risk wasting the day by having to come back empty-handed.

'Can I stay?' pleaded Maria when their mother said it was time to go.

'Can she?' asked Agnes. She would welcome the company and she knew she could trust her little sister to take the money and give the right change.

Her mother looked doubtful.

'I worked hard this morning,' Maria said, 'and I hate going to that warehouse. It stinks!'

Their mother nodded. 'All right,' she agreed, taking hold of Peter's hand. 'I'll see you both later.'

'She's been complaining about you all morning,'

Maria told Agnes after their mother had gone. 'She keeps saying you'll ruin us. You won't, will you?'

'No, of course not!' Agnes reassured her, hoping that she sounded more confident than she felt. Despite her frustration with her mother's lack of enthusiasm for her enterprise, she had to admit that she had her own worries. Even though her morning had been rewarding, fun almost, she knew she must make a profit today, and every day after, because there would be no coins put into her hand by Mr Reynolds at the end of each week.

Business was steady and by the time the market closed Agnes was pleased that she'd taken more money than she had hoped. But the next day was a Thursday and there would be no market here. She wondered what to do. Should she take Mr Anderton's advice, get up very early, and walk to Preston to stand on the market there?

## 31

Even though Agnes felt exhausted after her first day as a market trader, she was determined to get up very early the next morning to go to Preston.

'I'm going to bed as well,' she told her mother as she watched her tuck Peter in. 'Don't let Maria wake me when she comes up.'

'What time are you planning to leave?' asked her mother.

'About four-ish.'

'That early?'

'I think so,' replied Agnes. 'It's a long walk.'

'Wouldn't you be better off just staying in Blackburn?'

'I'll sell more on the market than going door to door.'

'You could still sell around the market square here.'

'Not many people go into town on a Thursday,' said Agnes. 'I'll make more money in Preston.'

'You'll wear yourself out,' said her mother. It sounded like a reprimand, but Agnes knew it was because her mother was worried about her. She knew that all her objections to the cheese selling business were because she worried, but Agnes wished that her mother had more faith in her. It would be so much easier with her support.

'It'll be worth it,' she promised. 'You'll see. You'll be

able to put the rag gathering behind you when I get my cheese shop.'

'Maybe. I've quite grown to like it though,' her mother replied. 'It can be rewarding when you find good things.'

Agnes nodded and kissed her mother's cheek. It wasn't something she'd ever have expected her mother to admit. It certainly wasn't the life she'd envisaged when they boarded that ship from Ireland.

Knowing that she would never wake up without some sort of help, Agnes took a precious candle and estimated where she needed to push a pin into it to wake up on time. When the candle burned down, the pin would clatter into the bowl of the metal candlestick and alert her that it was time to leave her bed and go to sell her wares.

When the noise wakened Agnes it was still dark outside and she almost groaned at the thought of getting up. Her mother had wakened with the falling pin too, although Maria, lying between them, was still sound asleep.

'Eat and drink something,' said her mother. 'It'll be a long, hard day.'

'I will,' promised Agnes as she dressed herself. She was glad that her mother wasn't still trying to persuade her not to go. She hoped it was the start of her accepting her desire to make a success of the business.

Downstairs, Agnes packed some bread. Any crumbs of cheese that she might have left over would be better put on a sandwich than swept to the floor for the birds to peck. Despite her promise to her mother, she took no time to eat, but drank a little of the thin blue milk that was stored in a pottery jug on the cold slab. Then she manoeuvred the barrow out of the front door and hurried to and fro loading it up. Agnes checked her purse was secured around her waist beneath her gown then pulled a shawl around her shoulders. Even after a full day outside it still smelt of the warehouse. She was glad that she wasn't going there. Even though she'd enjoyed the work, Agnes was enjoying being her own boss more.

The streets were deserted as she wheeled the barrow along, trying to be quiet and not disturb those who were still sleeping. She turned out of Mary Ellen Street and tackled the steep hill up to the Preston road. She'd remembered her gloves, and a clean apron was tucked under the freshly washed cloth that covered her goods. When she reached the top, she paused to get her breath back and then set off at a smart pace towards her destination.

The morning was fine and warm, and a chorus of early birdsong filled her with optimism as she walked briskly on. The way was familiar to her now. She went along, glancing up towards Mellor where the first smoke of the day was beginning to plume upwards from the chimneys of the cottages and the cotton mill. On she went until she reached the Halfway House, and then down towards the river.

When she reached the track that would take her to Goosefoot Farm she hesitated. The urge to go that way and see Jonas again was strong and she wondered if she had the time. All she wanted to do was check that his father was recovering and ask if the cows really had gone. But Agnes was unsure if she would be welcome. Mr Marsden had made it clear he didn't approve of her, and although she'd half-expected and hoped that Jonas would seek her out in Blackburn, as he had done once before, he hadn't come.

Perhaps her mother was right about one thing, she mused as she went on her way. It would be easier to marry a boy from her own community, even if it wasn't Patrick Ryan. To wed someone who had nothing in common with her, and whose parents disliked her, would bring about so many difficulties. It wouldn't be a good way to begin a marriage. It might be better if she tried to forget Jonas Marsden.

The sun was shining on the Ribble when she reached it and crossed the bridge. Not far now, she thought as she urged herself on. Just one last hill to climb and then it would be level all the way.

Her arms and legs were already aching and Agnes tried not to think about the return journey. She'd been walking for hours before she approached the centre of Preston. The streets were busy with carts and horses, even though it was too early for the carriages of the gentry. They would still be in their homes, enjoying their breakfasts.

Agnes heard the sound of the market before she saw it. Trading had already begun and the vendors were calling their wares to the early shoppers. She wondered if she needed permission to sell here, but not knowing who to ask and eager not to lose any sales, she decided she would set out her wares and explain herself later if any superintendent approached her.

She pushed the barrow around the edge of the stalls, wondering where would be the best place to set up. She saw that there were several cheese stalls here already, vying against one another, and she decided that it would be better to stay in the vicinity. There was no sense in tucking herself away in some obscure corner where the stallholders were only selling pots and pans.

Agnes found a small space and rested the barrow on its legs. She folded her shawl away, took off the gloves that had kept her hands clean and blister-free and tied the apron around herself. No one paid her any attention as she folded back the cloth, set up her scales alongside the barrow and took a breath.

'Cheese! Fresh Lancashire cheese!' she shouted. 'Only thruppence a half-pound!'

'It's ready cut,' complained a woman who paused by the barrow, attracted by the bargain price.

'I'll pop it on the scales so you can see you're not being cheated,' said Agnes, lifting a portion and balancing it against the half-pound weight. 'The scales are true,' she added. 'The weights are verified as accurate.'

'Go on then,' conceded the woman as Agnes transferred the cheese to her outstretched shopping basket and took the three pennies payment. Her first Preston sale, she thought as she transferred the money to her purse.

None of the other sellers seemed interested in her although they all seemed to know one another, calling out greetings and asking after relatives and friends. Some of them had already wandered over to the public houses that surrounded the square and had come back with refreshments in their hands. The sight made Agnes realize how thirsty she was after her long walk, but she didn't dare to leave her things to go to buy a drink; besides, she craved a pitcher of fresh, clean water from an Irish stream, not the cloudy ale that the men drank which made them shout even louder. Next time, she must remember to bring something with her.

As the market became busier, Agnes was pleased to welcome a steady flow of customers who were keen for a bargain. She saw some of the other stallholders eyeing her suspiciously and hoped that none would make a complaint about her. During a few minutes' respite when no one was at her barrow, Agnes took the opportunity to assess how many others were selling cheese and to try to hear the prices they were charging.

It seemed that Preston market had quite a few cheese-mongers, although some were selling other goods as well. Many of them looked like farmers. There was something about the ruddiness of their weatherworn cheeks that set them apart from the pale-faced millworkers who rarely saw daylight except for on a Sunday.

Most were selling at a similar price to her and Agnes wondered if it was because she was new that customers were approaching her. Still, she wasn't about to complain. The weight in her purse was increasing reassuringly.

As the crowds parted for a moment, Agnes had a glimpse of a stall further along the square and her heart leapt a somersault as she thought that she saw Jonas Marsden. She wondered if she had been mistaken when her view was blocked again, so she moved out from behind her barrow, unaware of being jostled by the shoppers, and stood on tiptoe to try to get a better look. She was sure it was Jonas.

Agnes tried to make sense of it. The stall in question had several wheels of cheese, but how could it be? Whose cheese was Jonas selling if his mother had stopped working in her dairy?

Her first instinct was to push the shoppers aside and run over to where he was standing, but good sense caused her to hesitate. She had no one to watch over her goods. She should have asked to bring Maria with her, she thought. At some point she might need to leave the barrow unattended, if only to relieve herself at a nearby inn.

'Do you know that cheese seller?' she asked her nearest neighbour. 'Is it Jonas Marsden?'

The man gazed in the direction she was pointing.

'Aye. It's the Marsdens' lad,' he agreed. 'Do you know him?'

'I do. I need to speak to him,' Agnes said. She looked at the man. He was middle-aged, florid, with bushy whiskers springing from his cheeks and chin. He looked trustworthy, she decided. 'Would you watch my barrow for a moment?' she asked.

Agnes knew that it was a risk, leaving her goods with a complete stranger, but her desire to speak to Jonas was overwhelming, and even if the man had said no she thought she probably would have gone anyway.

She wended her way through the crowd. Jonas had a few people at his stall and was busy serving someone. Agnes had no option but to join the queue, as the sharp elbows of the housewives prevented her approaching ahead of them. Jonas was reckoning up the cost of several items for a young girl who looked like a kitchen maid on an errand. There was an endearing furrow above his half-closed eyes until he opened them wide and said his price. The girl smiled shyly as she handed over the money and Jonas returned it with a wide smile of his own. An unexpected stab of jealousy pained Agnes as much as a physical blow, and unable to stop herself, she called out his name.

'Jonas!'

He jumped as if struck, and turned to look for her. Agnes waved her hand and his eyes found hers. His expression was pure astonishment.

'Agnes!' he called. 'What are you doing here?'

The women at the stall looked from her to Jonas and back. They nudged one another and tried to move closer to hear what would be said. The market was often a good place to witness scandals and gossip, they knew. But Agnes was barely aware of them. She pushed her way to the edge of the stall to reach Jonas.

'What are you doing here?' she asked him without answering his question. 'Whose cheese are you selling?'

'My mother's,' he said, as if puzzled by her question.

'But I thought you'd got rid of the cows?'

'No.' He shook his head. 'I can't explain now,' he said. 'Will you stay a while? You could help me out,' he suggested, looking at the women who were now crowding around the stall.

'I can't. I have my own stall – well, I'm selling from my barrow today,' she tried to explain. 'I can't leave it.'

He looked disappointed and Agnes was torn. She didn't want to leave him. She could think of nothing better than standing beside him to sell cheese, but she couldn't just abandon her own, not when she'd worked so hard and come so far.

Then the solution came to her. It was so obvious.

'I'll wheel my barrow across here,' she told him. 'I'll be back in a minute.'

Agnes made her way back through the gathering crowd to where she'd left her barrow. She half expected to find it gone, but it was still there, under the watchful eye of her bewhiskered neighbour.

'Thanks for watching it,' she said as she loaded the

scales and picked up the barrow's handles. 'I'm going to stand near my friend.'

The man nodded at her and Agnes called out, 'Excuse me! Excuse me!' as she struggled to get through the shoppers.

Jonas smiled when he saw her coming.

'Stack your cheese on here,' he said, moving some of his own to make space for hers. Eagerly, Agnes transferred her stock from the barrow on to the stall.

'Is that the same cheese?' asked a customer.

'No. This is from Oozebooth Farm in Blackburn. It's good cheese though. Each portion is a full half-pound,' she added, putting one on her scales to prove her claim.

'I'll try some,' said the woman and Agnes hoped that Jonas wouldn't mind her taking some of his trade.

'Did you say it's from Oozebooth Farm?' he asked her when there was a break between customers. 'What made you buy from them?'

'It's nearer home – and some of the other farmers wouldn't sell to me.'

He nodded. 'I was sorry when you didn't come down to Goosefoot again,' he said.

'I would have come if I'd known you had cheese,' Agnes told him. 'I thought you'd got rid of the cows.'

She had to wait for an answer as Jonas turned away to serve a customer.

'Did you not hear?' he asked when he came back to her. 'My father died.'

Agnes was upset by the news. 'I'm so sorry. I didn't know.'

'He seemed to be improving, but then he died quite suddenly. The doctor thought it must have been internal injuries because the bruises we could see were fading and he'd been getting better.'

'It must have been a shock,' said Agnes, wanting to offer more sympathy than just words. 'How's your mother?'

'Traumatized,' Jonas admitted. 'She cried and cried.'

He turned away to serve another customer and Agnes watched him with tears in her own eyes. She'd been thinking that he didn't care because he hadn't come to find her. Now that she knew it was because he'd been dealing with such a terrible bereavement, she felt guilty and selfish.

'It's all fallen on me,' he told her when there was another opportunity. 'I wasn't sure what to do at first, but in the end I told my mother I was keeping the cows. My father had been making more money from the dairy than from the crops and it seemed foolish to let them go. My mother was against it at first, but it was my decision because the farm is mine now.'

Agnes served a customer of her own. She was selling less cheese than if she'd stayed on her own patch because all the regulars approached Jonas first and only came to her if he looked too busy or if there was a lengthy queue. But she didn't care. She'd thought that she might never see him again, and although his news had been stark and she was sorry for it, she was happy to be in his company once more.

'My mother won't go near the cows,' he went on, 'but she's agreed to continue with making the cheese. It's been hard work though,' he added. 'They still need to be milked twice a day and I'm having to employ a lass as a milkmaid so I can get out to the markets in good time.'

'You've never been back to Blackburn market,' said Agnes. If he'd come there then she would have known all this sooner, she thought.

'I never did very well there. It didn't seem worth it.'

'That cheesemonger who undercut you was cheating his customers,' Agnes told him, and explained what had happened.

'You were brave to take him on,' Jonas remarked.

'I suppose I was. He went up before the magistrate and I heard he was sent to court here in Preston.'

Jonas nodded. 'It serves him right,' he said. 'I don't believe he thought his weights were accurate. So,' he went on after a moment, 'are you selling on Blackburn market now?'

'I've just started to. I've given up my job at the warehouse.'

'That was brave as well. What did your mother say?'

'She's not happy,' Agnes admitted.

'I can believe it.'

As Agnes watched Jonas cut another piece of cheese it struck her that neither of their mothers were happy with the choices they'd made. It made her feel yet more affinity with him, as if it was a battle they both had to face.

'Did you push that barrow all the way here?' he asked.

'Yes.'

'You must have set off very early.'

'It was only just coming light when I left.'

'It's just about light at this time of year, but you'll not be able to do it through the winter,' he told her.

It was something Agnes hadn't considered, but she realized that he was right. Pushing a barrow in the dark was out of the question. It would be too dangerous on the road with the carriages rushing past – they would never see her.

'Well, there's all the summer to come,' she told him. 'I might be able to afford a pony and cart before then.'

'I'll give you a lift back if you like, as far as Goose-foot anyway.'

'I'd like that!'

He smiled. 'I'm glad you came,' he said. 'I thought I might not see you again.'

When the market was finished for the day, Jonas collected his cart from the inn and Agnes helped him to load it. Then she climbed up on to the bench seat beside him and they set off towards Samlesbury.

'Are you going to buy from Oozebooth Farm again?' he asked as they headed downhill towards the river.

'I'd like to buy from you again,' she told him. 'My customers like your cheese. But will you have enough if you're going to Preston market?'

'I'm planning to expand,' he said. 'I want more cows so that I can cut down on the crops and concentrate on making cheese and butter – and maybe I'll sell some eggs too, if I can persuade my mother to add to her flock of chickens. But I can only do that if I'm confident I can sell what we make.'

Agnes nodded. She did want to buy from Jonas, but she didn't relish the long walk and the journey home with a heavy barrow. The truth was that Oozebooth Farm was much nearer and more convenient.

'I know it's a long way for you to come out here,' said Jonas, as if he were reading her thoughts. 'But I could deliver it to you.'

'Would you? That would be wonderful!' she told him. She was grateful that he was willing to go out of his way to make things easier for her.

'There would be a condition though.'

'What?' asked Agnes, hoping it wouldn't be something to spoil her enthusiasm.

'I wouldn't want you to come to the other markets with it. I don't want competition for my own cheese.' He laughed awkwardly. 'You would just have to sell it locally, in Blackburn.'

Agnes felt a bit disappointed, but she wasn't surprised. She'd enjoyed spending the day with him and would have liked to do it again, but she could see his point. It was no use to him having two people selling his cheese in the same places. Besides, it would be pointless for him to deliver the cheese to her if she was going to take it all the way back again to Preston. The trouble was, she wasn't sure if she could make enough money if she was only able to sell three days a week on the Blackburn market, and she was reluctant to go back to the street selling.

'Think about it,' he said. He sounded slightly gloomy that she hadn't agreed straight away. 'Would you like to come in for a cup of tea?' he asked when they reached the lane that led down to Goosefoot Farm.

Agnes hesitated. She wanted to spend more time with Jonas, but she wasn't sure that his mother would welcome her intrusion at such a difficult time.

'I'd better get home,' she said. 'My mother will be looking out for me.'

'All right.'

Jonas reined the pony in and they both got down from the cart. He lifted her barrow down and loaded it with the scales and the unsold cheese.

'Perhaps you'll walk down on Sunday morning again, like you did before?' he asked. 'I'll take you home in the cart with any cheese you want to buy.'

Agnes was still conflicted. Much as she wanted to see him again, she knew that she mustn't let her desire to see Jonas overcome her good sense. She must do what would be the best for her business and herself – and she wondered if that might be buying the local cheese and taking it round to all the markets rather than being limited to selling only in Blackburn.

'I'll see,' she told him, trying not to let her emotions get the better of her.

She put on her gloves and took up the handles of the barrow and turned it towards home.

'Goodbye,' he said, sounding disappointed, as if he thought she might not come back.

Agnes gave him what she hoped was a reassuring smile. 'Goodbye, for now,' she replied before she began to walk up the hill. She thought she could feel Jonas watching her and when she reached the top of the hill she stopped and looked back. Sure enough, the pony and cart was still at the head of the lane. Agnes waved, although she wasn't sure Jonas could see her in the gathering dusk. As she watched, the cart moved off and disappeared so she thought he must have done. She sighed, rearranged her shawl and pressed on. Things had changed in the course of a day but she still wasn't certain if they'd changed for better or for worse.

## 32

Agnes turned the developments over and over in her mind – as she walked home, in bed that night – and even on the market the following day she was distracted by the decision she needed to make.

Before the close of the market on Saturday she'd sold every portion of her cheese and she packed up early so she could go home to count her money and take what she owed to Mr Anderton. She would ask his advice, she decided. He was the only one she trusted to give it impartially because she knew her mother would advise her to have nothing more to do with Jonas Marsden.

Agnes had kept some cheese back for Dorothy and she knocked at the kitchen door.

'Mr and Mrs Anderton are still eating. Would tha like summat whilst tha waits?' asked the maid.

Having been busy all day, Agnes hadn't eaten since early that morning. She was hungry and the smell of the bacon and potatoes was too much for her to refuse.

Dorothy filled a plate and sat her down at the table.

'Tha looks like tha needs feeding up,' she observed. 'Tha's such a skinny little thing. Get that inside thee.'

Agnes thought it was the best meal she'd ever eaten,

although she recalled having something similar the night the Andertons had brought them back here to sleep. The thought of the feather bed upstairs prompted her to yawn and she realized how very tired she was. She would have loved to have a restful day the next day, but there was business to be done both tonight and tomorrow. As Mr Reynolds had warned her, it wasn't easy.

Later, upstairs in the parlour, drinking tea with the Andertons, Agnes told them about her encounter with Jonas on the market at Preston and how he was planning to expand his dairy business.

'Of course you must buy from him again!' exclaimed Mrs Anderton when she finished. 'I think it's wonderful that you've met up with him again.'

'Not so hasty!' laughed Mr Anderton. 'It all seems very romantic, I agree, but Miss Cavanah and I are here to discuss what will benefit her business.'

'And what better business arrangement could she make than to buy cheese from the best cheesemaker in the county – if not the country?' demanded his wife. 'Even you complained that the cheese we've had recently hasn't been so tasty as that from Goosefoot Farm.'

'If Miss Cavanah was sure it was the right thing to do, she wouldn't be here asking for my opinion,' replied Mr Anderton. He turned his full attention back to Agnes. 'What do you see as the flaw in this plan?' he asked. 'What bothers you about it?'

'I'm not sure I could make a living selling on the

outdoor market just three days a week,' Agnes explained. 'I could look for other work when it isn't market day, I suppose, but I doubt Mr Reynolds would take me back for only three days when I was so keen to persuade him to let me go.'

Mr Anderton nodded as he listened carefully. 'I think there are a couple of things you could do,' he said after he'd given the matter some thought. 'You could rent a stall in the market house, which is open for five days. Or you could get a shop, which you could keep open as many hours as you liked, except for Sundays.'

Agnes considered the options. She'd already thought about the first herself and had her doubts.

'The rental on the market house stalls is more expensive,' she said, 'and I'm not sure that people would go in there to buy cheese. They expect the cheese stall to be outside, where it's always been – and if they don't see it there they might never think to look any further. Jonas hardly sold anything when he had a stall inside. And I couldn't afford the rent on a shop! It would be much more than a market house stall.'

'You could continue street selling on the other days,' Mr Anderton suggested.

Agnes nodded. It was something she'd thought about too. She wasn't keen on the idea but it seemed the only solution if she was to buy cheese from Jonas.

The next morning it took Agnes an enormous effort to waken up. She yawned and rubbed at her aching eyes, whilst wishing for more sleep, but she eventually roused herself, determined to make the most of the day.

She knew that the sensible thing would be to go to mass and then walk up to Oozebooth Farm after dinner for some cheese. But as she splashed her face with cold water and dressed herself in her Sunday gown, despite knowing that the track to Goosefoot Farm would still be muddy, the thought of seeing Jonas helped her decide to walk to Samlesbury and hope that he would keep his promise to bring her home on his cart.

Agnes waited until they were all ready to leave the house before she told her mother that she wasn't going with them to St Alban's. She didn't wait to hear her mother's objections, but hurried off in the opposite direction.

The sunny morning dispelled her lingering weariness and she walked at a good pace, watching out for the familiar landmarks that punctuated her way. It had seemed so far the first time she'd walked to Samlesbury, but she was growing used to it now, and the additional food that her mother was able to buy with the extra contribution to their budget from the cheese sales had helped increase her strength and stamina.

Her excitement built as she approached Goosefoot Farm. Agnes found it impossible to quell the fluttering of anticipation and nerves in her stomach as she heard the dog begin to bark.

'Quiet!' called a voice she recognized as Jonas's, and by the time she reached the gate, he was holding it open to admit her.

'I hoped you would come,' he said, looking pleased.

'I've come to buy some cheese,' Agnes told him.

He smiled at her.

'Come inside,' he invited. 'I'm sure you'll enjoy a cup of tea and some toasted bread after your long walk.'

Agnes followed him into the farmhouse kitchen. It was the same as she remembered it, except that today Mrs Marsden was sitting in a rocking chair by the fire. She looked pale and thin and gazed at Agnes as if she didn't recognize her.

'You remember Agnes, don't you?' said Jonas. 'She's been before, for cheese.'

'I'm sorry about your husband,' Agnes said to her. She wanted to take the woman's hand to comfort her but wasn't sure if the gesture would be welcomed.

'You're the Irish girl,' said Mrs Marsden.

'That's right,' said Agnes as she accepted the chair Jonas brought forward for her and sat down near to his mother. 'I used to buy your cheese. It's the best cheese I've tasted – all my customers like it. I only stopped coming because I didn't think you were making it any more,' she explained. 'But I would like to buy it again.'

'If Agnes buys our cheese to sell on the market in Blackburn it means I can concentrate on Preston and the other markets,' explained Jonas.

His mother nodded and Agnes was shocked to see that she didn't stir from her chair but allowed her son to brew some tea and pour it into cups. Jonas reached for the bread knife and sliced thick portions from a loaf and handed one to Agnes, impaled on a toasting fork for her to hold in front of the fire.

'I wanted him to get rid of those cows but he wouldn't hear of it,' his mother told Agnes as she watched the bread turn a golden brown. 'Dangerous beasts!' She visibly shivered and Agnes wondered where she was finding the strength to make the cheese. She looked so frail and weak.

After they'd eaten, Jonas took her across to the cold store to show her the cheeses. There were plenty stacked up and Agnes was surprised.

'Your mother looks ill,' she said as she wondered whether to take the freshest or the more matured ones.

'Losing my father has devastated her,' he admitted.

'But is she still able to make the cheese?'

He nodded. 'It's all she can do. When she comes across to the dairy she seems much more like herself, but in the house all she does is sit by the fire.'

'Do you have to do everything else?' Agnes asked, appreciating the heaviness of the weight that had fallen on Jonas's shoulders.

'Aye, including the milking on a Sunday. I have to give Lizzie, the lass who helps us out, a day off. Would you like to have a go?'

'At what?'

'Milking a cow.'

'No.' Agnes thought about poor Mr Marsden lying in his grave and decided that she'd rather keep her distance from the huge black and white beasts. 'Your mother says they're dangerous!'

'I got rid of Buttercup,' Jonas told her. 'It was a pity because she was a good milker, but it was a concession to my mother. She couldn't sleep whilst that cow was still on the farm. The rest are docile. They're friendly beasts and would rather lick you than take a kick at you. Come on!' He reached out and grasped her hand, pulling her after him into the yard and across to the byre where some of the cows were tied in the stalls. 'These are the ones still waiting,' he explained.

As Agnes watched, Jonas picked up a three-legged milking stool and sat down near the cow's flank. Then he positioned a bucket under the beast and reached forward to take the teats in his hands. He squeezed and pulled them and the milk shot out in spurts, frothing into the bucket and steaming slightly in the cold air.

'Come and try,' he said.

Hesitantly, Agnes lowered herself on to the stool, flinching as the cow shifted its weight. Under Jonas's guidance she reached for the teats, finding them warm and stiff beneath her hands. Her head was pressed against the warmth of the animal's flank and she could smell the ripe scent of its skin and the sweet aroma of the milk. As she squeezed, carefully aiming the spurts of milk into the pail, she had a vivid memory of having experienced something similar.

'I think I've done this before, or seen it done,' she

said, surprised by the recollection. 'It must have been at home, in Ireland.'

'Well, you certainly have a flair for it,' Jonas replied. 'I'd employ you as a milkmaid.'

He watched as Agnes filled the bucket with the creamy milk that would become the cheese she would sell. Was this what it would be like to be a farmer's wife? she wondered. Could she imagine herself doing this every day, or twice a day, before learning from Mrs Marsden how to separate the curds from the whey, then add the rennet and press the cheese into finished wheels? Agnes suddenly realized that the prospect appalled her. She wanted to be a cheesemonger and she couldn't see how she could do that if she was stuck out here in the countryside on this farm.

She let the teats go and stood up, briefly patting the cow's back.

'I think there's more to come,' Jonas encouraged.

'I'll let you finish it,' she said.

'Are you afraid?'

'A little,' she admitted. 'It's a long time since I left Ireland. I've become a town girl.'

She rubbed her hands together and checked that her skirts hadn't been soiled. Wearing her Sunday best again had been foolish, she thought. She should have known better after the last time.

Agnes watched as Jonas finished milking the cows. Then he turned them out, one by one, into the field and they walked back to the cheese store.

'Take as many as you think you can sell,' he advised. 'I'll load them on the cart and take you home. There's no need for you to walk all that way.'

Agnes was relieved that he'd remembered his promise. Mr Anderton had lent her extra money this week, saying that she would probably need to buy more now that she was working at her business full-time. She chose four cheeses – two freshly made and two matured. It would give her customers a choice and the matured ones would keep if she couldn't sell them all.

'I can deliver the same amount to you next week,' Jonas offered as they rode along the leafy road back into Blackburn. 'There's no need to come out to the farm every week. And maybe we could take a walk together afterwards – although I'll have to get back for milking time.'

Agnes thought about the couples who paraded on a Sunday afternoon along the Preston road.

'I'd enjoy that,' she told him.

## 33

Kitty was surprised to hear the wheels of a cart outside the house, especially as it was a Sunday. She put her sewing down and lifted the curtain at the window to see who it was, hoping that no one had sent for a burial cart. She knew that old Ma Quinn at number ten was ailing. Father Kaye had asked for prayers for her that very morning. But Kitty was astounded to see Agnes climbing down and she dropped the curtain to hurry to the door, Maria following her closely.

Kitty stepped outside to see her daughter with a wheel of cheese in her arms. She wasn't surprised by that, but she was disturbed to see the lad from the farm at Samlesbury lifting more down from the cart.

'Mind out. This is heavy,' complained Agnes as she came to the door with the cheese.

'Good afternoon, Mrs Cavanah,' said the lad. He had nice manners, Kitty had to admit that, but she was worried to see him here again. She'd hoped that Agnes had stopped meeting him.

'I thought you'd started buying your cheese up at Oozebooth,' she said to Agnes as she followed her inside.

'I was, until I found out Mrs Marsden was still making hers. It's much nicer,' said Agnes as she set her load down with a thump on the kitchen table.

Before she could reply, the lad, Jonas, came in with another huge round of cheese and then went back out to the cart.

Kitty grasped her daughter's arm as soon as he'd gone. 'What's *he* doing here?' she demanded.

'He gave me a lift home. I'd never have been able to carry it all otherwise.'

Kitty watched with growing concern as Agnes collected another wheel of cheese, and then Jonas brought the last one.

'That's four!' she cried as she stared at them piled up on her table. 'What do you want so much for?'

'I need plenty if I'm selling it every day,' Agnes told her.

Kitty didn't know how to reply. It was true that Agnes had given her more money this week than she had when she was working at the rag warehouse, but it was the uncertainty of it that worried her.

'What if you can't sell it all?' she asked, thinking that it would only take one week with all this cheese turning green on the slab to ruin them.

'Some of it will keep. It's matured,' Agnes assured her before offering Jonas a cup of tea.

Kitty watched as she brewed it and Jonas sat down. She wanted him gone. She didn't want him getting his feet under the table and thinking that he was welcome – not when he could never be considered as a husband for Agnes. It was out of the question.

'Jonas is getting more cows. He's planning to have a huge dairy making cheeses as well as butter,' Agnes told her.

'And where will you sell it all?' Kitty asked Jonas, wondering if there could really be such a demand for cheese.

'On the markets to begin with. But I'd like to open a shop eventually,' he explained. 'It would mean the cheese could be stored there rather than having to keep driving it around every day.'

'Mr Anderton keeps suggesting a shop to me,' Agnes told him as she poured the tea and sliced a crust off the loaf of bread to butter and give to her friend. 'Jonas must be hungry,' she said to her mother when she saw her frown. 'He did me a favour by harnessing up the pony to bring me back.'

Kitty wanted to remind her daughter that their food was precious, but she said nothing, not wanting to seem miserly. If it had been Patrick Ryan, or some other suitable boy, she would have fed him gladly.

'A shop here would be ideal for you,' said Jonas. He seemed very enthusiastic and Kitty's heart plummeted. A shop would mean paying out even more rental than it was costing for the market stall, and she was terrified by the thought of Agnes getting into a lot of debt.

'That would never work. Agnes will be marrying soon and then she'll have to stop!' Kitty burst out, unable to prevent herself. It was clear now that this lad had ideas that needed to be cut short. It was no good him thinking that he could have any sort of a future with her daughter when he wasn't even a Catholic.

'Mam!' exploded Agnes. Kitty could see her daughter was furious with her, but she wasn't sorry for speaking out. It was better to be straight about it now than let either of them continue with false hopes and get into something that they couldn't afford.

'I'd best be on my way,' muttered Jonas, putting his tea down on the table and standing up.

Agnes watched as Jonas climbed back on to his cart.

'I'm sorry – about what my mother said. She thinks she's protecting me,' she explained.

He nodded, but Agnes could see that he was hurt and she knew how it felt. His father's words had wounded her as well.

'She doesn't speak for me though,' Agnes told him, disappointed that he was leaving without keeping his promise to walk with her. 'Please bring more cheeses next week,' she said after he'd turned the cart in the narrow street. She hoped he wouldn't refuse.

'Are you sure?' he asked.

'Of course I'm sure! I'm not giving up my business – not when I've only just started it.'

'I'll look forward to it then,' he said, and his anxious expression relaxed into a smile.

After he'd gone, Agnes went back inside.

'Why did you say that?' she demanded of her mother as she moved the cheeses one by one to the slab. She would have to cut one of them here for her door-to-door sales, and she knew that it would be much harder than using Dorothy's spacious kitchen.

'Because it's true,' replied her mother. 'You can't marry him, so it's no good setting yourself up for a disappointment.'

Agnes washed her hands and then began to slice the cheese into portions, weighing each one as she did.

'What makes you think I was considering marrying him?' she asked provocatively.

'Why else would you be friendly with him?'

'Because I do business with him.'

'And is that all it is?' asked her mother.

Agnes didn't answer. They both knew it wasn't. Agnes was sure that she loved Jonas. She'd never felt the same about anyone before. She thought about him almost all the time. She dreamt of him at night. Her whole body erupted with joy when she saw him, and when she was with him she wanted them to stay together for ever. If her mother had asked her earlier that day if she wanted to marry him, she would have replied 'Yes' without hesitation, but Agnes had to admit to herself, as she worked silently at the table, that since then something had changed. A doubt had set seed in her mind and although she did still love him, she knew that if Jonas were to propose to her she would hesitate. It wasn't because he went to the wrong church. She didn't care

349

about that. It was when she was milking the cow with her face pressed against its smelly body that she'd had a moment of insight.

Agnes had realized that if she married Jonas she would have to live at Goosefoot Farm and that as well as all the cooking and cleaning, she would be expected to help with the animals. Marriage would bring babies too, and babies needed to be looked after and brought up. She wasn't ready for it. She was too young. She wanted to concentrate on her business first.

# 34

Agnes went from door to door with her basket for the first two days of the week. She even called at the rag warehouse early on Tuesday morning and sold to her regular customers there, but she knew she could have sold more on a market stall – or in a shop.

'We miss thee,' Mr Reynolds told her as he made a purchase of his own. 'But it looks like tha's doin' all right.' He smiled approvingly at her. 'Serves me right for encouraging thee,' he said again. At least he'd stopped asking her if she was walking out with a lad yet, thought Agnes with some relief. If he'd seen her riding on the cart with Jonas he would have been expecting an invitation to a wedding before the month was out.

On Wednesday she took a stall on the market again and did a brisk trade.

'It's from Goosefoot Farm today,' she told her customers and they smiled approvingly and bought eagerly.

Thursday was always a quiet day in Blackburn. Agnes yearned to walk to Preston to see Jonas but she decided she must keep her promise not to trade there. Instead, she filled her basket and went out around the streets again to see if she could make any more sales. She would give up at dinnertime if she found it wasn't worth it, she decided. She deserved an afternoon off.

She was coming up Darwen Street when she saw Mr Anderton coming towards her.

'Agnes!' he called out. 'I'm pleased to see you. I have something to show you. Come with me.'

Intrigued, she followed him up to the junction at the top of King Street, but rather than turning for his home, as she'd expected, he led her into Church Street.

'Down here,' he said.

At first Agnes thought they were going to the post office where Timothy worked, but Mr Anderton hurried her past it.

'Further along,' he urged her. 'Here!' he announced after they'd walked a few more yards. 'What do you think of this?'

He grinned as Agnes stared around, not sure what she was supposed to be admiring. 'The shop!' he said. 'What do you think of the shop? It's recently empty so I'm looking for a new tenant and I thought it would be ideal as a cheesemonger's!'

Agnes turned her attention to the empty building, snuggled in the middle of a brick-built terraced row between the ropemaker's offices and a printer's. There were newspapers pasted across the windows and the black door was firmly closed.

'It was a grocer's, but they've moved on to bigger premises,' Mr Anderton explained.

Agnes thought it would be ideal, but she knew that she could never afford the rental.

Mr Anderton felt in his pocket and brought out some keys on a ring. 'Come and take a look,' he encouraged her.

He unlocked the door. Agnes followed him in and put her basket down on the counter. It was topped with white marble that would be ideal for cutting cheese. It was only small inside, but several rows of sturdy shelves were fixed to the back wall and Agnes imagined them stocked with eggs, butter and maybe some jars of pickles and preserves.

'There's another room behind that you could use for storage,' said Mr Anderton. 'It's empty at the moment,' he said as he led her through, 'but it's cool and you could bring in a cold slab and store some buckets of water underneath for washing things – there's even a tap outside the back door.' He unlocked it to show her and Agnes stepped into a tiny yard, surrounded by walls so high she couldn't see over them. 'There's no way out here, so it's very secure,' Mr Anderton told her. 'What do you think of it?'

Agnes loved it. It would benefit from a scrub and some limewash. Apart from that it was perfect, but she couldn't see how she could afford it.

'Dorothy told me you'd been round on Monday with cheese from Goosefoot Farm again,' said Mr Anderton after he'd relocked the back door. 'Mrs Anderton was very pleased about it.' He laughed. 'It's not so much the cheese as the idea of getting you married off to Jonas Marsden that she likes.'

'I don't think there'll be a wedding just yet,' replied Agnes.

'But you have decided to buy from Jonas again, rather than the local farmers?'

'I have,' she told him. 'He's offered to deliver the cheese to me each Sunday so it was an easy decision in the end.'

'Good. That's why I wanted to show you the shop,' Mr Anderton explained. 'I know you couldn't afford to rent it on your own, but from what you've told me, Jonas seems a keen young businessman, and if he increases his production he'll need more outlets to sell it. I wondered if you might be interested in taking it on together.'

It was an intriguing idea and one Agnes hadn't considered. She'd been so focussed on having a shop of her own that it hadn't occurred to her that she could achieve her dream by sharing one with Jonas.

'Do you think he might be interested?' Mr Anderton asked.

'He might,' Agnes agreed. It was an exciting idea and she hoped that Jonas would be agreeable. She would love to be able to sell cheese here rather than on the market, and it would mean there would be no need for her to trudge around the streets any more.

'Perhaps you could ask him,' Mr Anderton suggested. 'When will you see him again?'

'On Sunday. He's bringing more cheese.'

'Tell him to come and call on me if he's interested,' said Mr Anderton. 'I'd be mighty pleased to make his acquaintance again.'

When Jonas arrived at Mary Ellen Street with cheese on the Sunday afternoon, Agnes's mother greeted him courteously, if not warmly, and offered him tea. She seemed resigned to the idea that he would be bringing cheese each week, and her acceptance of the situation had been helped along by the two shillings that Agnes had given her from her takings. It was a step in the right direction, thought Agnes with relief.

She waited until her mother had gone out to the pump to fetch more water before she mentioned the possibility of the shop to Jonas.

'Mr Anderton has asked us to call on him,' she said as they drank their tea. 'It's about a shop. You said you wanted to open one,' she reminded him. 'Mr Anderton has a property that's come vacant and he suggested we could share it. I've been to see it and it would be ideal as a cheesemonger's. It's on a busy street and I'm sure it would do well. Will you come with me, to see him?' she asked, hoping he would agree. 'Just to find out more about the cost of the rent and the terms.'

'Can I come?' asked Maria hopefully. She'd put her mending aside as soon as she heard Jonas's cart at the door.

'Not today.' Agnes felt sorry for her little sister, but

355

this was to be a business meeting, not a social call. 'But you could mind the pony until we come back,' she said and was pleased to see her sister's face light up.

'What do you think?' she asked Jonas and was gratified to see that he looked interested.

'I can't promise to take it on,' he told her. 'I've already spent a lot on the farm, but if the price is right I'd be willing to consider it.'

'We could rent it between us and split the profits,' suggested Agnes.

He nodded. 'Well, let's hear what this Mr Anderton has to say before we decide.'

They walked down to King Street together. On the way they passed a few other couples walking out in the spring sunshine, and when Agnes saw Patrick and Hanora on the other side of the street she slipped her hand inside Jonas's elbow and passed them with her head held high.

She took Jonas to the front door of the Andertons' house and rang the bell. They were here to talk business, she reasoned. They weren't tradespeople to be sent around the back.

Dorothy opened the door and her face creased into a knowing smile when she saw them standing side by side on the step. It caused Agnes a moment of irritation. Why did people think only of marriage?

'Come inside,' Dorothy urged. 'Mr Anderton said he was hoping you would come. I'll tell him you're here.'

Jonas stared around the hallway as they waited.

Agnes could see that he was impressed by what he saw. Then Dorothy ushered them into the parlour and Mr Anderton stood up to greet them.

'Mr Marsden! It's good to renew our acquaintance.' He held out a hand and Agnes was relieved when Jonas moved forward to shake it. 'Do sit down,' Mr Anderton invited.

'I'm guessing Agnes has already told you about the shop. It's well placed,' he said. 'It's been a grocer's and the previous tenants did so well they've taken a larger premises. I was charging them five shillings a week, but I'm prepared to let you have it at half the rental for the first six months. It's not a favour,' he added. 'It's better for me than having it stand empty with no rental at all coming in. And I know you would be good tenants. I'd rather rent to folks I know and trust than take a risk. Go and have a look at it,' he said, handing the key to Jonas. 'Then you can come back with your decision.'

When they left the house, Agnes eagerly showed Jonas the way. She took the key from him and unlocked the door to show him the counter, the shelves and the yard. He responded warmly to her enthusiasm.

'You could bring the cheese up on a Sunday and I could get everything ready to open on Monday mornings. There wouldn't be any competition even when it's market day unless someone else sets up a stall, and even then we'd hopefully have our own regular customers – and our cheese would be the best. *Cavanah's Cheeses*,' suggested Agnes, imagining the sign that would hang outside the shop.

'No,' replied Jonas, interrupting her dreams. 'If we go into partnership then it must be *Marsden and Cavanah – Cheesemongers.*'

'What's wrong with *Cavanah and Marsden*?' she asked.

'It doesn't sound as good,' he said. '*Marsden and Cavanah* has a better ring to it.'

She felt momentarily irritated until she saw that he was teasing her.

'There is another option,' he said hesitantly.

Agnes turned from where she was estimating the length of the shelves to see his face had taken on a serious if slightly anxious look.

'What?' she asked, hoping that he wasn't going to change his mind and decide he didn't want the shop after all.

'Agnes,' he said, coming towards her. He reached out and took her hand. 'You know how I feel about you. At least I hope you do,' he added. 'And I don't care about the difference in our churches. It doesn't matter to me. So I was wondering . . . Do we need the *Cavanah* bit?' He seemed suddenly flustered. 'Agnes,' he said hesitantly. 'Would you marry me?'

His question took Agnes completely by surprise. It seemed so sudden. She'd had no idea that he was planning to propose to her, so she hadn't considered how she would answer him. A couple of weeks ago she knew that she would have said yes straight away and fallen into his arms, overcome with joy, but now she held back even though she saw the hope fading from his eyes when she didn't respond immediately.

'It would be difficult,' she said slowly, unsure how to reply.

'My mother will welcome you,' he reassured her. 'I'm sure she will. She's not prejudiced like my father was and I know she likes you. And I'm sure we can persuade your mother to give her permission. She didn't glare at me quite as hard when I arrived at your house today.'

Agnes knew that he was right, but their religious differences weren't the only reason she was hesitating.

Jonas seemed puzzled by her reluctance. 'I love you,' he said.

'I know. I love you too,' she assured him. 'But I don't think I'm ready yet. We're both so young,' she reminded him. 'There's no hurry.'

Agnes knew that she was hurting him, but she'd achieved so much, come this far, and she didn't want to give it up just yet.

'We can still walk out together,' she said, offering a solution.

'I thought you wanted to marry me. I wouldn't have asked you otherwise.' He looked so disappointed that Agnes almost relented and agreed.

'I do. Jonas. I do.' She reached out and put her hand on his arm. 'It's just that now doesn't feel like the right time. Please,' she said, horrified by the sorrow in his eyes. 'I don't want to hurt you. I'm not saying no. I'm just saying, not yet.'

He turned away and Agnes felt panic rising in her. What had she done? Had she ruined everything? If he walked away from her now all her dreams would come tumbling down.

'*Marsden and Cavanah*,' she offered, trying to lighten the moment.

He turned back to her.

'And you promise that you'll think about the other? About getting married?' he asked.

'Of course I will!' she assured him. 'I'd love to be married to you, but I think we need to get this shop sorted out first, and you need to concentrate on the farm and setting up the dairy. It would be better to wait a while. Wouldn't it?'

He nodded reluctantly and she hoped it would satisfy him. She didn't want to lose him. Of course she didn't. But the only place she wanted to imagine herself for now was in a clean white apron, with spotless hands, behind that marble counter, wielding the cheese wire, whilst a queue of women waited patiently, knowing that they were about to buy the best cheese in the county.

# Acknowledgements

Thank you to my editor Hannah Smith for all her hard work and input. Also to Claire Bowron, to my copy editor Sarah Bance, my proofreader, to Emma Henderson and all the editorial management team, and everyone at Penguin Michael Joseph.

# *He just wanted a decent book to read ...*

Not too much to ask, is it? It was in 1935 when Allen Lane, Managing Director of Bodley Head Publishers, stood on a platform at Exeter railway station looking for something good to read on his journey back to London. His choice was limited to popular magazines and poor-quality paperbacks – the same choice faced every day by the vast majority of readers, few of whom could afford hardbacks. Lane's disappointment and subsequent anger at the range of books generally available led him to found a company – and change the world.

*'We believed in the existence in this country of a vast reading public for intelligent books at a low price, and staked everything on it'*
**Sir Allen Lane, 1902–1970, founder of Penguin Books**

The quality paperback had arrived – and not just in bookshops. Lane was adamant that his Penguins should appear in chain stores and tobacconists, and should cost no more than a packet of cigarettes.

Reading habits (and cigarette prices) have changed since 1935, but Penguin still believes in publishing the best books for everybody to enjoy. We still believe that good design costs no more than bad design, and we still believe that quality books published passionately and responsibly make the world a better place.

So wherever you see the little bird – whether it's on a piece of prize-winning literary fiction or a celebrity autobiography, political tour de force or historical masterpiece, a serial-killer thriller, reference book, world classic or a piece of pure escapism – you can bet that it represents the very best that the genre has to offer.

**Whatever you like to read – trust Penguin.**